DON'T WANT NO SUGAR

DON'T WANT NO SUGAR

J. D. Mason

 St. Martin's Griffin ♍ New York

www.stmartins.com

Library of Congress Cataloging-in-Publication Data

Mason, J. D.
    Don't want no sugar / J. D. Mason.
        p. cm.
    ISBN 0-312-30158-8 (hc)
    ISBN 0-312-34899-1 (pbk)
    EAN 978-0-312-34899-1
    1. Triangles (Interpersonal relations)—Fiction. 2. African-American fami-
lies—Fiction. 3. Married people—Fiction. 4. Deception—Fiction.
5. Murder—Fiction. I. Title.

PS3613.A817D66 2004
813'.6—dc22   2004048386

First St. Martin's Griffin Edition: December 2005

10 9 8 7 6 5 4 3 2 1

Acknowledgments

First and foremost, I'd like to thank the little people: my children, Brett and Aliyah. I can never thank you enough for being more impressed with me as your mom than as a writer. Your patience and support has been immeasurable, and I couldn't have written two better kids than both of you.

My voice of reason, my friend, and the agent of my dreams, Sara Camilli, you have been wonderful and caring and attentive since day one. When you decide to retire, I think I'll retire, too. And don't ever fire me. If you do, I'll probably stalk you until you agree to a new contract.

There is no better editor on the planet than Monique Patterson. I am thrilled to have you as a teammate (serving double duty as a cheerleader on occasion) and friend. Working with you, as always, is a learning experience for me, and with each project I feel myself growing as a writer. You know how to bring out the best in me, and for that I'm eternally grateful.

I've been blessed with a host of family and friends who've believed from the beginning that I'd see this dream of becoming come to light. To them, my gratitude runs deep and I couldn't ask for a better support system. I'm a better person for having known all of you.

DON'T WANT NO SUGAR

The Gravedigger Look Me in the Eye

1931

Bobby Lewis was charred coal-black when they found his body in the bed of Eula May Adams. The house had burned to the ground but no one but that child knew for sure how it had caught fire. Bobby had been a fool after that woman, sneaking out to her house thinking that nobody knew about the two of them, but everybody knew, including his wife. A woman always knows when her man is cheating.

Martha stared at the child, wondering if she'd actually seen her mother kill that man, then concluded that that child had probably seen a whole lot of things growing up in that house.

It was warm for April, and Martha Armstrong was convinced that summer was coming earlier than usual this year. She sat on her porch with Eloise Tyne, fanning herself with the cardboard fan she'd borrowed from the church, trying to stay cool and keep the flies off of her. Martha's old chair creaked eerily as she slowly rocked back and forth. Miss Tyne sat on the top step of the porch, glancing out at the little girl from time to time, fanning herself with her straw hat.

"They found her momma over by Cranson Creek yesterday," Martha explained to Eloise, who said she'd come by to check on the girl. But Martha knew better. Miss Tyne was a nosey woman, and she'd trekked her behind all the way over to Martha's just to get into her business. But that was fine. Martha didn't get too many visitors to her place way out on the outskirts of Bueller, so when she saw Miss Tyne coming down the road, it brought a smile to her face. Besides, she always did like Eloise, nosey or not.

Eloise watched Roberta playing with her doll, talking to it like it was a real baby. "She was drivin' that ol' Packard of his. Everybody know he been seein' that girl fo' years. His wife know too, but she act like she didn't. I don't know why she wanna act like she didn't know."

Martha sighed. "Folks know what they wanna know, I suspect. I think she had too many chil'ren to care one way or 'nother 'bout what he did."

Eloise turned to Martha. "I hear that gal shot herself in the heart. They found her with the gun layin' in her lap."

"There you go again, believin' everything you hear, Miss Tyne. The gal shot herself in the head and blew the back of it clean off. They found the gun on the ground outside the truck where she dropped it."

Martha glanced at Roberta, who'd stopped playing and stared at the two women. "Get outta my mouth, gal! Chil'ren don't belong in grown folk business!" she scolded. Roberta quickly went back to playing. "That woman wasn't right in the head nohow," Martha went on to explain to Miss Tyne. "Come up from Beaumont, I think, some years back. I think she had some Creole in her."

Eloise nodded. "She look like she might be Creole. Had that good hair."

Martha huffed. "It wasn't that good if you got up close 'nuff. It wasn't nowhere near that good, and like I said, she was only part Creole if she was any at all. But she sho' did have some strange ways 'bout her."

"Sho' 'nuff?"

"Runnin' 'round in her gown late at night, singin' and dancin' and twirlin' 'round in circles like she was havin' a party, and wasn't nobody else invited but her."

"Go on!"

"Chil'—I put my hand on the Bible and swear to it if I have to. Not that I paid no mind to all her carrying ons, you understand. Cain't nobody 'cuse me of stickin' my nose in otha folks' business. I jus' ain't got time for all that. I tends to my own business, which ain't much, mind you, but I ain't up in nobody else's neither." Martha cast her gaze on Miss Tyne, wondering if she'd caught the subtle hint she'd thrown in her direction. Miss Tyne seemed oblivious, of course. "I seen him goin' up to that woman's house all the time. Used to try and sneak past here in that truck, hopin' I wouldn't see him, but I saw him. And he'd smile all silly-like, tip his hat, and say 'Afternoon, Miss Martha,' like I didn't know what he was up to. He was up at that gal's house damn near every day."

"She probably put a root on him," Eloise said matter-of-factly.

Martha looked over at Roberta. "That li'l one look jus' like him. Jus' like him. Even mo' than his real chil'ren."

"Bobby Lewis was dead long 'fo that house burned to the ground. His heart gave out from what they say, probably 'cause of her."

Martha sucked her teeth and rolled her eyes. "Course 'cause of her. You know how these young women are. Steal away another woman's husband faster than you can blink, and don't give a damn neither." Martha nodded in the direction of Roberta. "That li'l gal didn't have nobody. She ain't got no notion of who her peoples is or where to find 'em. And 'sides, I needed some help 'round here anyhow, and she a big girl. Big 'nuff to be plenty of help."

"I been tellin' you to getchu some help."

"I told them county folk she could stay with me since she didn't have nowhere else to go. They was jus' gon' put her in some home somewhere—one of them orphanages. You know black folk don't need to be in no orphanages. White folks liable to do anything to a black chil' in one of them places."

"You sho' is got a good heart to you, Martha," Eloise said warmly. "Always did have a real good heart."

Martha smiled, swooshed a fly out of her face, and nodded.

Miss Martha was always talking about Mr. Bobby. Roberta would hear her, but most of the time she pretended not to.

"She keep talkin' 'bout that fat man with the black eyes," she whispered to her doll, BettAnn. "She keep askin' me 'bout him, but I ain't tellin'. It ain't none of her business."

"Move on over outta that sun, gal, 'fo you get sores in yo' head," Martha scolded from the porch.

Roberta did as she was told.

Miss Martha had strange ideas that hardly made any sense at all to Roberta. Ideas like the sun burning sores in a person's head. Roberta had never heard of such a thing.

You still scared? You scared to think about him?

Roberta blinked at BettAnn, who knew how to talk without moving her lips. She wished she could say things, too, without moving her lips. She'd tried to with Momma and even Mr. Bobby sometimes, but neither of them ever heard her the way she could hear BettAnn. Of course, they never seemed to hear BettAnn either, which meant that they just weren't listening.

"Maybe I was dreamin'?" she said to BettAnn.

Naw. It was real. Otherwise you wouldn't be livin' here with Miss Martha. It was real, 'Berta.

"Wake up, Bobby Lewis. Wake up—one mo' time, fo' me."

Roberta's mother begged him all the time to open his eyes and get up out of that bed, but he never did. Roberta wished for him to wake up too and take a bath because he didn't smell good at all. She wished he'd wake up so that her mother would finally stop crying long enough to fix Roberta something to eat.

"Getchu a biscuit, 'Berta," she'd told her. "Getchu a biscuit or somethin'."

The biscuits had been sitting on the table for days and were too hard to eat. The only thing they were probably good for was skipping on top of the water in the lake, like she'd learned to do with rocks. Her mother didn't care about all that, though. She never cared about anything or anybody but Mr. Bobby whenever he came by the house. This last time, though, he'd come by and stayed too long, refusing to wake up and put his pants back on to leave. He'd stayed past dark, twice, and he'd never stayed past dark before. In the back of her mind Roberta feared he'd stay forever, laying in her mother's bed, with his big belly blowing up like a balloon and smelling bad.

"He jus' need a good washin'," her mother murmured, carrying the tin basin filled with hot water back into the bedroom. Roberta watched as her mother scrubbed Mr. Bobby's skin so hard, she worried that she'd wash it right off of him.

"Lord! You got to fix him," her mother prayed. "Even though I ain't right, you got to fix my man!"

Yes, Lord, Roberta prayed too. Fix him so he can leave. So I can eat something besides hard biscuits.

Her mother stared at him like she was afraid that he'd disappear if *she blinked, and she leaned in to kiss his face. Roberta shivered at the thought of kissing Mr. Bobby because he smelled too bad too kiss.*

"What the hell you lookin' at?" her mother spat. Her eyes were swollen red from the tears that had burned trails down her cheeks. "Close my do' and get outta here. We don't want you here, 'Berta. Not today."

Roberta did as she was told. She stood on the other side of the door, listening to the sounds of her mother whimpering, "You can't be gone, Bobby. I won't let you leave me."

Eula May raised the hem of her skirt up around her waist and climbed on top of him. "Make me feel good, Bobby," she cried. "Make me feel good again."

Roberta peered through the keyhole, watching her mother rock back and forth on top of Mr. Bobby, hoping that it would work, that he'd grab hold of her like she'd seen him do before and grunt like one of Mr. Parker's hogs. Roberta waited and watched for any part of him to move, but he never did, so she grabbed BettAnn and went outside to play.

Hours later her mother called her from inside the house, " 'Berta! I need you to come on in now!"

"Yes, ma'am?" Roberta said, out of breath, running into the house.

"I got someplace I got to go, baby," Eula murmured, sliding on her gloves.

"Where we goin', Momma?"

Eula slowly bent down and kissed Roberta's forehead. "I need you to do somethin' fo' me, 'Berta."

Roberta beamed. "Should I put on my new shoes?"

"I'm goin' by myself. You got to stay here!"

Roberta followed her mother into her room. Eula stared down at Bobby, laying bloated in bed.

"I . . . couldn't wash it off, Bobby," she started to sob. "I tried *but . . . it wouldn't come . . . off.*" Eula turned to leave the room and nearly bumped into Roberta standing behind her.

"But I don't want to stay here by myself, Momma." Roberta's eyes filled with tears. "I'm gon' be scared."

Eula took Roberta by the hand, then slowly led her to where Bobby Lewis lay. "You ain't gon' be by yo'self. See him?" she said, motioning to Bobby's body. "You know who that is? That man is yo' daddy, 'Berta." Eula's voice quivered. "He yo' daddy, and . . . I got to go somewhere. And you . . . he need somebody to look after him, 'Berta."

Roberta waited for him to finally move.

"He still sleep?"

Eula nodded. "Yeah, he sleep." Roberta saw tears flood her mother's eyes. "He sleep, and as long as he sleep, he mine. He belong to both of us while he sleepin', 'Berta. But the minute he wake up, he ain't ours no mo'. We jus' need to let him rest."

Roberta sat in the chair across the room from where Mr. Bobby slept while her mother drove away in his old truck. She tried not to inhale him and she tried not to fall asleep, but Roberta couldn't help but to do either. When she opened her eyes again the house was dark, except for the light of the moon shining down on Mr. Bobby.

"Momma?" She called out. No one answered. Roberta got up from where she'd been sitting, found the lantern on the table next to the bed, and lit it. She raised it up to get a good look at Mr. Bobby.

"Mr. Bobby? You wake up yet?"

He hadn't moved and Roberta was beginning to believe he never would.

"Don't nobody ever sleep this long, Mr. Bobby." Roberta's heart beat slow and deep inside her. "But I don't think you sleepin'." She took a step toward the bed, then screamed at the top of her lungs, hoping that the noise would wake him up. "Aaaaaagh!"

Mr. Bobby didn't budge.

He ain't gon' wake up, Berta. Maybe he dead.

She looked at BettAnn. "You think so?"

Like that gray dog you saw on the side of the road. Remember? It wasn't movin' either, even after you kicked it.

"Maybe I should kick him?"

Roberta frowned. The odor coming from him tasted sickly sweet on her tongue and she gagged. She turned and started to run out of the room. Roberta turned to look at him again, in time to see his eyes suddenly open. He blinked up at the dark ceiling, then slowly he turned his head to where she stood and stared at her through eyes blacker than oil.

Roberta gasped, clutched tightly to BettAnn, and dropped the lantern on the floor. She ran faster than wind, through the house, and out the front door.

That first night Martha finished bathing Roberta, slipped a gown on over her head that was three sizes too big, then tucked her into the cot against the wall that would become her bed. She stood over with her hands on hips to survey the work she'd done. Roberta had been bathed, her hair greased, plaited, and tied with a rag to keep it in place during the night, and finally tucked into bed.

That was when Roberta asked, "When my momma comin' back?"

Martha sighed heavily, "I don't know when she comin' back, gal. So don't keep askin' me 'bout that."

Martha blew out the lantern on the kitchen table, went into her room, and slammed the door shut between them, leaving Roberta alone to wrestle with Mr. Bobby.

Night after night, he tiptoed around in the dark room, waiting until Miss Martha fell asleep before coming for Roberta. She'd begged Martha to please leave the light on, but Miss Martha dismissed her pleas as nonsense, mumbling under her breath about the high price of kerosene and how she'd be damned if she left the light on all night, in case it should fall over and burn her house down too. So, Roberta had no choice but to keep her eyes wide open, darting them from dark corner to dark corner, hoping to see him before he had a chance to get to her, and praying she'd never see him again, with his bloated belly and black eyes.

She sniffed hard, thinking that he smelled so bad the last time she'd seen him, maybe she'd smell him coming before he could get to her. Mr. Bobby moved too fast for her, though. She could never see him or even smell him, but she heard him, scurrying around on the floor in the kitchen. Roberta held her breath at the sound of him and stretched her eyes even wider to try and find him in the dark. She heard him again, scurrying across the floor like a mouse. Miss Martha had mice in the daylight, but at night Roberta knew that mice slept, so it had to be Mr. Bobby running around in the dark. He was coming after her and Roberta broke out in a sweat at the thought of him, tall and dark, hovering over her bed. His eyes had been blacker than night, so she knew she wouldn't be able to see his eyes. Not until it was too late. She'd see his long white teeth, though, snarling at her like a wild animal, reaching out to her and—she caught her breath again. He was getting closer. She could feel him. He was getting closer to her bed, and soon he'd be on her, all over her, tearing at her, eating her—

Roberta! She heard her name in the whisper of his breath. And then, suddenly, there he was, rising high above her like a dark cloud rose in the sky just before a storm broke. His shadow swallowed the entire room, and then it swallowed her. Roberta's heart pounded fiercely in her chest at the sight of him and she knew she was going to die. He raised his massive hand and reached out to her, his white teeth gleaming like teeth of a wolf. Roberta opened her mouth to scream, but no sound would come out. She opened her mouth and tried again, and again, and—

"Wake up, gal!" Martha shook the girl so hard she'd thought for sure she'd break. "I said, wake up!"

Roberta forced open her eyes and stared into the angry face of Miss Martha.

"What the hell is wrong witchu? Now you know I don't take kindly to bein' scared outta my wits in the middle of the night by no screamin' chil'!"

Roberta sat up and quickly looked around the room. She rubbed her eyes. "Ma'am?"

"This is the las' time you gon' wake me up like this, Roberta. You hear me? I ain't havin' it. I mean it. Mornin' come too soon fo' me to be gettin' up all through the night 'cause of yo' nonsense!" Martha went over to the table and lit the lantern. " 'Bout scared me half to death," she muttered before blowing out the match.

Roberta breathed a silent sigh of relief. He'd almost gotten her. This time he'd come closer than he had the last time, but Miss Martha had saved her life, she thought, smiling appreciatively at the woman.

Martha scowled, "Whatchu grinnin' 'bout? Ain't no cause fo' you to be grinnin' 'bout nothin'."

Roberta hadn't realized she was grinning, so she stopped.

Martha paced slowly back and forth, rubbing her lower back. The floor creaked beneath her weight with each step, sounding more pronounced at night than it did when the sun was up. She stopped and looked at Roberta. "I'm tired, gal. And I'm too ol' to be up at this time of the night if I ain't gotta be."

"Yes, ma'am." Roberta muttered.

The girl had circles under her eyes. Martha seemed to notice them for the first time. She walked over to Roberta, put her hand under her chin, and raised her face up to get a good look at her. Roberta's eyes looked like an old woman's eyes. Martha hadn't paid much attention before, but the crescent moons under them told Martha that something was going on with this girl. Roberta was a quiet child. She hadn't mentioned her momma much at all after the first night she'd spent with Martha, so she figured it must not have bothered her, knowing her momma wouldn't be back.

'Course it bother her, Martha, she said in her mind. *She a li'l gal, and she miss her momma.* Suddenly sympathy washed over Martha, and she gently patted Roberta on the cheek. Martha walked over the kitchen table, pulled a chair out from under it, and sat down near Roberta's cot. Maybe she hadn't been, as sympathetic to the girl as she should've been, she thought. It's just that she had never had children or spent much time around them, and sometimes she forgot that they weren't like grown folks. They needed more tenderness than she sometimes knew how to give. This child had been caught up in a twister without even trying, and it had dropped her right down in Martha's lap for her to tend to. It wasn't her fault that her momma was a whore and that her daddy was a no-good cheater. Roberta was an innocent, Martha concluded. That was all she was.

"I know you miss yo' momma, baby," she said tenderly.

Roberta cast her eyes down to BettAnn that she was holding in her arms. She pulled the doll close to her chest and nodded. "Yes, ma'am. I do."

Martha smiled warmly. "It's alright if you wanna cry, Roberta. We all gots to cry sometime to let it out."

Roberta stared at Martha quizzically. "Let what out, Miss Martha?"

This child just wasn't right, Martha thought, staring into Roberta's small face. The whole time the girl had been there she hadn't cried once, and now she didn't even know how to cry, even when Martha had given her permission.

"Our grief, chil'. Our sadness."

Roberta thought for a moment. Yes, she was sad that her momma wouldn't be back. But she didn't know what grief meant, and she certainly didn't understand why Miss Martha wanted to see her cry all of a sudden.

"You been dreamin' 'bout yo' momma, ain't you, chil'?" Martha patted Roberta's thigh. "Is that what's been givin' you all these bad dreams? You dreamin' 'bout yo' momma?" She smiled at her own insightfulness, and at how good a mother she would've made had she ever had children of her own.

Roberta hesitated and then shook her head. "No, ma'am. I ain't been dreamin' 'bout my momma at all."

The smile faded from Martha's lips and disappointment quickly replaced the morsel of maternal instinct she'd scavenged inside her. "Then what the hell you doin' all that screamin' fo'!" she snapped, startling Roberta.

The little girl shivered at the thought of her tormentor. She forced herself not to think of him if she didn't have to. At night though, when the house was dark and quiet and Miss Martha was asleep, she ran from him.

"Answer me, gal!"

"I screamed 'cause—" she swallowed hard. Martha glared at her. "he come after me."

Martha studied Roberta for a moment. She turned slowly and looked around the room, finally resting her gaze back onto Roberta. "Ain't nobody here, gal, 'cept us."

"He come after you go to sleep," Roberta whispered.

He come when all the lights go out, Roberta heard BettAnn whisper, but as usual, Miss Martha ignored her.

Martha shook her head and rubbed the sleep from her eyes, realizing that this child was crazy just like her momma. She looked concerned at Roberta, worried that maybe taking the little girl in hadn't been such a good idea after all.

Thinking back, Martha remembered the night she swung open to door and saw Roberta standing there out of breath the night that house burned down. Instinct had warned her back then not to let the girl in, but she'd ignored it because she'd felt sorry for her, which wasn't like Martha at all. She'd always put a lot of faith into instinct because when nothing else in the world made sense, instinct always did. That's what her granny muh had taught her when she was small.

"Who come after you, gal?"

Roberta leaned close to Martha and whispered, "Mr. Bobby."

Martha sat back perplexed and crossed her arms over her chest. "Mr. who? Mr. Bobby? Bobby Lewis?"

Roberta nodded.

Martha thought for a moment and then laughed. "Chil', that man dead and gone. He ain't comin' after you. He dead. In the ground and buried—dead."

"No, Miss Martha," Roberta said anxiously. "He ain't dead. I saw him. I saw him and he opened his eyes and looked right at me."

"You bein' foolish, Roberta," Martha scolded. "I ain't gon' sit up here and listen to this mess."

"But it ain't mess, Miss Martha. I saw him open his eyes and he looked right at me. They was black eyes, Miss Martha. They was black and they looked right at me." Roberta felt herself start to cry.

Martha blinked back fear at what this child had just said. There was no need for her to get all worked up over Roberta or her bad dreams. That's all they were, just bad dreams. She snapped her fingers in Roberta's face. "Wake up, gal! I told you to wake yo'self up this instant!"

Roberta frowned, "I am up!"

"And you talkin' out the side of yo' head, too. Lyin'! That's what you must be doin', then. Lyin' right to my face!"

"No, Miss Martha," Roberta sniffed. "I ain't even lyin'. I saw him look at me, I did. Momma left me to watch him and I did, and then he turned his head and he looked right at me with eyes that was black. Black like night—black!"

Martha sat back and stared at Roberta for a moment. It wasn't hard to see the fear in this child because there was plenty of it, and it was rubbing off on Martha, too. She didn't want to believe Roberta's tale, but she couldn't help it. Dead people were liable to do just about anything, sometimes. She'd seen them herself, twitching and opening their eyes when they were supposed to be closed, or refusing to close them altogether. Once, when she was a child lying in bed late one night with her sisters, she saw her dead granny muh floating above the bed, pointing at all three of them, telling them that they'd better be good—or else she'd get a switch to them. She'd have thought she was dreaming until the next morning, when her sister Mary said she'd seen their granny muh, too. But her granny muh had loved them, so she wouldn't have hurt any of them. Not all spirits were so kind. Martha knew that some spirits, snatched away from life before their time, could be mean and nasty when they wanted to be. Maybe Bobby Lewis hadn't been ready to go. Maybe this girl was telling the truth.

"You say he had black eyes when he seen you?"

Roberta nodded.

"Don't never disrespect the dead. If'n they wanna cross ova, they will. If'n they don't, they ain't gonna," her granny muh had said once. She'd taught Martha that dead folks weren't really dead. They were just a different kind of living.

Black eyes could've meant his soul had left him. It could've meant he was just empty, and that there was nothing left in his place but an empty shell of the man he'd been.

"He say anything to you?" Martha asked cautiously.

Roberta thought for a moment, then quietly answered. "No, ma'am. I don't recall him sayin' nothin'."

Martha sank back into her chair and closed her eyes. Her mind was reeling with thought, wondering too many things all at once. Roberta had no call to lie about something so terrible. But children lied sometimes. This girl looked afraid, though. She looked like she believed that what she'd seen was real. And what if it had been real? What if Bobby Lewis had opened up his eyes and looked that girl right in hers? What would've caused him to do it? After all, he'd probably been dead at that point. Roberta hadn't said, but Martha had heard the man could've been dead for days before that house burned. This meant Eula Adams had let that dead man stay in her house with her and this girl the whole time he should've been buried. Lord, that woman must've been crazy. And maybe she'd driven Bobby Lewis crazy, too, and left his soul wandering around too long, without peace or rest. She'd angered him, or worse. She'd sent his soul straight to hell. Eula Adams might've put a spell on him. That woman might've put a root on that man so powerful that there was no way heaven would take him. Martha slowly opened her eyes and stared back into Roberta's.

Curses fell on whole families, Martha knew this. Eula May Adams was cursed, and she'd cursed that man, and he'd seen curses all over this little girl before that house burned down. Martha stared so hard at Roberta that there was a moment when she swore she could see the curses, too.

"Sometimes I ain't so sho' I shoulda took you in," she said, almost as if Roberta weren't there. "Maybe I shoulda let them county folk take you."

Roberta swallowed hard. There were times that Miss Martha was a lot like her momma. She hurled words at Roberta like other people hurled rocks, and hit her upside the head with them hard enough until they hurt someplace deep down inside.

"Dead men don't too often look at folk. You understand me?"

The girl nodded.

"Black eyes mean that man might've went straight to hell when he died, and if he looked at you 'fo he went, then maybe he wanna take you with him." Martha's voice sent a chill up Roberta's spine and she shivered.

"Either that," she paused, "or maybe—maybe he thought you was yo' momma." The child favored her mother, and in his dead state maybe Bobby Lewis couldn't tell the difference. Now that made sense to Martha. The man had had black eyes when he'd seen the girl, which meant that he probably couldn't quite make out who she really was, or it could've even meant that the devil was stingin' him so with his fire that he'd lost his mind and good judgment in the midst of his torment. Whatever the reason, Bobby Lewis had seen that girl from the other side of life, which meant only one thing to Martha. Roberta was cursed—by her own daddy.

"If he seen you, then he might think you was yo' momma, 'cause you favor her so."

Roberta shuddered again.

"And if he thought you was her, it might be that he marked you, gal. Thinkin' you was Eula May, he might think he need to come after you fo' what she done to him."

The little girl's eyes grew wide with terror.

All of a sudden Martha raised her hands and wailed, "Lawd! Jesus! I hope I ain't here when he come after you! I hope I ain't the one here witchu!" With that, Martha rushed into her room and slammed the door shut, praying out loud until the sun finally rose.

Time faded memories of Bobby Lewis, and years later Roberta's nightmares of him played out in shadows and whispers of dreams she didn't even remember, replaced by the luxury of growing up, even poor, into a young woman. Even Martha seemed to forget him and the curse she was so sure he'd put on this girl. Neither of them spoke of that night again, content to let life take its full course.

BLUES ALL AROUND MY HEAD

Lord, He's Got That Sweet Somethin'

1939

Charles Brooks squinted through the smoke from his cigarette, smiling at the sight of Nadine Cooper pacing back and forth in the doorway of the abandoned barn. She was looking for him. Charles leaned against the side of his gray pickup truck parked less than half a mile away in a wooded area, out of view. Nadine had no idea how close he was. If she did, she'd have surely cussed him up one side and down the other. Even from where he stood, it was easy to see how mad she was, with her lips poked out and hanging low enough to damn near drag on the ground.

Charles laughed and muttered to himself, "Don't trip on 'em, girl."

He'd played this game for months with Nadine Cooper, and he'd learned to play it well. It was the kind of game a man made up the rules to as he went along and kept them all to himself, because that was the only way to win. But Charles knew better than to take too much for granted. Nadine Cooper played games of her own, and despite his best efforts Charles usually found himself a step behind, licking his wounds, and wondering what the hell had happened.

Nadine was the kind of woman who would stomp a man under her heels if he let her. When they'd first started seeing each other, she crushed him too many times, belittling him when the opportunity presented itself in those rare moments when he let his guard down. Nadine was poisonous, like a snake that would bite the hell out of him if he wasn't paying attention. All it took was one word from her—"boy," her usual weapon of choice—to shrink him down into his boots. It was the way she used it that cut into him like a razor, the tone she took, like a mother takes with her son when she wants him to know he's never too grown or too big for her to tear his ass up if she wants to. Nadine called him boy like white men called him boy, making sure he knew that in her eyes he was less than a man. Never mind that he might spend an hour being a man all up inside her.

Women came easy to Charles, especially as he got older. There wasn't a day that went by that he didn't have a woman close to him if he wanted. Pretty women like Heddie May Walker, quoting scripture out one side of her mouth and pushing her tongue out the other side and down his throat, nearly choking him to death. And Linda Dobson, the smart girl who always had her nose stuck in a book and carried another one under her arm. She got on his nerves sometimes because all she wanted to do was to teach him how to read. Hell, he worked in the sawmill and would probably always work in the sawmill, so Charles could see no point to reading. And neither did Linda Dobson, once he slipped his hand up her skirt. Then that girl would forget all about Benjamin Franklin and George Washington and anybody else she'd been reading about in those books.

"Charles! Pay attention! You ain't even tryin' to—Oh? Oh my! Oh—Charles!"

He enjoyed their company well enough, but neither of them could make him feel the way Nadine made him feel. She'd left a mark on him, one that singed his insides. No other woman he'd known had ever left an impression on him like Nadine had. She hadn't been the first women he'd been with, but she'd certainly been the best, opening herself up to him, filling his plate with her every time he'd licked it clean, like it was Thanksgiving and Nadine was the meal. He'd eat so much of her, he thought he'd bust open if he took one more bite. And he always wanted just one more.

But that smart mouth of hers tended to get in the way most times. Nadine was only five years older than he was, but she went out of her way to act as if she were so much older.

"What do I want with a boy like you, Charles Brooks? You think you grown, but you ain't. You ain't no kind of man . . . yet," she'd say with a twinkle in her eye and a curl at the corners of her mouth. Touching her, making love to her, was his chance to prove her wrong and show her how much of a man he really was.

She sure is a pretty woman, he thought, watching her from his hiding place.

Nadine had a whole lot of pride that blinded her to the truth most times. Like the kind of truth that dragged her out here to see him every chance she got. Charles figured that Nadine had probably turned a deaf ear to that truth a long time ago, but he hadn't. Charles knew it and relished the reality that she needed him just as much, if not more, than he needed her. He could admit and accept that but knew good and damn well Nadine never would. He'd made the mistake of telling Nadine that he loved her and Nadine had chewed him up and spit him out because of it.

"You are such a fool, Charles," she laughed in his face. "But I ain't the least bit surprised. Of course you love me, boy. But me and you—we ain't nothin' more than a fleetin' thought. Just a notion, that's all. I couldn't bring myself to love someone like you, though."

"Why not?" he'd asked, trying to hide the offense he felt. "You meet me here all the time. If that ain't love, then what is it?"

"It's a good time, Charles. I like to have a good time every now and again. But love ain't got nothin' to do with it. Never will. So stop actin' silly."

He never mentioned the word around her again.

She insulted him like that all the time in the beginning. Eventually he got tired of it and decided that he'd had enough of Nadine and her disrespect. Charles had decided not to meet her one afternoon and left Nadine waiting all that time, knowing full well that she'd probably never speak to him again. A few weeks later, though, he caught a glimpse of her automobile following his down Smith Road. Charles slowly pulled over to the side, expecting Nadine to keep on driving and turn up her nose at him when she passed. Or to stop long enough to cuss him out and then leave him choking on the dust left behind as she drove off. Sure enough, like any good snake, Nadine surprised him and pulled her car up right next to his.

She batted her pretty brown eyes and spoke sweetly, "I missed you the other day."

Charles hesitated before answering, then shrugged indifferently. "I had some bus'ness to tend to."

Nadine just smiled and asked, "Will I be seein' you next time 'round?" He was stunned, and the look on his face told her as much. Nadine laughed. "I really would like to see you again, Charles. That is, if you don't have no bus'ness to tend to."

"I'll be there," he remembered saying just before she drove away.

That had been almost six months ago, the most important lesson in his life. Women like Nadine didn't appreciate a man being too good to them. They were quick to take him for granted, mistaking his kindness for weakness and walking all over him like he was the ground. From then on Charles learned to be accommodating enough to keep her coming back for more, but not so accommodating that she could ever get too comfortable.

The two of them met at that barn the third Wednesday of every month at three-thirty in the afternoon. That's when Nadine's husband Edward Cooper made the rounds of his sharecroppers to inspect his property and collect his money. Cooper wasn't much better than a white man in Charles's eyes. In some ways he was worse—a colored man taking what little they had from other colored men. No, he had no respect for Cooper. Nadine claimed she loved the old man, but Charles knew better. Nadine was in love all right, but only with the old man's money.

There were days when Charles would've robbed a bank if he thought he could get enough money to buy her like Cooper had bought her. As fine as she was, though, some other fool out there was probably thinking the same thing. It would've been a matter of time before a hundred banks were robbed in Nadine's name, and she'd eventually leave Charles behind for the next man who had more than he did. The best he could hope for was that she'd forget about money for a few minutes, long enough to fall in love with Charles, making it real easy on him to steal her away from Cooper, take her off to Louisiana or someplace, and marry her.

She'd been waiting in that barn for Charles for ten minutes longer than she'd planned on waiting, and she'd wait ten minutes more if he had anything to say about it. Charles dropped his cigarette on the ground, then snuffed it out with his boot. He pulled another one out of his pocket, lit it up, and slowly inhaled. He'd get to her soon enough—right after he finished this last cigarette.

*   *   *

She was so angry she didn't even hear him come in, and she nearly jumped out of her shoes, when he slipped his arms around her waist.

"Charles Brooks!" she screamed, pulling away from him and shoving him hard in his chest. "How dare you sneak up on me like that! You crazy?"

Charles stood back, rubbing his chest, grinning mischievously from ear to ear. "I gotchu good, didn't I, honey?" he laughed. "I gotchu real good."

He'd fallen in love with her when he was a boy. He ran around with her brother, playing the whole time, hoping to get a glimpse of her. She'd been beautiful back then, but was even more breathtaking now. Nadine was dark and the shade of black that people sometimes made fun of—blue-black, the color of midnight. But Charles had always been enchanted by her. Growing up, he'd often wondered if she tasted like blackberries or something else dark and sweet. He'd dreamed of running his fingers through the thick mane of hair she'd worn braided and hanging down her shoulders when she was a girl. Even back then Nadine's full hips held captive the attention of boys and men. She swayed them from side to side like a cat-o'-nine-tails, caught up in a rhythm all their own and threatening to lure some unsuspecting soul to a place where he'd be lost forever and wouldn't give a damn, either.

Nadine glared at him. "You too full of yo'self, Charles, and you know what?" she said, turning up her nose. "You can be full of yo'self by yo'self, 'cause I'm leavin'."

"Now, Nadine," Charles groaned, pulling her close to him. He kissed her softly on the neck. "I'm sorry, darlin'. You know I am."

"Get off me, Charles," Nadine fussed, trying to pull away from him. "I'm goin' home."

Charles refused to let go. "Didn't you miss me, girl? 'Cause I sho' missed you."

"Oh." Nadine stopped struggling and turned to look him directly in the eyes. "You miss me so much you more than twenty minutes late?"

"I got held up down at the mill," he lied.

"That ain't my problem, Charles. Now let go of me." She started to struggle again.

Charles squeezed her closer to him and melted into her eyes. "I'm sorry, Deen. You know I was comin'. You know I was gon' be here."

"You late, Charles," she said, exasperated.

"But," he smiled radiantly, "I'm here now, honey."

Nadine felt herself weaken in his arms. Yes, he was here, and that was all she'd wanted. She'd wanted him since the last time they were together, and she'd want him even more the next time.

"You know better than to keep me waitin', Charles." Nadine pouted.

"But it's always worth it, sweetheart," he said before kissing her. "It always is."

Nadine slowly began to unbutton his shirt. Charles slid his hands down her thighs and slowly raised her skirt up around her hips. He cupped her bare behind, then chuckled at the fact that she'd already removed her undergarments.

"Damn! I missed you too, Nadine." Charles backed her over to the blanket she'd laid out on the ground and eased her down onto it. He stood over her and slowly removed his shirt.

"Hurry, Charles." She moaned, writhing at his feet, arching her back as she unbuttoned the front of her dress. He smiled at the sight of dark nipples jutting up at him, then Charles knelt down and took one of them in his mouth, then the other, nibbling on them gently with his teeth.

"Mmmm," Nadine moaned, and then bit down on her bottom lip. Charles fumbled with his zipper until he freed himself. Nadine slid his pants down and gripped him with both hands, pulling him to her. He nestled himself comfortably between her warm thighs.

"Slow down, honey," he muttered between kisses. "We got time. Ain't no need to hurry."

But there was a need to hurry. Charles had a way of leaving her hungrier for him each time they were together. Muscles in his arms flexed as he raised himself up and hovered over her, and his shoulders spread like butterfly wings. He commanded Nadine to call his name out loud, and she did as tears slid down the sides of her face. All the money in the world hadn't been able to satisfy her like this. Nadine ached for Charles. She ached because her own husband hadn't been capable of filling this void inside her, and she ached knowing he never would.

Fourteen-year-old Roberta crouched low in the loft above and watched silently while the couple made love. She loathed Nadine Cooper. As far as Roberta was concerned, the woman was a dirty, two-timing whore pinned down at the moment under the weight of Charles Brooks. Roberta loved Charles enough to run through fire and water for him if he asked. But he hadn't asked. Not yet, anyway. She stared mesmerized at the way Charles had of making Nadine look delicious, and she wished more than anything she could switch places with that woman. She wished she was beneath him like that with her legs spread wide open, running her fingers up and down his broad back and gripping his full behind, forcing him into her as far as he could go until he disappeared inside her.

"That's it, honey! That's . . . aaaaah!" Charles threw back his head and growled. Nadine grabbed on to him and raced to meet him with her own release before it was too late.

"Charles? Charles!" She clamped him between her legs and locked her ankles until, finally, she screamed too.

Charles collapsed on top of her and both of them lay breathless and empty.

Roberta slid back into the shadows of the loft.

Charles and Nadine rested for awhile and kissed each other tenderly. He ran his finger softly down the side of her face and whispered, "That sho' was some good lovin', Nadine Brown."

Nadine giggled and kissed his chest. "How many times I got to tell you that ain't my name no mo'? Brown was my maiden name, boy. I'm Mrs. Cooper now." Charles sighed and rolled off her.

The two lovers dressed quickly and prepared to leave. "I hope you ain't late next time, Charles. You know I don't like waitin'," Nadine said, adjusting her hat.

Charles laughed. "It's always better when I make you wait, Nadine. Why you think I do it?"

Nadine rolled her eyes. "One of these days, Charles, you the one gon' be waitin' on me."

Charles bent and kissed her one last time. "I'll wait fo'ever on you, girl," he said teasingly.

Nadine patted his face and left.

Roberta waited in the barn and watched them head off in their separate directions. Nadine Cooper drove away in her husband's fancy automobile, and Charles pulled off in his truck until eventually he disappeared over the horizon and faded away like a dream. Roberta dusted off her coveralls and shook her head.

"You ain't in yo' right mind, Charles Brooks," she muttered. "That tramp ain't good 'nuff fo' you. You jus' too dumb to know it."

Roberta buried her hands deep in the pockets of her coveralls and headed home. Nadine was foolish to think he wouldn't be late next time. As long as Roberta had been coming to that barn, Charles had never been on time. It just wasn't in him.

Oh It's Cloudy as Can Be

Don't be pushin' 'til I tell you to push, Claudine," Martha warned.

Claudine gripped the sheets on the bed, balling the material up in her fists. "But . . . I feel like I got to push! I got to push, Miss Martha!"

"You go pushin' 'fo I tell you, gal, and bust yo'self wide open if you want to."

Roberta absentmindedly wiped the sweat from Claudine's face with a cool rag and listened to the sound of the woman's other children playing outside, wishing she could be playing with them instead of helping Miss Martha deliver this baby. "Roberta! Did you hear me, gal? I said go get me that towel!"

Roberta hurried and did as she was told, then squatted down on the floor next to Martha at the foot of the bed. "Give me yo' hand, chil'." Martha took one of Roberta's hands in hers, straightened out the girl's fingers, and pushed them inside the woman's womb. "Feel that? Keep 'em straight, now. You feel it?" Roberta nodded her head, then anxiously tried to retrieve her hand, but Martha held it firmly in place. "That's how open a woman 'sposed to be 'fo you let her start pushin'. Baby ain't ready to come 'less she open like this. Understand?" Roberta nodded again.

Martha Armstrong learned to be a midwife from her mother, and she had been teaching Roberta for nearly a year. "I needs you to help me now, chil', and you way past bein' old enough. 'Sides, I ain't go be able to keep on too long. I'm gettin' old, and folks 'round here needs a good midwife. Don't matter how po' folks is, they don't never stop havin' babies."

"Awww, I got to push, Miss Martha, I got to," Claudine wailed.

"Then go on an' push, gal! Go on and start pushin'! I'll be sho' to catch it!" Martha laughed.

The woman raised her knees towards her chest.

"Go on and help her now, Roberta," Martha snapped. "Don't jus' sit here."

Roberta hurried to Claudine's side and helped her to press her knees back towards her chest. Claudine took a deep breath, held it, and strained against the pressure of pushing out her third child.

"Lord, he crownin' already. Roberta! Come here and put that towel on my lap. Hurry up!" Roberta hurried again to Martha's side, then watched intently as Martha took her index finger and gently pushed back the skin of the woman's womb from around the top of the baby's head. "Big baby. Got a big head," she muttered to herself. Claudine took a deep breath, then started to push again. "Naw! Don't push now. You got yo'self a big 'un here. Ain't gon' be no rushin' him out. This ain't like shittin', gal."

"Oh, Martha! He too big for me to—he too big!"

"Too late to think 'bout that now. You got him up there. You damn sho' gon' have to get him out." Martha glanced at Roberta. "See how big he is?"

"Yes, ma'am."

"He stuck at the shoulders. Got some big shoulders. Who baby this is, Claudine?" Martha grinned. "Sho' can't be Lou's. Everybody know he ain't got no shoulders this wide."

Claudine glared at Martha and strained to push again.

"I told you to hol' still now!" Martha scolded. "You ain't pushin' this one out, 'cause he don't fit!" Martha shook her head. "Naw . . . his shoulders too wide. I'm gon' have to break him," she said, matter-of-factly.

Horrified, Roberta stared at Martha, wondering what she meant by breaking this baby.

"What?" Claudine gasped. "Whatchu mean? Whatchu gon' do to my baby, Miss Martha?"

"Lessin' you wanna walk 'round with this chil' halfway 'tween yo' ass and the world, I got to break him. That's the only way I'm gon' get him out," Martha scolded.

The woman bit down on her bottom lip against the pain of her contraction, then stared at Martha and nodded. "I don't wantchu hurtin' my chil', Martha! I ain't—gon' let you—ooooh Lord!"

"Hush now, Claudine, and lemme do this!" Martha commanded.

"Whatchu gon' do, Miss Martha?" Roberta asked, staring at the child stuck between Claudine's thighs. "Whatchu gon' do to him?"

Claudine huffed and puffed against the the endless contractions. "Martha! Martha!" she cried. "Don't you dare—" she growled.

"Hush, I said!"

"Uh-ugh, Miss Martha! Nooo!" Claudine gulped in air through the pain of her contraction. "Don't—you—dare—hurt my—chil'! Don't—you—awwwww!"

"He gon' really holla." Martha muttered, then reached inside

Claudine, grasped the baby's shoulders, and pressed them inwards towards each other until he screamed.

Claudine screamed too. "Oh—Jesus! Jesus!"

Fluid poured out from behind him once he was free, spilling all over Martha's feet.

"Gal! Where the bucket?" Martha yelled at Roberta. The boy slid out effortlessly from his mother. Roberta held up the towel so that Martha could lay him in it, "His collar bone broke, Roberta. Be careful with him."

"He alright?" Claudine cried breathlessly. "Please let my baby be alright!"

Martha wrapped the child's arm tightly across his chest to set it.

"He gon' be alright, Miss Martha?" Claudine asked again, her hands trembling uncontrollably.

Martha smiled, folded a blanket around him, and gently laid him in his mother's arms. "He gon' be jus' fine, chil'. Chil'ren heal faster than grown folk and babies heal faster than most everybody."

It was late when Roberta and Martha headed back to the house. The two walked slowly, not saying much at all. Martha was always quiet after delivering a baby. The older woman stared straight ahead, lost in thoughts that had nothing to do with Roberta. Roberta glanced over at her profile from time to time, thinking once again how hard it was to tell how old Miss Martha was. Even Miss Martha didn't know for certain.

"Where I come from, black folk didn't keep thoughts to things like that. Don't none of my brothers and sisters know how old they is. But I imagine I got to be 'round sixty or so, and I say that 'cause my friend Miss Tyne is fifty-seven, and I think I mus' be older than what she is."

Martha was hazelnut brown with high cheekbones and wavy

black hair sprinkled with gray that she wore braided down both sides of her head and pinned together at the nape of her neck. She was a heavyset woman, half Sioux on her mother's side. Her great-grandmother on her father's side had been African. Martha couldn't remember where she'd come from back in Africa, but she'd bought over wisdom with her that some called black magic. As far as Martha was concerned, the only thing black about her grandmother's magic was the fact that a black woman performed it.

"Wasn't nothin' wrong with my granny muh or the things she taught me and my sisters, neither. What she taught us was how to help folk and how to make 'em better, no matter what was ailin' 'em."

Martha began demanding her bath as soon as she and Roberta made it home, and peeled off her clothes as soon as the large steel tub in the middle of the kitchen was half-filled with hot water. "Is it boilin' yet?" she called to Roberta who was standing over another pot of water heating on the stove.

"Almost."

"Well, hurry up with it, gal! This ain't hot enough," she demanded, scrubbing her skin briskly until it was red and raw, stopping only long enough to let Roberta fill her tub again. "Birthin' babies is nasty," she muttered. "Nasty business puttin' yo' hands all up in some other woman's stuff. Give me yo' hand, chil'." Martha grabbed the hand of Roberta's that she'd put inside Claudine, then submersed it in her bath. Her large breasts weighted heavily on Roberta's arm.

"That's too hot, Miss Martha!" Roberta cried, trying to pull her hand out of the scalding water. Martha held on tight and rubbed soap on her hand and in between her fingers. "Miss Martha—!"

"Shut up!" Martha screamed, then glared into Roberta's eyes. "Shut up and let me wash that mess offa you, gal! You got another woman's pussy on ya! That's nastiness! Jus' plain dirty!" Martha finished scrubbing Roberta's hand, then let go and went back to washing herself. "Nasty! It's jus' . . . so filthy," she muttered.

Delivering babies was what the women in her family did. They'd done it for generations, but it was something Martha had never wanted to do. She'd begged her mother to let her go to school so she could learn to read and become a teacher.

"You ain't smart 'nuff to be no teacher, gal!" her mother fussed. "This here is what we do, an' it's what you gon' do too!"

Roberta came in from filling up the pot with more well water for Martha's bath. "You get that afterbirth in the ground?" Martha yelled over her shoulder.

"No, ma'am. Not yet."

"Get that shit in the ground, Roberta! How many times I got to tell you that? Get that shit in the ground fo' it stink up my house and draw flies! Put that water on the stove and do like I tol' you." Roberta hurried to the birthing room and gathered up the tin basin filled with the crimson mass. "And bury it out by the woods this time. Last time yo' ass buried it too close to my damn house and that smell 'bout drove me out my mind," she fussed as Roberta started to leave.

"That wouldn't be so hard to do, I reckon," Roberta mumbled under her breath.

"Come back here, Roberta!"

Roberta stopped in the doorway, afraid Martha had heard what she'd said.

Martha took a deep breath, then spoke calmly to the girl, "Don't fo'get to do what I taught ya. I ain't never gon' fo'give ya if you don't do like I taught ya."

Roberta sighed. "Yes, Miss Martha."

* * *

Roberta stood at the edge of the wooded area in back of the house and stared down at the *X* she'd drawn with a stick on the top of the mound of dirt covering Claudine's afterbirth, shaking her head at Martha and her silly notions before performing this strange ritual. Martha collected the afterbirth of every baby she delivered and made Roberta carry it back to the house in a sack, then insisted on having the girl bury it before they went to bed. Martha couldn't sleep until she knew it was safely in the ground where it belonged.

Roberta walked around the grave three times while reciting the Lord's Prayer like Martha had taught her.

"Our Father who art in heaven, hallowed be thy name."

Roberta recounted the story Martha had told her about this ritual.

"Ain't too many spirits as angry as spirits of dead chil'ren. They's mad 'cause they time done ended 'fo it even started and they's mad at the person who brung 'em here into this world. The only way to put 'em to res' is to bury they souls, and they souls is hid in the afterbirth."

"Well, what 'bout the ones that ain't dead when they born? You gotta bury theirs too?"

"'Course you do. They could die after I leave the house from birthin' 'em, or they could die later on when they big chil'ren, walkin' and talkin' and playin' by the pond with they friends, and I ain't takin' no chances. They might turn 'round and be mad at me fo' birthin' 'em even if they should die a ol' man or woman. I ain't takin' no chances," Martha explained. "Bein' the midwife, I don't trus' nobody. I learnt a long time ago to always bring it with you and put it in the ground yo'self, case that woman who's the momma might lie and tell you she buried it when she didn't. Then you say the Lord's Prayer and walk around the grave while you say it so he can send his angels to look afta you."

Roberta patted the loose dirt on top of the mound and stood over it, wondering if any dead babies really did haunt Martha.

"Roberta!" Martha called from inside the house.

Roberta heard her, then shrugged her shoulders and sat down near the fresh grave, oblivious to serenading crickets and dancing fireflies circling above her head. BettAnn was buried out here somewhere. Roberta had buried her years ago because she'd grown too big to play with dolls. Besides, BettAnn had lost both her eyes and most of her hair, and she'd just become ugly to Roberta. She saw no sense in dragging the ugly doll around behind her all the time, so she buried her out where Miss Martha always buried things that were of no use to her anymore.

"That ol' woman sho' do get on my damn nerves," Roberta mumbled, drawing her knees up to her chest and wrapping her arms around them. Snakes slithered into the wooded area in front of her, but Roberta wasn't afraid of snakes. They terrified Martha, though, and sometimes Roberta would find a little garter snake and sneak it into Martha's dresser drawer where she kept her undergarments. She giggled at the memory of seeing fat old Martha running from her bedroom screaming, wearing a pair of white bleached cotton drawers and nothing else.

Martha had always been strange, relishing religion and superstition, mixing the two together like a flavorful gumbo. She had replaced Roberta's mother and taken care of her after she'd died. Martha had fed her and given her a place to sleep, took her to church, and kept her hair pressed. But love never had a place between the two of them, and Roberta preferred it that way. She'd loved Eula, and loving anyone else seemed to betray the memory of her mother. Eula hadn't always been easy to love, though. The nights when Roberta had crept out of bed and watched her mother playing outside in front of the house all alone, or running around the yard chasing toads, were the times Roberta remembered falling in love with Eula all over again.

Other times Eula didn't want to be bothered, choosing instead to close herself up in her room for days, leaving Roberta to fend for herself. Roberta often stood on the other side of Eula's bedroom door, listening to her crying and talking. Sometimes she'd peek through the keyhole only to find out Eula wasn't talking to anybody at all, except herself. Eula wouldn't eat or bathe when she got like that, and she glared at Roberta from behind bloodshot eyes.

"You don't care nothin' 'bout me! I ain't nothin' to you!"

"That ain't true, Momma. I love you more than I love anybody in the whole world," she'd say, pressing her hands together and pleading with her eyes.

Eula would turn away in tears. "No," she'd whisper sadly. "You don't love me. You don't know what it is to love me. Don't nobody know. But that's alright, 'Berta, 'cause sometimes . . . I don't love you much neither."

Roberta learned to blink away her tears long before they had a chance to fall to the ground.

Eula was at her happiest when Mr. Bobby came over. As the years went by, Roberta had grown cold to the fear she'd once felt for him. Bobby Lewis had haunted her relentlessly when she was small, but not anymore. Roberta had lain awake at night, waiting for Miss Martha's prophecy to come true and for Mr. Bobby to reach up from under her bed and snatch her out of it before she even had a chance to scream. After awhile, though, she got tired of waiting on him all night and figured he must've forgotten about her and gone on about his business.

Eula turned into a new person whenever he'd come by the house. Roberta smiled remembering how her momma would put on her best dress and douse powder between her breasts, then put a fresh pressing around the edges of her hair, getting ready for him.

She missed Eula May, but Roberta figured Eula probably knew she couldn't be happy without Mr. Bobby to love her. In retrospect, Roberta realized that he'd been the only person in the world to matter to Eula anyway.

Men had coveted Eula May Adams. Every time she and Roberta went into town, men snapped their necks back and forth just to get a good look at her. Eula shone like copper when it was buffed and polished, and she had a head full of thick, reddish brown hair that she wore pulled back and braided at the nape of her neck when she was out in public. But at home she set it free and wore it wild all over her head. Her light brown eyes were shaped like pecans, framed by perfectly arched brows. She had a way of look-ing surprised, even when she wasn't, and her full lips were filled with warm kisses that left a tingle on Roberta's cheeks long after the kiss had disappeared.

Men loved her mother for all these reasons, but women hated her. Most of them still did, and they hated Roberta, too, for being the child of the whore who'd stolen Ethel Lewis's husband. Eula was the whore who'd killed him. At least, that's what they'd said. Maybe she did. Roberta didn't know for certain, but if that was so, then Eula had loved him to death. Folks said her mother had been crazy, but Roberta knew better. Eula hadn't been crazy at all. She just knew things that other people were afraid to know, or admit to knowing. Eula knew that love, real love, was strong enough to make a woman turn herself inside out for a man, or even put a bullet in her head over him, if need be.

Eula had explained it to her once. Late one night when Roberta was small, Eula had come to her. "Wake up, 'Berta. I got somethin' to tell you." The light from the moon shone through the window and illuminated Eula's face, making her glow like an angel. Roberta crawled out of bed, followed her mother to the front porch, and sat down next to her on the steps. It was late, and Roberta rubbed the sleep from her eyes and tried not to yawn.

Eula grinned from ear to ear and gazed up at the stars. "I think me and Mr. Bobby gon' get married." She looked down at Roberta. "Whatchu think 'bout that? You think me and him should get married?"

Roberta shrugged. If her mother and Mr. Bobby got married, would they let her stay too?

"I ain't never love no one like I love him. He's all I want in the whole world, and ain't nothin' I wouldn't do fo' him."

Roberta thought for a moment at what her mother had just said. "Would you jump off the top of the house fo' him?"

Eula laughed. "That's a silly question, girl. 'Course I would. I'd jump off a mountain fo' him. I'd chop down a tree with my bare hand fo' him. I'd pull out all my hair fo' him, 'cause that's how much I love him. When a woman love a man, ain't nothin' she won't do fo' him. Nothin' at all."

As far as Roberta was concerned, that was the only kind of love worth having. Anything less was a waste of time and wasn't really love in the first place. That's the kind of love she had for Charles Brooks. And she prayed every night that one day he'd have that kind of love for her too. Roberta craved love like that, the way most people craved a cool glass of water or a hot, home-cooked meal. Eula had shared her love with Roberta in small pieces, like candy, giving her just enough to remind her of how sweet it could taste, but never enough to fill her up. Roberta wanted barrels of it, until she could hardly stand it. She wanted to have to beg that man to stop loving her so much, because it was more than she knew what to do with. That's how her momma had loved Mr. Bobby, and how she'd never loved Roberta. And he'd had so much of Eula May that the only way he could get away from her was to die. Roberta wanted Charles to love her like that.

"Roberta!" Martha called again from the house. Roberta sighed and shook her head. She dreaded going back inside that house. Living with Martha wasn't easy. She always made it clear that her house wasn't home for Roberta, which was fine with her, because Martha was right. Her house wasn't Roberta's home, and maybe Bueller wasn't her home either. She had a plan, though. One of these days she'd find someplace where she could make her own home and fill it with all the things she liked. She'd plant flowers all around her house, filling her yard with black-eyed Susans, bluebells, butterfly weed, and bluebonnets. Then she'd fill the inside of her house with snakes, to keep people away she didn't like. Folks like Martha and Nadine Cooper.

"Roberta! Get yo' ass in this house, gal! I know you hear me!" Martha yelled again from the front porch. Roberta picked up the shovel and grudgingly walked back to the house.

Glancing in Martha's direction, she smiled at the sight of the teacup the woman held in her hand. "Shine," Roberta she mouthed. Martha always drank moonshine from that teacup with the yellow daisies after delivering babies. Shine cast its own spell on the midwife, carrying her along kicking and screaming into fits of laughter, crying utterances in some language Martha probably made up, though she insisted on calling it "tongues" or the language of angels. She'd spend hours fussing about men and how "none of them weren't good for much besides digging ditches and fixing things around the house." According to Martha, a man was destined to do a woman wrong, break her heart and sometimes her spirit.

Martha had never been married and had never had children of her own. She didn't talk much about her past to Roberta except when she was drunk, and Roberta had fitted bits and pieces of Martha's life together from her rambling. Martha had given birth to babies born dead. She'd fooled around with other women's husbands, with men who stole from her, beat her, and never loved her.

"A man ain't good fo' shit, gal!" she'd slur. "Don't ever let a man fool ya' or talk you outta yo' draws, 'cause they ain't good fo' shit 'cept breakin' you. Lord know they done broke me 'nuff times."

Martha would get so drunk sometimes she'd pee on herself, then fuss at Roberta and demand that she "clean that mess up." Once she went so far as to pull Roberta's face to hers, kiss her on the lips, and slip her tongue into the girl's mouth. Roberta snatched away and stared wide-eyed at the old woman, who was laughing hard enough to cry.

"I scared ya, didn't I? I knowed I did!" Martha fell back onto the sofa, drying her eyes with the collar of her dress. "I scared me too, gal!" she said solemnly. Martha gulped down the last of her drink, leaned her head back, and drifted off to sleep. Roberta hadn't spit so much in her life and still she was afraid she'd never get the taste of Martha out of her mouth.

The best thing about shine was that Martha would be out cold until late the next day. So Roberta made sure to keep her cup filled to the rim until the woman passed out.

She'd had a long day and still had plenty of work to do before she could eat and go to bed. She had to empty the water from Martha's bath, grease the old woman's head, and plait her stiff, gray hair.

"Where you been? You gettin' smart with me, heffa? I know it ain't take you all night to bury that mess! You hearin' me, gal?"

"Yes, ma'am. I heard you."

Don't You Hear Me, Baby, Knockin' on Your Door?

The light from the tiny candle flickered in the dark corner, casting shadows that to Roberta looked like wings flapping on a moth. To anyone else it might not have looked like that at all, but then, her perspective had always been different than most. People in general had a tendency to stop looking past the surface, letting their eyes rest there, drawing conclusions that were all too obvious and usually wrong. There was nothing interesting in the obvious. Roberta learned years ago that the truth lay buried in the layers beneath the surface, especially in people. She looked for the kinds of things people kept hidden in memories. Things like Martha's regret over never being able to give birth to living children, or the hesitation in Claudine's eyes when her husband came in and saw the new baby boy that wasn't his. Then there was the truth about her best friend Danny, who was a boy on the outside, but on the inside he was more girl than she was. He claimed his stepdaddy did things to him to make him that way, but Roberta suspected Danny had been that way all along and just needed to blame somebody.

She crouched down on her knees in the corner of the small room next to her bed. A tiny candle provided just enough light for her to perform her ceremony. The faint sound of Martha's snoring could be heard coming from behind her bedroom door. This house was too small to hold secrets, but Roberta had managed to keep this one to herself. Martha had the only bedroom, while Roberta slept in the main room on a small cot pushed against the wall across from the sofa. The kitchen was just beyond that. The house was filled with hand-me-downs and junk that Martha insisted on referring to as her "inheritance."

"Looka here what I inherited from Barbara Jean Simpson. She was gon' throw it out, but I tol' her I could take it and fix up this hole and it be good as new."

Roberta couldn't help but shake her head and laugh. Maybe Martha looked beyond the surface, too, and saw things other folks didn't see. But with all the junk they had in the house, Roberta wasn't so convinced that was always a good thing.

Roberta knelt next to one of Martha's spitting jars that she placed throughout the house for convenient spitting whenever she dipped her snuff.

It was after midnight. Martha would have a fit if she caught her up this late and found out what Roberta had been up to for the past three months.

"I ever catch you doin' anything that ain't right, I'm gon' put my hands 'round yo' neck and squeeze the life outta you! I mean that."

Roberta never doubted that she did mean it, but the older she got, and the more feeble Martha became, the less it mattered. Still, she wasn't in the mood to listen to the old woman's mouth, so she kept most matters to herself.

*　*　*

"My great-granny muh in Africa taught everything she know 'bout herbs and spells to my granny muh, who brung 'em from back yonder and passed 'em down to me and my sisters. That's how I know 'bout these matters. Spells work best when the moon is full, chil'. Don't let nobody tell you different. And if it's a hallowed moon? Ooowee! Lawd have mercy on that poor soul who got a spell put on 'em. Hallowed moons got conjurin' you can see. They got so much conjurin' they can't even hol' it all, which is why it look like a sun at night. The sun got sun rays, but a hallowed moon got powerful moon rays that spill out all ova everything when the earth is sleep. Most folk don't even know it, 'cause most folk don't know nothin' 'bout makin' no spells. But the folk that do—we the ones know how to take that conjurin' and make it work fo' us. 'Course, bein' a Christian woman, I know better than to work a spell without the Lawd's blessin' on it. My granny muh didn't know nothin' 'bout that, 'cause she come from Africa and they didn't know nothin' 'bout Jesus, God rest her soul. But a spell ain't nothin' but the work of the devil if you don't pray ova it. It ain't no good lessin' the Lawd hisself bless it. That's why every time I work one of my spells, I says a prayer behind it. That way, the Lawd blesses it and I ain't no sinner and I knows my spell gon' work. Long as the Lawd bless it, it ain't no sin. Jus' God's work."

In a tin can Roberta combined a lock of her hair, a small scrap of material from one of Charles Brooks's shirts she'd stolen while it hung on the line behind his house to dry, some horsemint, and a few drops of her own urine. She mixed it all together using a twig from a red oak tree, then she whispered a prayer she'd heard Martha make Miss Lula repeat when she'd performed the same ritual for her. "Callin' on his holy name," she said with her eyes closed and her hands clasped together. "Lordy, Lordy, Lordy be.

Make this man Charles Brooks fall in love with me." Roberta repeated this seven times, then lit a match and dropped it into the can, watching the smoke from her spell ascend into heaven, knowing it was looking for him because his name was written on it.

"Roberta?" Martha called groggily from her room. Roberta hurried and blew out what was left of the fire and then pushed the jar back against the wall. She quickly crawled into bed, pulled the sheets up around her neck, and answered sleepily.

"Ma'am?"

"I thought I heard somethin'."

"I didn't hear nothin'."

"I coulda swore I—you sho'?"

"I'm sho."

A few minutes later the sound of Martha snoring filled the house again. Roberta lay awake staring out of the window at the blue-black sky, filled with the moon shining down on Bueller, Texas. That moon had gathered up the delightful aroma of her love spell and carried it off to Charles Brooks. Roberta's eyes narrowed as she imagined seeing a mist rising up to kiss the moon that would kiss it back and blow it on him. She was too excited to sleep that night. It was only a matter of time, she thought. One of these days Charles Brooks would look at her and notice her for the first time. Nadine Cooper would become a vague memory to him, and she'd pass him on the street and wonder why he didn't smile at her like he always did when he thought no one was looking.

"What in the world done got into you, Charles?" Nadine would ask, astonished by his lack of attention. Charles's gaze would fall on Roberta, admiring her in the pretty dress she was wearing, the mint green one she'd seen in the Sears catalog. He'd push past Nadine like she wasn't even there and slowly make his way over to where Roberta demurely stood, and he'd be mesmerized by her innocence and beauty. He'd fall in love with her in an instant and realize how empty his life had always been without Roberta in it. Naturally, she'd pretend to be astounded by it all. His sudden devotion and declaration would catch her completely by surprise. She might even go as far as to appear appalled and perturbed by his attention, and swat him away like an annoying housefly of no consequence. Then, after he'd made a complete fool of himself over her and shamelessly courted her in front of the whole town, she'd offer up a smile in appreciation for his diligence and possibly even a kiss, on his cheek, of course. That is, until they were married. Then she'd love him the way she'd seen her mother love Mr. Bobby. Women did things like that for the men they loved. They sacrificed their virtue for the men they loved. Eula had done it. She'd done it all the time, even naked sometimes. Roberta had seen her.

She'd seen Charles a thousand times, but it only took one time for her to fall in love with him. It was the day she passed him when he smiled and said in a voice that warmed her like the sun, "How you doin' li'l lady?" The sky split in two that day and opened up to rain light all over Charles Brooks. It was the day her heart stopped beating every time she saw his face, even when her eyes were closed. Where had he been? she'd wondered. Where had he come from? And what in the world had he done to her? More than likely he'd done the same thing to her that he'd done to all the other women flitting around him like gnats. Charles had a way of casting his own spell on women who probably all thought they loved him, too. But none of them could possibly love him as much as she did. Not even Nadine Cooper.

Roberta was fourteen, running around in coveralls and pigtails like the tomboy she'd been most of her life, but Charles Brooks had made her a woman just by smiling at her. Butterfly wings lapped the insides of her belly like they did when she swung high in the air from that old tire tied to the oak tree behind the house. He'd stolen her heart that day, and Roberta was convinced he still had it tucked deep inside his pocket.

Loving Is the Thing I Crave

Spring swirled in circles above their heads, stirring the leaves of the cottonwood tree Roberta and Danny lay beneath. The hem of Roberta's dress rested slightly above her knees, and she lay barefoot with her legs crossed at the ankles. If she'd been with any other boy, she'd have pulled her dress down and maybe even slapped him upside the head for staring. But she didn't have to worry about that with Danny, because he wasn't like the other boys. Danny was what folks in town called an "abomination," meaning he was wrong for having been born at all. But they only called him that behind his back because saying it to his face would've been disrespectful to his momma, who was a kindhearted, generous woman and willing to lend a helping hand to anyone else in town who needed it.

Danny was a small boy for his age. He was fourteen, like Roberta, but he looked more like he was eleven or twelve. He was as skinny as a child could be, with a head full of thick black curly hair that Roberta liked to twist between her fingers, and he walked more like a girl than a boy. Robert had tried to teach him to walk the way boys do, but Danny never seemed to get it, so she left him alone to walk any old way he wanted.

"You ever wish somethin' was so true sometimes, you believe in it befo' it even happens?" Roberta asked, staring up at the powder blue sky.

"Naw, I don't think I have."

"Well, I'm gon' marry Charles Brooks, even though he don't know who I am. But it's somethin' I know deep down inside and can't nobody tell me different."

"Sound more like you dreamin' to me," Danny replied. "But dreamin' is what make things happen if you want 'em bad 'nuff, I s'pose. Like . . . I wish I was a girl, Roberta. A real girl with titties and long pretty hair." Danny's light brown eyes sparkled at the thought. He looked like a girl to her, only his hair was cut short like a boy's, but his lips were full and heart shaped, and his lashes were long like feathers on a bird. Boys teased Danny but not around Roberta because she could whoop a behind with the best of them when she set her mind to it.

"Titties ain't no big deal, Danny. Look at mine." Roberta said, unbuttoning the top of her dress.

Danny gazed admiringly at Roberta's breasts, wanting more than anything to put one in his mouth. But he knew better than that. Roberta would beat him up like nobody's business if he did that.

"Go 'head. Squeeze 'em. Ain't nothin' special 'bout 'em."

Danny did as he was told and gently kneaded each of her breasts. "Do that hurt?" he asked, his eyes wide with fascination.

Roberta shook her head. "Naw, boy. If they hurt, I wouldn't let you touch 'em."

Danny giggled. "I wish I had titties. Then I'd be sittin' 'round squeezin' on 'em all the time."

"And you'd look like a fool too. Girls don't squeeze on they own titties like that, Danny. It jus' ain't proper. And I think it's a sin too, but don't hold me to it. It jus' seems like somethin' that might be a sin."

Danny rolled his eyes and sighed. "How come everything that feels good is a sin? Every thought in my head is a sin." Danny lay back and rested his head on his arms raised behind his head. "You think I'm goin' to hell fo' feelin' like I do?"

Roberta shrugged. "I think you jus' might, Danny. 'Less you repent and change yo' mind 'bout wantin' to be a girl."

"I do repent, Roberta. I repent every day, but no matter how hard I try and change my mind, I can't do it."

"Could be the devil done got into you. That's what some folks say. If I was you, I'd get down on my knees every night and ask Jesus to take that demon outta me."

"You think I don't do that?" Danny stared at her. " 'Cause I do."

"Well, you mus' be doin' it wrong or else it shoulda worked. Jus' keep on doin' it, and believe it too. That's real important. You got to have faith, or else it ain't never gon' work." Roberta leaned over and kissed his cheek. "It really ain't even yo' fault, Danny. 'Cordin' to Martha, most things that people like is sinnin'. Like you wantin' to be a girl 'stead of a boy."

Danny sighed. "Well, sinnin' or not, I can't help it."

"That's fine. But that's why the Lord made repentance, and that's why he sent Jesus here too. So we can repent . . . which means, tell him how sorry we are—"

"I know what repent means, Roberta," Danny interrupted.

"And that way, He won't hold nothin' we do wrong against us." "You ever sin?"

"Oh, all the time." Roberta said matter-of-factly. "I wouldn't be human if I didn't."

"What kind of sin you do?" Danny asked.

"I do lots of sinnin'."

"Like what?"

"Well, like lyin' to Miss Martha. I do that all the time, 'cause it's so easy to do, and sometimes I jus' feel it's necessary. Martha don't understand a lot of things, and lyin' is more for her well-bein' than my own, you understand."

"What other kinda sinnin' do you do?"

Roberta shrugged. "Lustin' mostly."

Danny laughed. "After Charles Brooks."

She sighed and rolled her eyes. "Of course after Charles Brooks. Who else am I gon' lust after?"

"He ain't all that handsome if you ask me."

"Well, I ain't asked you, now did I? Charles Brooks is the finest man in Bueller. He might even be the finest man in all of Texas, and that's all I care 'bout."

"So, what do you be thinkin' 'bout him when you lustin'?" Danny probed.

"The usual things, I suppose."

"You ever think about his thang?"

"All the time." Roberta smiled. "I don't think it would be lust if I didn't. Do you?"

"Naw. I don't think so. You think his looks like mine?"

Roberta had seen Danny's penis, lots of times. "Naw, boy!" she laughed. "His thang don't look nothin' like yours."

Danny was offended. "How you know?"

"'Cause . . . I seen his thang, and it's big and black, and long. Real long, like from here to the house," she exaggerated.

"You lyin'."

Roberta laughed. "I'm a sinner, Danny. I'm s'posed to lie."

"So you ain't really seen it then?"

"I did too see it. I saw it pokin' in and out of Nadine Cooper's black behind, jus' the other day as a matter of fact."

Danny gasped. "Oooh! I know you lyin' now! Nadine Cooper? Why would she—"

" 'Cause she's a old married tramp, that's why. And if you think I'm lyin', then come with me every third Wednesday of the month to the old Smith place and see fo' yo'self. 'Cause that's where they do it."

"You seen 'em do it?"

"Sho' I have. They do it all the time, like dogs."

"So why you so in love with him if he doin' it to Nadine? And what 'bout all them other women I hear he been with? I know you heard 'bout the rest of 'em, even Linda Dobson, and she smarter than all y'all put together."

Roberta sighed. "Oh, I ain't worried 'bout them other fools. 'Sides, my lovin' him ain't got nothin' to do with any of them hussies, boy. Charles is a man, and everybody knows that a man can hardly keep his thang in his pants if a woman comes by and throws up her skirt at him."

"Hmph! I can."

"That's 'cause you ain't a real man, Danny. Anyway, he can't help doin' what he do with that woman. She spread her legs for him like peach preserves, and he jus' does what any man would do. That don't mean he love her. It jus' mean she hot in the draws, that's all. Charles is jus' takin' advantage of an opportunity."

"Miss Martha tell you that?"

"Miss Martha don't know nothin' 'bout it. I figured it out on my own. Like yo' stepdaddy, for instance. You think he don't see the girl in you?"

Danny turned away. "I told you not to talk about that."

*   *   *

Danny's stepfather had never really married his mother. But he'd lived with them for the last three years, and they'd just told everyone they were married.

"You baby that boy too much, Betty. He ain't nothin' but a momma's boy and if you don't stop coddlin' him the way you do, you gon' turn him into pure sissy," he fussed like that around Danny's mother, but in private he was even more cruel.

"You sissy!" he'd growl in a low voice so that only Danny could hear him. He'd swat Danny's behind, and laugh. *"You mo' of a girl, ain't you, boy? Nothin' but girl. Look atcha. Swishin' 'round here mo' than yo' momma do."*

One day Danny's mother had insisted he go fishing with his stepdaddy.

"Ain't no sense in doin' all that whinin', Danny," she'd scolded. "You need to get out and do things that other boys do, like fishin' and playin' ball. He jus' gon' show you how to be a man. And I don't wanna hear no mo' 'bout it. You goin' and that's all they is to it."

They drove out to a lake in Sherman, Texas. Before he knew what was happening, Danny's stepdaddy pulled him out of the truck by his collar, dragged him over behind some trees, and threw him down on the ground. He slid his suspenders off his shoulders and unzipped his pants.

"You wanna be a girl, boy? I'm gon' sho you what it is to be a girl."

Danny got up and tried to run away, but his stepdaddy grabbed him again and threw him face down on the ground, then forced down the boy's pants and pushed himself inside him. The sun glistened off the ripples in the lake, making it look as if diamonds were hidden in it. Danny stared out over the water, wishing he could reach out and hold the sparkling jewels in his hand.

"You ever tell yo' momma," his stepdaddy had said when he was finished. He zipped his pants. *"I'll kill you . . . and her too."*

"I'm tryin' to make a point." The sound of Roberta's voice interrupted his memories. "He see the girl in you, which is why he do the things he does and don't think nothin' 'bout it. It's like, if you was a girl, he'd still do them 'cause he a man and he want what he want, and he can't help hisself."

"It ain't the same thing, Roberta," he said quietly.

"Well, anyway . . . that's what Charles is doin'. He jus' doin' what come naturally to a man. But I'm goin' to make him fall in love with me. My spell is goin' to work, you mark my words. And one day, Charles Brooks is gon' be my husband."

"He don't even know you, Roberta. What make you think he gon' be yo' husband?"

"'Cause I got faith, that's why," Roberta said convincingly. "Faith is simple, Danny. If you believe in somethin' real strong, with all yo' heart and soul, then it's bound to happen. It can't help it. That's jus' how things work. Even the Bible say that if a man have faith the size of a mustard seed he can move mountains, or somethin' like that."

"Well, then, you'd better start gappin' open yo' legs like Nadine Cooper," Danny laughed, "'cause that might be the only way Charles Brooks is even gon' look at you."

"I ain't gappin' open my legs till I know he mine, Danny. 'Cause I got somethin' Nadine Cooper will never have."

"What's that?"

"Decency." Danny laughed again, but Roberta ignored him. "Laugh all you want to, dummy! I'm goin' to marry that man. You wait and see."

"Chil', I believe you. 'Cause you got *decency*, and yo' potions, and yo' faith . . . he don't stand a chance, Roberta."

Roberta watched Danny clutch his stomach and roll over in laughter. Let him laugh, she thought to herself. Danny was a stupid girl-boy who was probably going to burn in hell, anyway. Charles Brooks was going to belong to her, and when the time was right, Nadine Cooper had better not even try to stand in her way, or else.

I Wrung My Hands and I Wanted To Scream

She'd drifted off to sleep without blowing out the kerosene lantern next to her bed. Some folks closer to town had electricity, but Martha lived on the edge of Bueller, and electricity hadn't made it out her way just yet. Not that she would've taken it even if they'd given it to her. Some things were best left up to God in her mind, and light was one of them. A deep, tranquil sleep crept over her, beginning at the tips of her toes and working its way up to her knees, hips, shoulders, and finally her eyes. Martha felt herself smile contently. This was one of God's simplest and most precious gifts. Sleep. She'd be well rested in the morning, and looked forward to tending to her newly planted garden. She'd get out there early, just after dawn. That was the best time to do anything, when she would be brand-new and feel like a young girl again.

Roberta quietly tiptoed into Martha's room and walked over to the lantern near her bed. She blew out the light flickering inside, then stood over Martha while she slept, gazed down at her, and smiled.

What a pretty chil' she is, Martha thought while she slept. Her mind's eye gazed back at Roberta, taking in the loveliness of the girl. Roberta had grown into her dramatic features; wide, almond-shaped dark eyes, full lips. There were times when the girl was breathtaking and Martha had to force herself not to stare. Sometimes that girl looked so much like her momma, Eula May, it was frightening. It was as if Eula May had been reborn, or had never died. Of course Bobby Lewis was in her too, but the older she got, the more Eula May grew in her.

Roberta leaned down slowly and tenderly kissed Martha on the cheek, then she whispered something Martha couldn't quite make out. She strained to hear what Roberta had said, but Martha was too tired to open her eyes. They were shut tight and no matter how hard she tried, she couldn't seem to pry them open. Martha tried to ask Roberta what she'd said, but words wouldn't come from her mouth.

Roberta whispered the same thing over and over again. Martha began to feel uncomfortable at the closeness of this girl standing over her, whispering into her face. She tried to force herself awake and scold the girl, tell her to get back in that bed before Martha tanned her hide, but Martha couldn't move. She couldn't open her eyes. Roberta seemed to smile, and then she laughed. It was a wicked laugh, and Martha struggled to wake herself up and put an end to all of Roberta's nonsense right then and there. Somehow Roberta's hair had come unbraided and it fell past her face and into Martha's. It wasn't right. None of this was right in Martha's mind, and all she wanted to do was open her eyes and slap that girl's face.

Roberta's mouthed moved, whispering her secret over and over again until finally Martha heard it.

"The Devil done sent me afta you."

Martha's heart jumped into her throat. *Wake me up, Lawd!* she begged in her mind. *Please! Wake me up!*

Roberta's lips were close to Martha's, and she puckered them as if she were going to kiss her. The girl slowly began to inhale and a thin ribbon of breath flowed from Martha's mouth into Roberta's. Martha felt herself begin to drift even further into her sleep. She felt like she was sinking into something she couldn't explain. It was something forever, and far away, more than sleep. Martha was dying and Roberta was the thief sent to steal her soul.

Martha had dreams sometimes, prophetic and absurd dreams that woke her up in the middle of the night and took her breath away. She stood over Roberta lying asleep in bed, recalling the dream she'd just had, and shivered. She dreamed about the girl all the time and they were all similar, warning her of the evil lurking inside this child. *You bein' silly, Martha,* she'd say to herself. *She jus' a chil'. Ain't no way she could do such a thing.* But dead men with black eyes didn't waste time looking at people of no consequence. Bobby Lewis had seen something in her too, all those years ago. And that was the truth Martha embraced at the moment.

Martha held the long stiff switch firmly in her hand, then slowly raised it above her head. She stared down at Roberta sleeping innocently and peacefully. The girl had been burning spells. Martha had found the evidence behind her bed, next to the wall. She'd been burning spells to steal Martha's soul. "Get behind me, Satan!" Martha shouted, startling Roberta awake.

"Miss Martha?" the girl asked, stunned.

"Thou shalt worship the Lord thy God and Him only shalt thy serve!" Martha's eyes were wild, and before Roberta could react, the switch came down full force across her chest.

"Miss Martha!" Roberta screamed, trying to protect herself. "Miss Martha!"

Martha's eyes were glazed over and it was as if she was looking past Roberta at someone else. "Get behind me, Satan! Get back!"

Roberta jumped out of bed and ran towards the door. "What's wrong with you?" she shouted, trying to dodge Martha's attack. "What did I do?"

Fire shot from Martha's eyes as she glared at the demon, dressed up to look like Roberta. "How long you been burnin' spells? How long you been burnin' spells in my house, gal?"

Roberta shook her head, dismayed that Martha had discovered her secret. But what was she getting all riled up over? It was just a love potion, was all. A simple love potion to make Charles Brooks fall in love with her and ask her to marry him.

"I didn't mean no harm, Miss Martha," Roberta tried to reason. "I jus' wanted him to—"

"To take me to hell too, right along witchu and yo' crazy momma!" Martha growled.

Roberta looked confused. "No, Miss Martha!" she shouted, dodging from Martha on the other side of the table. "Whatchu talkin' 'bout? It's a love potion! I jus' want to get a man to—"

"Yo' momma was evil!" Martha sneered. "And you is too!"

"Wasn't nothin' wrong with my momma!" Roberta snapped. "And you need to wake up or somethin' 'cause you dreamin', Miss Martha. You need to wake up!" Roberta snapped her fingers at the old woman.

Martha lunged over the table at her and swung the switch, landing a blow to Roberta's arm. "Get back! Get back, I say in Jesus name!"

"You crazy!" Roberta screamed.

Martha hurried over to Roberta's bed, reached behind it, and picked up the can that held her potion for Charles. "Ain't gon' be no mo' conjurin' in my house!" she screamed, throwing the can at Roberta. "You hear me?"

Roberta cried as she watched the ashes fly across the room and scatter all over the floor. All her dreams had been in that can, her hope for love and for Charles, and Martha had destroyed it instantly in a rage of insanity.

"You out yo' mind!" Roberta shouted with tears in her eyes. "You a fool, ol' woman!"

Martha swung the switch again and landed it against Roberta's hip. "No! You the fool if you think I'm gon' let you do that mess in my house!" Martha's eyes narrowed. "You jus' like yo' old momma, gal! She put a spell on that man and then she killed him! Jus' like you tryin' to kill me! And I ain't havin' it! You can get the hell outta my house fo' I let you kill me, devil!" Roberta backed away towards the door, glaring at Martha. Martha's hand shivered. "And don't you be lookin' at me like that!" She swung the switch wildly in Roberta's direction. "Don't you be lookin' at me!"

Anger flared in her eyes. "Don't you say another word 'bout my momma!" Roberta said, gritting her teeth. "You hear me, ol' woman?"

Her gaze had suddenly grabbed hold of Martha's, and the woman stood frozen. A strange fire rose up behind Roberta's eyes, and Martha wanted no part of it.

"Get outta my house, gal'." Martha's voice quivered.

Roberta dried her face with the back of her hand, then ran out the door. It was still dark outside, but dawn slowly crept across the sky, and Roberta ran as fast as she could away from the house. She had no idea where she was going, but she ran barefoot down the dirt road leading away from town on her way to nowhere in particular and in a hurry to get there.

Charles knelt at the edge of the river, baiting his hook. The early sun flirted with him as it rose up from behind the trees. He spotted her out of the corner of his eye, the haunting image of a girl in white, walking on water. Thinking he must be hallucinating, Charles rubbed his eyes and looked again. He grinned, realizing that he wasn't dreaming after all. She obviously hadn't seen him as he was hidden from view behind the shrubbery just down the river from where she waded into the water. Charles couldn't take his eyes off the girl, watching her walk farther out into the river and raising the hem of her gown up to her thighs. A wild mane of thick black hair blew gently in the breeze, showing off the delicate features of her face as she stared across the river to the other side, as if she were looking at something in particular. The girl was young, not quite grown, but the sunlight revealed exactly what he'd suspected and Charles smiled at the sight of a woman's breasts, silhouetted beneath her gown.

Roberta was still fuming over Miss Martha's unexplained outburst that morning. She closed her eyes and took deep breaths to try and calm herself down. Miss Martha went too far sometimes with her silly ways, and she'd make Roberta suffer for them, then later on act as if nothing had happened. Once she'd locked the girl out of the house and refused to let her in until the next day, claiming that Roberta wasn't who she said she was but was somebody else entirely, dressed up to look like Roberta. Another time she'd made Roberta wash all the clothes and bedding in the house, even things that were already clean, because she claimed they smelled like some man she'd known years ago, a smell that didn't set well with Miss Martha.

"He smellt sour. Like lemons but without the sweet. Lemons is sour, but they got a sweet smell to 'em too if you take a good whiff—like fruit, 'cause that's what they is, you know. He didn't have the sweet. Jus' the sour," she explained, frowning.

Miss Martha was too strange sometimes to be right. She was always accusing Roberta of being peculiar, but she had no room to talk as far as Roberta was concerned. She'd seen the way folks sometimes looked at Miss Martha when she spoke of things that made no sense, raising their eyebrows, wondering if Miss Martha really understood the words that had just come from her mouth.

"That ol' fool!" Roberta muttered to herself. "I can't wait to leave that woman. One of these days—I swear—"

Roberta angrily kicked the water.

"'Mornin'."

The sound of his voice startled her, and Roberta turned to see Charles squatting at the bank of the river, smiling.

Lord, was she dreaming? Roberta blinked and stared without meaning to at his smile and the dimples on his cheeks, dimples deep enough to curl up in and go to sleep. There was no finer man in the world as far as she was concerned. She was frozen where she stood, knee-deep in the water, her words caught behind the lump that had welled up in her throat and threatened to choke her to death.

"It's a bit early for swimmin' ain't it?" he teased. "'Sides, you ain't dressed right for taken' a dip." Charles winked.

Roberta fought to keep her knees from buckling out from under her. Her heart raced in her chest, and with all the strength she had left, she willed her legs to move and get her out of the water before she fell over and drowned. Nothing would be more embarrassing than drowning right in front of the man she loved in two feet of water. She turned and slowly made her way back to the river bank.

This one here was light enough to turn a little red, he thought, watching her wade out of the water. He'd had her blushing, and he'd hardly said two words to the girl. Charles fought back the urge to laugh.

"You leavin' already? We ain't hardly even had a chance to talk," he said playfully.

Roberta let go of her gown and hesitated. She had no idea

what to do or say or even where to go at the moment. All she knew was that she'd never been so close to him before, and even though she'd dreamed this moment a hundred times, dreaming it could've never prepared her for when it actually happened.

"I—I didn't know nobody was here," she explained nervously. He must've thought she looked foolish with her hair all over her head, in her night clothes, standing in the middle of the river so early in the morning. Roberta rubbed her hand over her head, trying to smooth down her hair, cursing herself for not taking the time to braid it before she went to bed.

She looked familiar to him, and Charles thought for a moment about where he'd seen her before. Then it dawned on him. This was the girl who lived with the old midwife, Miss Martha. What was her name? Roberta. His mother and Miss Martha were friends, and he'd seen this girl running around town, dressed up like a boy in overalls and hats pulled down low on her head. He'd hardly even known she was a girl at all—until now. And right now, Charles didn't think he'd ever seen a woman more beautiful.

"I'm jus' gettin' some fishin' in this mornin', that's all," he said, unable to take his eyes off her.

Roberta stared down at her muddy feet, wishing she could disappear just long enough to comb her hair and wash her feet and put on some decent clothes.

"You the one who live with Miss Martha, ain't you?"

Roberta shrugged "I live with her—but we ain't no kin," she quickly interjected. "I'm jus' stayin' there 'till I can get off on my own." The last thing she wanted was for Charles to think she was actually related to Miss Martha. "I been livin' with her since I was little—right after my momma—" She stopped short, afraid that she might be saying too much.

He always did have a weak spot in his heart for shy girls, and this one was more shy than any he'd known in awhile. If he'd said boo, she'd have jumped right out of her skin. Charles didn't want to scare her, though. The morning breeze rose up and blew a strand of her hair into her face, and before he realized what he'd done, Charles had reached up and gently slid it back behind her ear.

Roberta stared at him, stunned. She took a step back, wondering why in the world he'd take it upon himself to do something like that, but then it slowly began to dawn on her that maybe her conjuring was starting to work. Roberta had dreamed for months that it would. It seemed that now her dreams were starting to come true after all.

It's workin', Roberta. He couldn't help hisself 'cause—it's workin', the small voice inside reminded her.

All those nights of praying and mixing potions—all that bragging she'd done to Danny—of course. Butterflies tickled her stomach. Roberta wanted to shout but swallowed hard instead.

When a man fall in love, he can't help hisself. He can't help hisself witchu now. Be careful, girl. Don't say nothin' foolish!

The look on her face made him uncomfortable, and Charles realized he'd been too forward. "I'm sorry. I didn't mean—"

"It's alright," Roberta smiled. "That's what I get fo' runnin' off without combin' my head."

Her smile caught him in a way he hadn't anticipated and it took his breath away. He cleared his throat. "Sho' is nice to see you outta them baggy pants. They big 'nuff to fit me." He grinned. "I had no idea you was this pretty."

Roberta blushed. "I ain't so pretty."

Hush Roberta! If he wanna think you pretty, let him!

"But thank you."

Bright wide eyes timidly looked up at him, and Charles couldn't help but laugh. "How ol' are you?"

He suspected he knew the answer to that question even before he'd asked it, but Charles prayed she'd surprise him with one he could live with.

She shrugged. "Fourteen—but I'll be fifteen in fo' months."

He was disappointed but refused to let her see it. She was too young for him—barely too young. Charles had made a rule not to mess with any girl younger than sixteen. Girls her age were children and he had no use for children, even children as pretty as this one was.

"Well, you best be gettin' on home now. I'm sho' Miss Martha must be lookin' fo' you," he said, trying not to sound disappointed.

Roberta cursed Miss Martha in her mind.

That ol' crazy heffa ain't lookin' fo' nobody. Least of all you. But, shhh . . . don't you dare tell him that, 'Berta!

"She usually let you go runnin' 'round this early by yo'self?"

Roberta crossed her arms over her chest, "I can do anything I wanna do, 'cause I'm jus' stayin' with her temporarily," she explained smugly. "Long 'nuff to get some money together so I can leave and get out on my own."

"Is that right?" Charles grinned. "You don't look ol' 'nuff to be out on yo' own to me."

Roberta shrugged, "Oh, I'm plenty ol' 'nuff to take care of myself. Actually, I'm the one who take care of me and Miss Martha, both. I do everything 'round that house. Miss Martha don't hardly lift a finger 'cause of me."

Charles nodded but didn't say a word, relishing the moment of this girl going out of her way to try and impress him.

His silence unnerved her, and Roberta decided she should leave before she felt compelled to give in to the love building up inside her. She hurried past him, then turned one last time, "Good luck with yo' fishin'."

He smiled and nodded his head. "Thank you. And tell Miss Martha Charles Brooks says hello."

Charles watched her disappear into the brush and shook his head. If she'd been a year or two older, he'd have probably let himself fall in love all over that girl. He found his fishing pole and sat down to finish baiting the hook, smiling at the image of Roberta lingering in his mind.

Roberta stopped in front of the house and inhaled deeply, filling her stomach with the delicious aroma of breakfast. She didn't know how mad Miss Martha would be and paced back and forth outside the house, wondering if it was safe to go inside, or if it was best to just keep on walking.

"You gon' stand out there all day, gal?" Martha called from the kitchen. "Breakfast 'bout done, and you need to get yo' fool behind in this house, 'stead of runnin' round town in yo' gown." Slowly Roberta ascended the steps and went inside. "Go wash yo' face and hands," Martha said, standing over the potbellied stove. "Then come get yo' breakfast."

Roberta obediently did as she was told, then sat down at the table while Martha set her plate down in front of her. She scratched her head, bewildered by Martha's behavior. Rarely had they been privileged to a feast like this—eggs and homemade biscuits.

"Don't use all my preserves, neither. It's gon' be awhile 'fo I can make some mo' so this got to last us."

"Yes, ma'am," Roberta whispered, staring down at the plate in front of her. Everything looked so delicious, and Roberta was hungry enough to eat all the food on her plate and Martha's too.

Miss Martha was a strange creature, Roberta thought, salt-and-peppering her eggs, fried sunny-side up just the way she liked them. Martha never cooked her eggs the way she liked them. Usually she scrambled them and slapped a mess of them in the middle of the plate.

"This sho' look good, Miss Martha," Roberta said, smiling.

"Jus' hurry up and eat fo' it get cold," Martha said quickly.

And that's when it dawned on her. "Poison," Roberta mouthed when Martha wasn't looking. Martha had probably fried her eggs in rat poison, or maybe she'd mixed together some of them herbs she had growing in the back of the house and made some kind of African potion out of them.

"Go on an' eat, chil'. I ain't put nothin in it." Martha stared at her as if she were reading Roberta's mind. She wiped her hands on her apron, then sat down at the table. "If I wanted you dead, I coulda done it a hundred times by now. Go on. Eat."

Roberta didn't move. Finally Martha shook her head and switched her plate with Roberta's, then started eating. "Pass the preserves." Martha took a sip of her coffee. "We got to go to the market tomorrow mornin', and Mary Edwards say we can come over and pick some greens outta her garden. She can't eat 'em 'cause they give her gas. I don't know why she bother growin' 'em every year. Least we can have us some greens. Remind me to pick up some mo' salt pork at the market. I'm 'bout out and Lawd know, I hate cookin' without salt pork. Roberta . . . get up and pour me a glass of buttermilk, baby. I forgot my buttermilk."

Blues All Around My Head

Roberta stopped sweeping the front porch and watched the candy-apple-red Ford Model A slow down and turn into the yard. Nadine stepped out of the car wearing a black floral silk dress with a long sweeping skirt and a matching sash cinched around her small waist. The matching black velvet hat sat perched strategically at an angle on her head.

"Miss Martha here?" she asked, standing at the bottom of the steps.

Roberta stared back at her, dismayed, but gathered enough strength to nod her head.

Nadine sighed, exasperated, making her frustration obvious. "Well?"

"Well . . . what?" Roberta shrugged.

"Can you tell her I'm here?" Nadine asked indignantly.

Roberta didn't budge. For the life of her, she couldn't figure out why Nadine would show up here. It just didn't make any sense at all.

Nadine sighed, stormed up the steps, and pushed past Roberta. "Oh, goodness gracious!" she huffed, pulling open the screen door, "Never mind."

Martha rocked slowly back and forth in her chair, watching Nadine Cooper barge uninvited into her house. It wasn't long ago that Martha would've taken a switch to her behind for storming into her home without knocking. But Mrs. Cooper didn't have much regard for anybody since she'd married that rich husband of hers. Nadine strutted around town with her nose turned up in the air, rolling her eyes in her head like she was the belle of the ball. She hadn't always been so stuck-up, though. Martha remembered how poor that child had been before he'd come along, flashing green dollars in her momma's face, all the while licking his lips at the sight of Nadine, young and tender. Nadine had been a decent enough girl back in those days, but Eddie and his money had turned her into the kind of woman most people didn't want to share company with.

Of course, Eddie Cooper was a liar, plain and simple in Martha's opinion. He bragged of how he'd worked so hard to buy the land he owned when the truth of the matter was, he'd inherited most of it from a white man who'd owned his great-grandmomma back when she was a slave. Mr. Lyons had been one of the few white men in Bueller who could afford slaves, and he'd fathered black babies right along next to the white ones. Before he died, he promised that all of his children would be taken care of, no matter what color they were. It was rumored that he'd actually loved Eddie Cooper's great-grandmomma, but if he did, the truth lay buried in the ground with him. From what Martha knew, the woman had never said much about it one way or another, and took her portion of what happened to the grave with her as well. Edward didn't get as much inheritance as the white children had, but he'd gotten enough.

Martha stopped rocking, glared at Nadine standing in her doorway, then picked up an old coffee can and spit thick brown liquid into it. *Thwat!* Nausea welled up in the back of Nadine's throat.

"Don't you know how to knock?" Martha asked venomously.

Nadine nervously wrung her hands together. She stood rigidly in front of Martha, unsure of what to say next, but quickly gathered up her composure and reluctantly apologized. "I'm . . . sorry."

Martha's eyes narrowed. "You is sorry if you don't knock 'fo comin' up in folks house. Like to get a bullet up in you if you ain't careful."

Nadine swallowed hard. She was in no mood to stand and listen to this old woman fuss all day about something as insignificant as knocking on that raggedy door, barely hanging on the hinges. But she was desperate and Martha was the only person in town who could help her.

"I do apologize, Miss Martha." Nadine said, trying to sound more convincing. "It's jus' that . . . well, I need yo' assistance."

Martha stared at her for a moment, then let out a burst of laughter. "My assistance? What kind of high-and-mighty talk is that, gal? That sound jus' like that white-folk talk to me."

Nadine was offended but tried not to show it. Martha was ignorant and she really hadn't been surprised at all by the woman's outburst.

"So whatchu want with me?" Martha asked, finally composing herself.

Nadine hesitated, choosing her words carefully before she spoke. "I hear you can give me somethin'."

"Give you somethin' . . . for what?" Martha asked suspiciously, already certain of the answer she'd known from the moment that woman had set foot in her house. Desperation shadowed the grave expression Nadine wore on her face. It was so obvious sometimes; Martha couldn't understand why other people couldn't see it. That's what panic looked like, fueled by a child of some other man not her own growing in her belly. Nadine Cooper was expecting a child, but she'd come running all the way out here to Martha's long before it was due, which meant that Eddie Cooper wasn't the daddy and she had no intention of keeping it.

Martha's eyes twinkled at the sight of this stylish woman standing in front of her, trapped in a predicament that stood in sharp contrast to Nadine's polished manner. All the money and fine clothes in the world couldn't hide what she really was—an adultress, careless enough to make a mountain out of an affair that she'd probably assumed should've been no bigger than a molehill.

Martha slowly got up from her chair and walked over to where Nadine was standing. She stood a head shorter than Nadine. Her eyes slowly traveled down the length of the woman and rested on her belly. "When's the last time you had yo' menses?"

Nadine nervously cleared her throat as she searched her memory. "I'm 'bout two weeks late."

Martha frowned. That would make her about a month along. "You shoulda come to me sooner."

"I came as soon as I . . . I didn't know fo' sho' till a few days ago." Nadine explained anxiously.

Martha turned and walked back to her chair and sat back down. "Mos' of the time it ain't a problem if you catch it early on. You might be too late," she said indifferently.

Nadine bit back her frustration. If she could've spit in Martha's face and slammed the door on her way out, she would've. This old fool was wasting time and Nadine didn't have time to waste. "I came as soon as I knew," she snapped. "Now are you gon' help me or what?"

Nadine couldn't have this child. Edward would know it wasn't his and he'd kill her before he'd let her give birth to it.

"Watcho tongue with me, gal." Martha warned, spitting in her can again. "You come here to me, I didn't come to you."

Nadine took a deep breath. She walked over to the chair closest to Martha and sat down. Tears threatened to fall from her eyes, but she refused to let them. "I need yo' help, Miss Martha," she said, calmly. "Can't you do somethin'?"

"'Course I can," Martha said matter-of-factly. "But we gon' have to get started soon 'fo too much mo' time pass. You done waited too long already, but I done had women come through here who waited longer than you. You gon' have to do 'xactly what I tell you, though."

"What do I have to do?" Nadine asked anxiously, feeling optimistic for the first time in days. If Martha told her she'd have to stand on her head in the middle of a cotton field, she'd do it. The last thing she needed was a baby by Charles Brooks. If he ever found out, it would be as bad as if her husband discovered the truth. Charles was in love, or so he said. And he'd probably have the nerve to think he could take care of her and this child. He'd show how silly he was and expect her to leave Edward and be with him because of this baby. The time she'd spent with Charles was nothing more than what it was. Despite all his promises about what he'd do for her, he had no idea of what it was to take care of a woman like Nadine. Not like Edward. Charles's only purpose in her life had been to give her the kind of pleasure Edward never could, but that was all. He'd never been good for much else, and having a child by him was out of the question.

"I'm gon' make you a tea. You follow my instructions and you be jus' fine."

"It's that simple?"

"Killin' a chil' ain't never simple, Mrs. Cooper." Martha said seriously.

"It ain't no chil' if it ain't born yet." She said defensively.

Martha laughed. "You ain't very bright. Is you, gal?"

Nadine's irritability was starting to show through and before she let her temper get the best of her, she hurried and asked, "How much is it gon' cost me, Miss Martha?"

"Yo' husband know you here?" Martha asked, knowing the answer before she'd posed the question.

"That ain't yo' business."

"His neither, apparently. He mus' not be the daddy." A mischeivous gleam sparkled in her eye.

Nadine glared at her. "It don't pay to get in other folks' business, Miss Martha."

"You brung yo' business to me, Mrs. Cooper." Martha said coyly. "But jus' so's you know, I can't help but get in folks' business doin' the kinda work I do. Bringin' life into the world and gettin' rid of one . . . make a woman nosey by necessity."

Nadine rose to her feet. Her business here was finished for now. The seed of relief was beginning to set in, knowing the midwife would help her with her problem. "When can I get my tea, Miss Martha?" Nadine asked, walking towards the door.

"I gotta make it up, gal, and that's gon' take a few days. I don't jus' keep that stuff layin' 'round the house fo' any fool to get. That mess can kill you if you ain't careful."

"So I got to come back?" Arrogance washed over her face.

"Only if you want it. But now . . . if you and the daddy . . . whoever that is, change yo' mind . . . then naw, baby." Martha smiled and winked. "You ain't got to come back."

Nadine shot her a look of warning, unable to hold her tongue any longer. "You need to mind who you talkin' to, ol' woman."

Martha leaned forward and locked her eyes onto Nadine's. "Who am I talkin' to, Nadine Cooper? A whore? I might go as far to say I respect yo' husband on occasion, but Lawd know I ain't got none fo' yo' cheatin' ass, gal." Nadine started to protest, but Martha interrupted her. "And don't bother gettin' smart with me neither. You needs me mo' than I'm ever gon' needs you. You come back in two days and I'll have yo' tea ready fo' you. It'll cost you twenty-five dollars and that's as cheap as you gon' get 'round these here parts, lessin' you wanna drive over to Tyler County and get Sincerely Baker to do it fo' you. But as far along as you is, she might be inclined to put you on a dirty table and take a rusty coat hanger to yo' ass," Martha taunted, knowing full well that that wasn't the case. Nadine looked frightened by the thought, which Martha relished. That girl needed to be afraid of something. "And you too pretty a girl to be layin' up on dirty tables."

Twenty-five dollars was an awful lot of money, and Martha's palms itched just thinking about it. Normally she would've never charged a woman that much money, but Nadine could afford it, and that was the difference.

On her way out of the house Nadine bumped into Roberta, who'd been listening on the other side of the door. "All y'all got a penchant for nosiness, I see," she said angrily.

Roberta's eyes twinkled as she watched Nadine hurry down the steps and practically run towards her car. "Yes, ma'am."

A Fire That Always Keeps on Burnin'

That voice inside her was always whispering to her about something or other. A long time ago, it used to sound like BettAnn. Ever since she'd buried BettAnn, though, it just sounded familiar, but like no one in particular. And right after Nadine Cooper drove off, it told her, *Finish up them chores, Roberta, so you can run and tell Danny 'bout that woman comin' over here. Hurry up, girl!* And that's exactly what she did. Roberta finished her work, then ran in the direction of Danny's house, taking the shortcut through the woods behind Ma Violet's old house. Ma Violet had been dead for two summers, and the sound of voices coming from the direction of the house surprised Roberta. As soon as she realized that it was Charles and Nadine, she quickly crouched behind the bushes before either of them saw her.

"Whatchu mean we ain't seein' each other no mo'?" Charles smirked. He reached over to Nadine and ran his finger up and down her arm. "Whatchu call what we doin' right now? I'd say we seein' each other jus' fine."

Nadine abruptly stepped back and folded her arms in front of her. "I said what I mean, Charles. After today, me and you is over! And that's it!"

Charles suddenly looked agitated. "What I do now, Deen? C'mon—tell me. I know I must've done somethin', but I can't fix it if you don't tell me what it is. What? You jus' want me to say I'm sorry?" Charles placed the palm of his hand against his chest, bowed slightly at the waist, and rendered a heartfelt, "I'm sorry, honey. I'm sorry fo' whatever it is I done. Now," he stepped closer to her, "is that better?"

"You ain't heard a word I jus' said. Have you, boy?"

Charles winced. Even from where Roberta hid, she saw it.

"I done tol' you 'bout callin' me boy, Deen," he said, sternly. "I tol' you I don't like it."

"Oh, you done tol' me, alright." Nadine dropped her arms to her sides, and this time she stepped into him. "But I don't know what else to call you since you don't act like nothin' else."

Agitation rained all over him, but Nadine didn't seem to care. Roberta would've cared. In fact, she did care, and if she could've gotten away with it, she'd have jumped up from where she was hiding and slapped that woman right across the mouth for talking to him like that.

"You tryin' me, Deen!" Charles pointed his finger in her face, but Nadine slapped his hand away.

"No, I'm tellin' you, Charles. From now on, you gon' stay away from me, and you gon' stay away from my husband, too."

"Whatcho husband got to do with this, Nadine? You ain't gave a shit 'bout yo' husband when we was together befo'! All of a sudden you givin' a shit 'bout him now?"

"Me and my husband ain't yo' bus'ness, Charles."

"Naw, he ain't my bus'ness. But you been my bus'ness in that barn over yonder. Ain't you, Nadine?"

Nadine slapped his face.

Roberta fell back on her bottom, but quickly sat up to see what he'd do.

Hit her back, Charles! she screamed in her mind. Why didn't he just hit her in her back?

Charles rubbed his cheek and then smiled. It wasn't a sweet smile, though. Roberta didn't like it, and she hoped she'd never see him smile at her like that.

"That ol' man buy you a new dress, honey? He get you a new ring, or that hat you wearin'?" His tone was cold. Nadine stood rigidly in front of him, balling up her fists like she was ready to hit him again.

"Or has he been born again and can give you what you been gettin' from me all this time?" He winked.

"Regardless of whatchu might think, Charles, I can live jus' fine without you all up on me, 'cause I got me a real man at home, who know how to take care of my needs. You ain't never gon' be able to take care of me the way he can—and you know it, jus' like I do." Charles was a hard-headed boy and Nadine knew that being cruel was the only way to get through to him sometimes. She'd remembered that from when his little nappy-headed ass was running around playing with her brother Jesse.

"Yeah . . . you tell yo'self that, Deen," he said, trying not to sound as hurt as he was. "Maybe you might believe it, but I know better. Deep down, you know better too." He pointed in the direction of the road. "Maybe it's best if you got back in yo' man's car and go home. Try and peel you off some of that good lovin' I been givin' you from his ol' ass, then come back when you realize what you missin' out on, 'cause all the money in the worl' can't buy what I can give you."

"To hell witchu, Charles!" Nadine swung again, but this time Charles caught her by the wrist before she could land the blow.

Hit her! Roberta wanted to jump up and yell.

"You gon' miss me, Deen," Charles leaned in close to her. "You gon' miss the hell outta me, and you know it." He kissed her, but Nadine quickly jerked away and ran back towards her car.

"I'll die befo' I miss the likes of yo' ass, boy!"

Charles laughed sarcastically, "Naw, girl! You gon' miss me long fo' that happens. And when you do, you know where I'll be. I ain't gon' hol' no grudges, honey. Not witchu, Deen. Not ever witchu, girl!"

Roberta could hardly believe her ears. She watched as Nadine disappeared into the brush, leaving Charles planted in the ground like a tree. Had Nadine told him about the child she was carrying? Roberta wondered. But why would she tell him about it if she'd come to Miss Martha's asking for her help to get rid of it? Roberta wouldn't put it past Nadine to tell him, though. She had some ugly ways about her, and Roberta wouldn't have been the least bit surprised if Nadine had told him that she was going to have his baby.

Whap! Without thinking, Roberta swatted at a mosquito on her arm.

"Who there?" he called out, startled, in her direction.

Roberta felt like her heart was stuck in her throat, and that she would choke on it for sure.

Charles slowly walked over to where she was hiding. "Who there, I said!"

Roberta squeezed her eyes shut, held her breath, and hesitantly came out of her hiding place.

Charles couldn't believe his eyes. He recognized the girl almost immediately. "What the hell you doin'?"

Roberta felt so ashamed, she could hardly bring herself to even look at him. "I wasn't doin' nothin'," she whispered.

He eyed her suspiciously. "How long you been here?"

"Not long."

"Whatchu hear?" Charles prodded angrily.

Roberta didn't answer.

"I said, whatchu hear, girl!"

She'd heard pretty much everything, but the last thing she wanted was for him to think she'd been eavesdropping, which she had been, but he didn't need to know that. Frustration filled her eyes with tears as Roberta struggled inside herself to come up with one good lie. For the first time in her life she couldn't find one, and Roberta stood face-to-face with Charles and the truth.

"I ain't heard much of nothin'!" Roberta said defensively.

"You didn't hear much of nothin'? Well, how *much* of nothin' didn't you hear?" Charles asked sharply.

She'd managed to get herself in a predicament that had no way out, except through him. There was no going around or over or under the situation, and she realized that that anything she had to gain or lose all came down to this moment. Roberta felt a knot swell in her stomach that reminded her of the one she used to get right before she got a whipping.

"I heard her say that she didn't want to be witchu no mo'." Her voice quivered, and Roberta defied him with a look to try and slap her face the way Nadine had slapped his. He might break her heart, but there was no way she'd stand there and let him hit her. "And I saw her hit you 'cross the face too. I sure did. I saw her try and hit you again, too, and I—"

"All right. Damn! All right." Between this girl and Nadine,

Charles decided he'd had about all he could stand of women for one day.

Charles sat down on the tree stump behind him, held his head in his hands, and sighed.

"Why you like that woman so much?" Roberta asked hesitantly.

Charles shook his head. "Why don't you mind yo' bus'ness?"

Roberta crossed her arms in front of her. "Nadine Cooper ain't even that pretty if you ask me."

"Yeah, well, didn't nobody ask you."

"Not to mention she got a husband. What kinda woman go runnin' 'round with another man if she got herself a husband?"

"Why don't you take yo' nosey ass home?"

Roberta was offended. "My ass ain't nosey. Everybody in town know she got a husband and they probably all know she cheatin' on him, too."

Women wrecked his nerves sometimes. There always seemed to be too much of them, or not enough. Nadine had lost her mind for no good reason, and this one, Roberta, had buried her nose in business that was his. All he could do was shake his head.

Whap! Whap! Roberta slapped her leg and her arm, then brushed off the bodies of dead mosquitoes.

"Ain't nothin' worse than a nosey woman," he muttered to himself, then looked at Roberta. "Can't nobody know what went on out here tonight—Roberta? That yo' name?"

She nodded and smiled that he'd remembered.

"There'd be a whole heap of mess goin' on if you tol'." Charles stared at her and decided just by looking at her that she had a big mouth and that before the sun came up in the morning, word of him and Nadine would be all over town.

"I won't say nothin', 'cause it ain't nobody's bus'ness no how," Roberta said anxiously. Her heart swelled because he trusted her.

She couldn't explain how she knew it, but she did. Roberta sat down next to him.

"That's right," he said quickly. "It ain't nobody's bus'ness. 'Specially yo's."

She was offended. "You act like that's all I do is scoot 'round in bushes listen' to folks carryin' on like y'all did," she spat back.

"Don't you?"

She rolled her eyes. "If you mus' know, I was on my way to my friend's house and this is the way I always go. You and Nadine Cooper ain't got no mo' rights to Ma Violet's yard than I do."

Charles couldn't help but laugh. "Oh, is that right? So who died and made you queen?"

"Ain't nobody have to die and make me nothin'," she said smartly. "I do what I wanna do, and when I wanna do it. But that don't mean I was out lookin' fo' you to see whatchu doin', 'cause I really don't care."

Charles listened to this girl and suddenly found her amusing. Two days ago she'd been too shy to barely look him in the eyes, and now she was sitting here trying to argue with him when she was the one who'd been wrong. It was hard for him not to laugh.

"Oh, I think you care. I think you care mo' than you lettin' on." His eyes twinkled. Instinct told him that she had a crush on him.

"She ain't even pretty if you ask me," she said, again quickly changing the subject. "Everybody think Nadine Cooper is so pretty but I think she look like a catfish."

Charles laughed. "A catfish? How you figure she look like a catfish?"

She shrugged. "She got them big bug-eyes way far apart on her head, and that wide mouth, and she sho' nuff the same color as one."

"Sound like jealousy talkin', if you ask me."

Roberta huffed. "Jealous? Of Nadine Cooper? Ain't nobody jealous of that old ugly woman! Shoot! Least I don't look like no fish."

Charles smiled at her antics. He stared at her for a moment. "Naw, girl. You sho' don't look like no fish," he said sincerely. "As a matter of fact, if you was a lil' bit older, I might be back here carryin' on witchu 'stead of Mrs. Cooper."

Charles cursed himself for toying with this girl. He knew better, but sometimes he couldn't help himself. Flirting came easy to him, which had always been his problem. He held back the urge to reach out and touch this girl, even to kiss her, before sending her home. The sun had set down, leaving dusk behind to envelop Roberta and remind him of how soft she looked.

She shrugged. "I think you too good fo' her."

"Oh, you do?"

"I think you a good man, Charles. Better than what she deserves. And 'stead of wastin' yo' time with her, you need a woman who know how good a man you are. That's all I'm sayin'," she explained apprehensively. "You could have any woman you wanted. I know that fo' a fact. I seen the way women look at you." She stared into his eyes, hoping he understood that he could have her if he wanted.

Charles nodded, and he understood. It was hard not to be tempted, but he knew better. At least, for the time being he knew better. Next time he might not be so wise. "It's gettin' late, sugah. You best get goin'."

Roberta glanced up at the darkening sky. It was too late to go to Danny's, and Miss Martha would have a fit if she weren't home soon, but the last thing she wanted to do was leave him.

"You want me to walk you home?" he asked, hoping she wouldn't, and he could avoid the temptation of kissing her goodnight.

She shook her head, smiled, and before he knew what was happening, Roberta leaned in and kissed him squarely on the lips, then ran away from him as fast as she could.

Charles sat where he was and watched Roberta disappear one more time.

I Don't Want No Sugar

Roberta watched intently as Martha chopped the squaw-root for Nadine Cooper's tea, which looked like nothing more than weeds to her. Martha had always said that that was the beauty of herbs.

"They don't look like much of nothin' growin' in the ground, but they full of all kinds of healin' powers mos' folks don't know nothin' 'bout."

"You learn to make this from yo' granny muh from Africa too?" Roberta asked.

"Naw, chil'," Martha explained patiently. "But my great-granny who was Sioux Injun taught it to my granny muh on my daddy's side. Injun's know 'bout potions too 'cause they wasn't much better off than black folk sometimes and had to figure out they own medicine too."

"Why you call it squawroot?"

Martha chuckled. "'Cause it's fo' sqaws, chil'. It's a women's root to fix all kind of things," she said, carefully measuring the herb into a bowl. "'Cludin' babies by a man who ain't yo' husband," she muttered.

There were times when Roberta despised the old woman and her blatant contradictions and views. As far as Roberta was concerned, Martha didn't know if she was coming or going and seemed perfectly content in some stale, gray place in between. But then there were times like this, when her confusion seemed to blend together perfectly, balanced, strangely enough, in a way that made more sense than any thinking Roberta could've ever imagined on her own.

"You think Mr. Cooper know she don't want this baby?" Roberta asked innocently, knowing full well that Nadine's husband wasn't the father of the child she was carrying.

If the midwife heard Roberta's question, she chose not to answer it. Martha turned to the stove to check the water. "Hand me them roots, gal," Martha said intently, and then carefully measured three teaspoons of black cohosh for every cup of water in the pot.

"Get me that mason jar on the flo' in the back of the pantry, Roberta."

Roberta did as she was told. There was nothing but crushed dried leaves in that jar and Roberta wrinkled up her nose, wondering what kind of power could possibly be held captive in them.

"What's this fo', Miss Martha?"

"These here is called pinny ro'." Martha carefully measured three teaspoons into the pot. "Don't mess 'round with no pinny ro'," she warned. "These here strong enough to kill a woman if it ain't used right. Make a woman bleed to death, 'specially the oil, and I keeps that in a special place, hidden away real careful, way on the back shelf in the cupboard so it don't end up in my greens." Martha laughed at her own joke. "Some fools go out there and try to mix together they own tea. End up bleedin' and can't stop it." Martha shook her head. "If'n you ask me, havin' a baby ain't never so bad as bleedin' to death."

Roberta couldn't argue with that.

"He might not want her to get rid of it," Roberta said, continuing to probe.

"What he don't know won't hurt 'em," she said indifferently. "She gon' be pickin' this up tomorrow evenin', but I ain't gon' be here. I got to go to Paris to sit with my cousin Faye. You know she ain't been feelin' too good. I told her I'd bring her some of my granny muh's soup to help her feel better. Ain't nothin' like granny muh's soup to fix what's ailin' you."

"What time is Mrs. Cooper comin'?"

"Sometime tomorrow is all I know. I'm gon' brew this up and put it in a jar. All you got to do is hand it to her and make sho' she hand you my twenty-five dollars." Martha turned to Roberta, propped her hand on her hip, and stared intently at her. "Now, make sho' you tell her to drank one cup, fo' times a day. No more, no less. You hear me?"

Roberta nodded.

"One cup, fo' times a day fo' fo' days and that's all," she repeated emphatically.

"Yes, ma'am." Roberta picked up the jar and stared at it, entranced by the power hidden in the unsuspecting herbs. How many times had she trampled over poisons like squawroot and pennyroyal, thinking they were nothing more than weeds? But then, that was how magic worked most of the time. It didn't look like much to the naked eye, but if a person had been privileged to have granny muhs in their lives, who knew the secrets of the earth, anything could happen.

*   *   *

Nadine sashayed arrogantly into the house and stared down her nose at Roberta. "Martha here?" She didn't like Martha and she didn't care much for Martha's child either, Nadine decided. Roberta had a disrespectful air about her that didn't set well with her.

"She had to leave," Roberta said quietly.

"She leave something for me?" Nadine asked, looking regal and fine and not at all like a woman in desperate need of an abortion. If Roberta didn't know better, she'd think maybe she'd dreamed the whole thing.

Roberta walked over to the table and returned to Nadine, holding the jar. Nadine reached out to take it, but Roberta abruptly pulled it away just in time. "You got the money?"

Nadine clenched her teeth, then reached deep into her handbag and handed Roberta a small roll of bills at the same time she snatched the merchandise from Roberta's hand. "I ain't got all day."

Roberta carefully counted the money. "Don't drink more than fo' cups a day for fo' days. That's very important."

"Or else what?" she asked impatiently.

"It'll make you sick. Real sick." Roberta stated simply, holding Nadine's gaze with her own. Nadine shifted uncomfortably, then turned towards the door.

The moss-colored mixture in the jar looked harmless enough, but that crazy old woman had mixed up a concoction strong enough to rid her of the child she was carrying, and Nadine shuddered uncontrollably at the thought.

Just before leaving, she turned to Roberta. "How will I know it worked?"

Roberta shrugged. "You can't help but to know. Miss Martha say that when you start yo' menses . . . it's workin'. And she say you might bleed quite a bit . . . but jus' take it like I tol' you and you ought to be fine."

Roberta smiled as Nadine let the door close behind her.

* * *

Roberta gasped at the transformation. Nadine Cooper didn't even look like herself anymore. The fancy woman who'd stepped out of that red car looking flawless in her silk dress, just the other day, had melted into a pitiful heap right in front of Roberta's eyes. It was such a shame, Roberta thought, shaking her head. A shame that Mrs. Cooper would let herself go like that. And what about Charles? What would he think if he saw her looking this way?

Roberta slowly approached Nadine, who was bent over a large tin. Beads of sweat glistened on Nadine's forehead, while she scrubbed *the* white garments feverishly against the ribbed washboard. Slowly she raised her eyes in Roberta's direction. Nadine blinked several times, then squinted, trying to clear the blurred image of the face making its way towards her.

"Afternoon, Mrs. Cooper," Roberta said, smiling and standing with her hands buried deep in the pockets of her coveralls. "Miss Martha sent me over here to check on you".

Nadine wiped her brow with the back of her hand, and stared up at the girl hidden behind that tomboy façade. This one was sneaky, she thought, looking past Roberta's baggy blue jeans and baseball cap. A woman lurked behind those clothes, no doubt, as treacherous as women could be, but this one was sinister because she worked so hard to appear unassuming. Her eyes gave her away, though. Something ominous lurked behind them. Nadine caught her breath as panic began to well up inside her.

Madness. That's all it is, Nadine thought she heard Roberta say.

"What?" She blinked, unsure of whether Roberta had really said it, or if she'd imagined it.

"I said, Miss Martha want to know how you feelin'? She sent me over to see 'bout you," Roberta lied.

Nadine's bottom lip quivered as she fought to hold on to her frustration. "How come she didn't tell me that shit was gon' make me so sick?"

She ain't such a pretty woman at all, Roberta thought, studying her hair that was matted on her head and the ashiness of her skin, once dark and shimmering like polished black leather shoes. She couldn't help but wonder what a handsome man like Charles had ever seen in this woman. Roberta glanced at two piles of white garments lying at Nadine's feet. In one pile lay rolls of freshly washed undergarments, rung out and ready to hang up on the line. In the other pile lay crumpled stained underpants, smelling like something that wasn't natural.

"You takin' the tea like I told you?" Roberta asked innocently.

"'Course I am!" Nadine said through gritted teeth. "And why'd she send you over here? How come she didn't come her damn self?" Nadine's hands trembled. Martha should have come to see about her personally, not send a impish little girl in her place.

Roberta shrugged. "She said to tell you she'd be by soon. Jus' ain't no need right now. You still got another day or two to go. She gon' come by after you drink it all up."

"You tell that ol' woman I done bled this chile' out by now and I need her to tell me how to stop it!" Nadine growled. "You tell her she need to tell me—" Nadine trembled.

Roberta placed her hand sympathetically on the woman's shoulder. Nadine cringed uncontrollably. "I'll talk to Miss Martha fo' you and tell her you ain't feelin' well. Maybe she can do somethin'," she assured her. Roberta smiled sweetly, then turned and started to walk away. She turned to Nadine one last time and smiled. "By the way, Mrs. Cooper. Yo' nose is bleedin'."

Without thinking, Nadine quickly snatched up a pair of soiled undergarments, pressed them to her nose, and hurried past Roberta into the house.

*   *   *

One thing was for certain, Roberta thought, smiling as she strolled in the direction of Danny's house. There was no way she'd ever be as dumb as that fool, Nadine. What woman with any sense at all would get herself into that kind of predicament? All of her suffering could've been avoided if she'd have just been a wife to her husband instead of being a whore to Charles. Marriage was a sacred thing, and God punished fools for treading on sacred things. That had been Nadine's whole problem. Whatever happened to that woman served her right, and she had it coming.

She'd only added about a teaspoon of that pennyroyal oil to the tea Martha had made, enough to make sure that Nadine never had that baby. Charles might decide he couldn't leave that woman alone if he ever found out she had his child. Fate. That's all it was.

And Jump into the Ocean

N adine Brown . . . Nadine Brown," Charles muttered to himself. "Whatchu done to me, girl?" Charles knew the answer to that question. Nadine had torn him up inside, that's all she'd done.

He'd intended to drive right by the place and keep on going, but before he knew what was happening, Charles had stopped his truck and parked outside the barn where he and Nadine had been meeting. He hadn't seen or heard from her in days, and at first all he could think was, "Good riddance." Charles sat on the ground, leaning his head back against the wall, reliving images of him and Nadine entwined on the blanket that still lay crumpled across the floor. He slowly opened his eyes and smiled at the vision of her, dark and smooth and slippery wet beneath him.

"Don't stop, Charles," he heard her moan. *"Don't ever stop."*

And he never would've stopped, either. Not in a million years. But Nadine had been the one to stop it, Charles thought grimly.

"To hell with that woman," he muttered.

Charles took a deep breath and held it for a moment. When he let it go, he'd hoped thoughts of her would go with it, but Nadine lingered on him like she tended to do sometimes. He had no business fretting over that woman because she'd proven she just wasn't worth it. Nadine Brown might've been worth it, but Nadine Cooper wasn't worth a damn. Not anymore. That girl wouldn't have known what a real man was if he'd walked up and spit in her eye. She'd had the nerve to to call him a boy every chance she got, when in fact she was nothing more than a girl—a greedy girl, dripping all over Old Man Cooper because he had a little money. Charles chuckled to himself at the thought of Nadine sitting on top of that old man, trying to squeeze lemonade out of nothing but dried lemons. She had told him, *"Edward don't know the first thing 'bout makin' a woman feel good, Charles. Not like you. He can't do it the way you do—the way I like."*

But that girl had dug her own grave, Charles concluded. She'd tossed him aside as if he'd never mattered at all. Never mind how he felt or what he might've wanted. Nadine didn't care and she'd made that clear.

Charles lit up another cigarette. Yeah, to hell with her. He'd always put her too high up on a pedestal, anyway. Higher than she deserved to be, and she'd jumped down from it real ugly, right on top of his head. She'd come around, though, and Charles knew it wouldn't take long. Nadine was hot in the drawers, and no amount of money in the world could replace what she needed to cool them off. That old man couldn't do it. She was a fool to even think he could. It wouldn't be long before Nadine came back, batting her eyes and switching those big-ass hips of hers in front of him, expecting him to come running like he was thirsty and she was a cool glass of water. Charles smiled. Of course he'd take her back, but not too soon and not so easily as she probably expected. He'd take his time and make her wait awhile. He'd make her work for him, and when it was all over, Nadine would be back in his arms again where she belonged. Maybe this time that woman would come to her senses and realize she needed to stay put. That's what usually happened when people came close to losing something good—they appreciated it more and took better care of it the next time around, and they'd do whatever it took to keep it.

Roberta's heart raced ahead of her. The closer she got to the barn, the more certain she was that it was Charles's truck parked outside. Roberta stopped for a moment and searched frantically for Nadine's car. Was she there too? She didn't see Nadine's car, but if she'd parked in back like she usually did, then—

She cut through the open field, hardly noticing the wildflowers and weeds whipping against her bare calves. Roberta's eyes scanned up and down the dirt road ahead of her, expecting at any moment to see Nadine Cooper speeding towards her, racing to get to Charles before Roberta could.

She'd given up on this old barn, thinking that Charles had given up on it, too, since he wasn't seeing Nadine anymore. Besides, the last time Roberta had seen Nadine, she didn't look to be in any shape to traipse around in barns or woods with anybody. But maybe she'd gotten better, Roberta thought. Maybe Nadine had given up that child she was carrying and felt good enough to meet Charles out here after all.

Wild images ran through her mind that Roberta wished she could swat away like flies. Images of Nadine dressed up fancy and clean, gleaming like a new penny, throwing her arms around Charles's neck and kissing him square on the lips.

"Oh, Charles!" Nadine would exclaim, grinning from ear to ear. "I feel so much better now, and I missed you terribly! I did! I really did!"

She was flooded with images of Charles tearing away at Nadine's pretty dress until it fell away and his eyes lit up like she was the only present under the Christmas tree and she was all his.

No! That can't happen, Roberta! You can't let that happen!

She hurried as fast as she could to get to him before Nadine did. "I hope I ain't too late! I hope I ain't—"

Roberta stopped for a moment, breathless and anxious, and raised her fingertips to her lips. The warmth of his lips was still on hers. It had stayed there there and sometimes, she'd swear, his lips were still pressed against hers. Her stomach fluttered at the thought. She'd hardly been able to think about anything else but him since the last time she'd seen him. Roberta had surprised herself more than Charles by kissing him so abruptly, but she couldn't have stopped herself if she'd wanted to. Her only regret was that she'd hurried off so quickly after it happened. One kiss hadn't been enough. It had only whet her appetite for him more, and now he was all that mattered. Roberta picked up her pace, hurrying towards the barn. She had to get to him before Nadine Cooper did. She'd lose him if Nadine got to him first, and whatever it took to keep him, Roberta would do it. She'd sacrifice herself for him; throw herself at his feet if she had to. Nadine wasn't getting him back.

Charles hurried to his feet at the sight of Roberta bursting through the door. "What the—"

Roberta stopped a few feet in front of him, breathless from running so far and so fast. She looked around the barn, then let out a sigh of relief, knowing she'd got there first, and rested her eyes on him.

The Good Lawd help those who help themselves.

How many times had Miss Martha told her that? And how many more times had she dismissed those words as meaningless because they'd come from Miss Martha? And why were they prevalent in her mind now, standing in front of this man she loved more than her own life?

Roberta had prayed to a hallowed moon and any other moon that would listen, and burned potions in the middle of the night for this man. She'd helped to put his unborn child to rest, and maybe even Nadine Cooper along with it. She'd tossed and turned, dreaming of him and of being in his arms, and now it was finally time for her to "help herself" and be the woman she knew he needed.

Charles looked over her shoulder and then finally at Roberta, who was standing in front of him, looking like a wild animal. There was something in her eyes he'd never seen before, something he couldn't explain, and it made him uneasy.

"You alright, Roberta?" he asked hesitantly. Charles slowly stepped towards her, then reached out his hand and rested it on her shoulder. "Maybe I need to getchu home?"

Roberta shook her head, then swallowed. "I jus'—need you, Charles."

He looked confused and concerned. "Whatchu need, sugah? Whatchu need me to do?"

She stepped into his arms, kissed his cheeks and chest, and whispered, "Love me, Charles."

Charles suddenly stepped back and gently pushed her away. He didn't like this, not one bit. Then it came to him that maybe someone was playing a trick on him. He pushed past Roberta, swung open the barn door, and looked outside to see who was out there, waiting—laughing. Could've been Grady, his best friend. Grady was always playing around like this. Or maybe—it could've even been Nadine, testing him to see how far he'd go with another woman. Like she even gave a damn. Roberta tugged on his arm and pulled him back inside.

"What's wrong witchu, girl? Who you come here with?"

"I didn't come with nobody," she said desperately. "I'm here—'cause I saw yo' truck, and I—"

"You what?" he snapped.

Before he knew what was happening, Roberta quickly began unbuttoning the front of her dress and let it slide down her shoulders to the floor.

"Roberta? Girl, what the hell you call yo'self doin'?"

Next she slipped off her shoes, and all that was left was her slip.

"Put yo' clothes back on, Roberta!" he demanded. "You hear me?"

Roberta's breast pressed against her slip. It was hard not to notice her nipples peeking back at him.

There would be no turning back and no running away this time. Roberta had made it up in her mind that she'd see it through, no matter what, to the end this time. She wanted Charles Brooks and she could see in his eyes that he wanted her too. Not Nadine Cooper but Roberta Brooks, standing in front of him, alone and nearly naked. She was giving herself to him. All he had to do was reach out and take her.

Charles watched in awe as this girl's slip slid down her body. Whatever he'd had to say had lost its way somewhere in his throat and all he could do was stare. Roberta was perfect and all that perfection made him grow hard in his pants.

Roberta slowly approached him and wrapped her arms around his waist, then stood on the tips of her toes and kissed him softly, slowly, on the lips

No turnin' back, Roberta. It's too late.

Charles meant to push her away, but as soon as his hands touched the soft skin on her arms, they greedily found their way to her back. He pulled her closer to him and gradually eased his tongue in between her lips. That was all it took.

Roberta grimaced beneath him, but Charles didn't seem to

notice. She'd willed herself there, under him in the same place she'd seen Nadine, and all the pain in the world didn't matter. It had all been worth it, she thought, looking up at him through the tears that had pooled in her eyes. He'd been worth it, and she'd suffer all her days for his namesake. Where had she heard that before—Miss Martha? It was probably biblical too, and Charles was certainly worthy of biblical.

"You sho' you alright?" he'd asked one last time before dropping her off. Roberta had insisted that he let her out of the truck far enough down the road from the house, out of sight from Miss Martha.

She smiled. "I'm alright."

Charles nodded. He had no idea what else to say. They'd ridden side by side without hardly saying anything at all to each other. He hadn't expected ever to be with this girl like that, and if he had anything to say about it, it would never happen again. Roberta had just caught him off guard, and he hadn't been in his right mind lately. She sure was a sweet girl, though, he thought, gently running his finger down her cheek. Too sweet for him. Too sweet for most men. He'd been her first, and there were some parts of him that wished he could be her last, but he wasn't the man for Roberta. In time she'd realize this. Right now he knew it, and that was enough.

"Well," he said, smiling, "you get on home now."

Roberta quickly leaned in and kissed his cheek. "I'll see you later?"

Charles just smiled. "Be good."

She waited and watched his truck disappear into the horizon, then Roberta did what she'd wanted to do since it happened and pinched herself on the arm to make sure she hadn't dreamed the whole afternoon.

Miss Martha's house waited for her in the distance. As Roberta approached it, she realized how small it looked all of a sudden. Had it always been so small? she wondered. That house hadn't changed, she realized, but she had. Roberta had grown from a girl to a woman in the span of an afternoon, and she couldn't wait to tell Danny. He hadn't believed in her love for Charles or her spells. But he'd have to believe her now.

Never More to Call Your Name

I t wasn't easy living up to the facade of Edward Cooper, the wealthiest black man in Bueller, Texas, and the surrounding three counties. But he'd played the part well, for a time at least. Edward drove home, worn out from keeping up appearances—driving around in his fancy car, dressed in European suits, going that extra effort to stand taller than other men, with his shoulders pulled back and his chin up. Rich men never slouched. Rich men wore pride like it was their birthright and measured it by the size of the wad of bills in their money clip. Edward had been poor as a child, but he'd been a rich white man's bastard nigger son, who reluctantly held out his hand and took whatever Dole Lyons decided to give him. Most people never thought he deserved the things he had. They never believed he'd worked for it, earned it. But what the hell did they know? He'd earned every dime, having to suffer through nights when that white sonuvabitch would come to the house, take his mother by the elbow, and lead her to the back room. She couldn't look Edward in the eyes for days after Lyons would leave, trying to hide her shame and humiliation, but Edward had never needed to see it to know it was there.

"You my boy," Lyons would call out to him from his car before he left. He'd wink and cast a ghostly smile in the boy's direction. Edward never returned it. Lyons had given him a small fortune just before he died, eight hundred acres and the kind of money even most white men dreamed of having.

"Put yo' money in the bank, boy," he told him from his deathbed. "Be smart 'bout yo' business, and keep yo' money in a financial institution."

Edward had taken his advice and lived to regret it. The Depression had stolen his money, his land. But Edward had kept silent about it, and he'd continued to try to live up to the legacy he'd built for himself. Thank God he didn't have heirs. His first wife hadn't been able to bear children and Nadine . . . he'd never wanted children with her. By the time he'd married that girl, Edward was too old to think about raising children. Besides, Nadine was enough of a child herself, always holding out her hand and batting big brown eyes at him, smiling and going on and on about some new dress she wanted. If she'd known he was broke, she'd have left him. He knew that for certain. So, he kept up appearances, leaving the house every morning just after sunrise to take care of his "business." The truth was, he didn't have any. Edward spent most of his day driving, stopping in some juke joint for a few drinks, sitting by the river growing old, thinking of ways to keep enough money to fill that girl's hands. He'd sold off land so dirt cheap the only thing he owned now was the plot his house sat on, and he suspected that soon enough he'd have to sell that, too. And what next? Would he have to get himself a job, working for someone who'd possibly worked for him at one time?

The notion weighed heavy on him. After all, what would Edward Cooper look like, working for some fool who hardly had a pot to piss in? Who might've even called him boss? Death would be more welcomed.

Edward slowly pulled the car up in front of his house and turned off the engine. He considered what might be waiting for him when he went in. All the lights downstairs were out. Sadie, the housekeeper, had been gone for hours by then. He noticed a dim light coming from the bedroom upstairs where Nadine was probably waiting for him. A tender fondness touched his heart at the thought. He'd come to care for her in the eight years they'd been married. Nadine hadn't been much more than a child when he'd first met her, and in many ways he'd raised her and taught her how a man should be treated. She'd been hard-headed in the beginning, stubborn and defiant, threatening to leave and go back to that bordello she'd been raised in. It hadn't been easy, but he'd broken that wild spirit of hers and molded her into a woman perfectly suited for him.

"Do you love me, Edward?" she'd asked him once.

He couldn't help but laugh at her innocence. "No, Nadine. But I care deeply fo' you, honey."

Edward could tell by the expression on her face that he'd hurt her feelings, but that was fine. Sometimes he had to do that. It was what kept her pride in order, and what kept her submissive to him.

What worried him, though, was how poorly she'd been feeling lately. For the past several days he'd watched her deteriorate in front of his eyes, and no one had been able to tell him why. Nadine insisted that she was fine.

"It's a womanly issue, Edward," she'd said, trying to reassure him. "Men don't know nothin' 'bout things like this. I 'member my momma had the same thing once, maybe even twice when I was a li'l girl, and she turned out to be jus' fine."

He let himself in and hung his hat on the mahogany coatrack in the foyer before quietly walking up the stairs to the bedroom. Edward had made up his mind to put her in the car in the morning and drive her over to a doctor friend of his in Dallas. The local Doctor Walker knew more about doctoring on pigs and cows than he did people. Edward had told him so, right after he'd left a few days ago after examining Nadine.

"Nadine?" he called as he ascended the stairs. Edward strained to hear her response, but none came.

He opened the door to the dimly lit bedroom and saw her lying in bed, covered up to her chin. Edward walked over to where she was and gently touched her shoulder. "Nadine, honey. Wake up and lemme know, how you feelin'?"

Nadine never budged. Edward stared at her for several minutes, expecting her to stir at the sound of his voice. Nadine had grown obedient to him over the years, even in her sleep. But she didn't move. An unexplainable chill washed over him, and Edward's voice became trapped in his chest as he watched her lie motionless in bed. A womanly issue . . . that's how she'd explained it, but a quiet alarm had been nagging in him for days.

"Don't worry, Edward. I'm feelin' much better today."

She'd told him that this morning, just before he kissed her cheek, climbed into his car, and drove off. Catching an image of her in his rearview mirror, somehow he suspected she wasn't being truthful with him. Edward tried pushing aside the dread growing inside him and insisted on convincing himself that everything was fine. She was just sleeping, that was all. Nadine had been ill and tired, and she probably needed a good night's sleep to make her feel better. He stood for a moment and thought he'd leave her alone and let her sleep, but without thinking, Edward pulled back the quilt covering his wife. All the strength in his legs gave way and Edward stumbled back, and fell into the chair across the room. Nadine lay naked from the waist down, drowned in a claret pool.

"Nadine," he whimpered as the vision of her blurred in his eyes as tears formed in them, but the image of her bloodied sheets burned in his mind forever.

"Miss Martha," Roberta called from inside the house. "Time fo' supper. Miss Martha. You need to eat somethin'."

Martha had never made it into the house. She had planted herself in the chair on the porch right after the funeral and had stayed there, still wearing her hat and gloves, staring straight ahead. She'd been drinking since they'd gotten home, wallowing in guilt. All of a sudden Martha had lost faith in the things she'd been taught all of her life. Ever since she'd heard of Nadine's death, Martha had given into uncertainty about having done something terribly wrong. She sat with her eyes closed, measuring and remeasuring the ingredients of the tea she'd made for Nadine over again in her mind. Lord, had she somehow made a mistake? Had she missed something? What? What had she done wrong?

"Miss Martha?" Roberta said again, opening the screen door. "It's gettin' late and supper is gettin' cold."

"How I kill that girl?" Martha asked earnestly. "How in the world did I kill that girl?"

Roberta stared at the woman and felt sorry for her. Martha's eyes were glazed over from tears she'd shed at the funeral and since they'd been home.

"You didn't kill her, Miss Martha. Some things jus' happen sometimes and we can't do nothin' 'bout it. You ought to know that," she said, trying to reassure her.

Martha muttered to herself, "Two tablespoons squawroot.

Three tablespoons tickweed . . . tickweed. Did I do that right?"
She took a sip from her cup and wiped her mouth with the back
of her hand. "Did I boil the squawroot in a quart of water for five
minutes, no mo', no less? Tickweed and tansy in a—tansy. Did I
forget the tansy?"

Roberta left Martha to struggle with her memories and anguish,
and went back inside. Nadine Cooper hadn't deserved that kind of
attention, as far as Roberta was concerned. She didn't deserve Mr.
Cooper's tears or Miss Martha's heartbreak. She certainly hadn't
deserved Charles, who sat in the back of the church, occasionally
rubbing his eyes before his own tears had a chance to fall.

Roberta sat down at the table and began toying with the food
on her plate. She hadn't intended for that woman to die. Roberta
just wanted to make sure Miss Martha's potion worked, that was
all. She took a bite from her fork but tasted nothing and forced
herself to swallow. She felt bad about what had happened, not
that she hadn't wished Nadine Cooper dead enough times, but
she'd never really intended for any of her wishes to come true.
Nadine just wasn't as strong as she looked. That had to have been
it. Maybe she was already kind of a sickly woman, and Miss
Martha's tea only made matters worse. Her death had everybody
crying and falling out at the funeral, even though most of those
folks there didn't even like Nadine Cooper and talked about her
like she was a dog when she was alive. Roberta had heard them
plenty of times, calling her out her name and shaking their heads
about how shameful she was. Nadine was just supposed to drink
that tea and be done with it. But leave it to her to make a mess of
everything.

Suddenly Martha burst through the door and stared wide-eyed
at Roberta. "What did you do, chil'?" she shouted.

"Miss Martha?" Roberta asked innocently.

Martha slammed her cup down on the table and stormed in

Roberta's direction, then grabbed her by the shoulders. "What did you do to that woman?"

Roberta struggled to get free from Martha's grip. "What's wrong with you, Miss Martha?"

"What the hell did you do, I said?"

"You done had enough shine fo' one evenin', Miss Martha," Roberta reasoned.

"That woman didn't die 'cause of me! I know she didn't! I been makin' that tea since I was a chil' and I know she didn't die 'cause of me!"

"I don't know what you talkin' 'bout! I didn't do nothin'!"

Martha pleaded with her eyes for answers to questions that would ease her condemnation. "Did you do like I tol' you and rub the oil on the bottom of her feet?"

"Yes, ma'am," Roberta lied.

"Did you rub her heels?"

"Yes, Miss Martha! I did everything you tol' me."

"Her stomach, Roberta! Did you rub the oil on her—"

"I did everything you told me! I swear I did!"

"You lyin'!" Martha slapped her hard against the face. "You lyin'! You lyin'!" she screamed and shook the girl as hard as she could.

Roberta jerked free from Martha's grip. "Leave me alone!" She shouted. "I didn't do nothin'! You killed that woman, not me!"

She stumbled as she pushed past Martha and ran out the door.

"Oh, Lawd!" She heard Martha wail, drowning in penitence. "Oh, Lawd! Fo'give me, Lawd! Please—"

Roberta ran away, racing against the setting sun towards Danny's house.

She'd caught her breath by the time she arrived, composed herself, and knocked on the door. Danny's stepfather answered.

Leroy Simpson had always been an intimidating-looking man to Roberta—tall, dark, and as wide as the Red River. But Roberta couldn't help but notice fraility about him this time. A timorous shadow covered his face, and his once broad, square shoulders seemed weighted down by burdens nearly too heavy for him to bear.

"Evenin', Mr. Simpson," she said politely, composing herself. "Danny here?"

"It's late, gal. Ain't you s'posed to be home this time of day?" Even his voice lacked that threatening tone it usually carried. Before she could answer, Danny's mother pushed past him.

"Roberta?" she asked, looking concerned. "You alright?"

"Yes, ma'am. I'm jus' lookin' to talk to Danny fo' a minute or two, if you don't mind."

Danny's mother took a deep breath and squared her narrow shoulders. Leroy Simpson seemed to shrink even more in comparison. Roles had been reversed in this house. Something had happened, and the souls of these two people had switched places.

"Danny ain't here, Roberta," she said firmly, glancing accusingly at her husband out of the corner of her eye. "I sent him to stay with my brotha and his wife in Tennison, and I'm afraid he ain't comin' back no time soon."

Mrs. Simpson smiled politely and closed the door with Roberta still standing there. Roberta wasn't very far away from the house when the arguing started up:

"Of course she know! You think he didn't tell her?"

"To hell witchu, Leroy! And don't you put yo' got damned hands on me, or I swear—"

"How a man do that to a boy? How you do that and call yo'self a man?"

"Cry, motha' fucka! Cry like you made my baby cry! I don't give a shit 'bout you no' mo'!"

Danny must've told, Roberta concluded. "Why'd he have to say anything?" she muttered, walking away. Warm tears filled her eyes and escaped down her cheeks. Now who could she talk to? Danny had been her friend, but like she'd known all along, Danny had been weak. Weak enough to let his stepdaddy do those things to him and too weak to keep his mouth shut about it.

Roberta picked up her pace and began to run as fast as she could, knowing she'd probably never lay eyes on Danny again, even if he did get the courage to come back.

Close yo' eyes and turn yo' head the next time you see him, and act like you don't know who he is anymo'.

"That'll teach him!" Roberta cried. "That'll teach him to leave me here!"

Eventually she made it to the barn where she and Charles had been together, and inside sat Charles. The two were startled to see each other, and without hesitating Roberta ran over to him and wrapped her arms around him. Tears streamed down her face from the pain and sadness of losing her best friend. Roberta had never heard of Tennison, but it might as well have been the moon because she had no chance of getting there, either. And Roberta was still seething from her encounter with Martha who had no right to hit her like she did, or accuse her of lying about Nadine Cooper. She hadn't lied to Nadine, and that woman had died by her own hand.

"Roberta?" Charles asked, confused.

She raised her lips to his and kissed him. "Make love to me, Charles. Please? Please make love to me like you did the other day," she kissed his neck and shoulders.

Right or wrong, he missed Nadine. And right or wrong, he lay Roberta down on the ground, raised the hem of her skirt around her waist, and eased himself between her legs.

Oh, I've Got What It Takes

The changes that had been taking place the past few months in Roberta hadn't gone unnoticed by Martha. The awkward and indifferent tomboy Martha had become accustomed to had grown into a woman, and she had been foolish enough to think Martha would be too dumb to notice, or too drunk. But even a blind man could've seen what was happening, though Martha didn't know the boy's name. Not that it mattered. She stood over the stove, stirring the simmering pot of grits and savoring the smell of freshly brewed coffee rising up to greet her. Martha glanced out of the corner of her eye at Roberta, swaying slightly back and forth at the table, trying to hold down the contents of an empty stomach.

Martha relished the moment she'd come to know the source of the girl's ailment.

"I think I might be comin' down with somethin', Miss Martha," Roberta had told her. She'd come down with something alright,

Martha concluded. The kind of something that came from rolling around with some hot-in-the-pants boy who probably didn't know anything about nothing, which was more than this dumb-ass girl had known.

Martha filled her bowl with grits, poured herself a cup of coffee, and sat down at the table across from Roberta. She glanced up at Roberta, who had turned the color of boiled cabbage, and salt-and-peppered her grits.

"You still feelin' poorly?" Martha asked casually. "You sho' you don't want a cup of coffee? Might settle yo' stomach."

Roberta took a deep breath, then twisted her nose at the scent of Martha's strong black coffee. "No, ma'am. I think I jus' need to lay down fo' awhile."

Martha fought back laughter. *Jus' how dumb is this girl?* she thought to herself. Roberta started to get up from the table. "Set here with me fo' a spell," Martha suggested, filling her mouth with a spoonful of grits.

"I really ain't feelin' too good." Roberta stared, hypnotized by particles of Martha's breakfast pooled in one corner of her mouth. All of a sudden Roberta ran out the front door, leaned over the porch, and threw up in Martha's flower bushes.

A few minutes later she came back inside. "You feelin' better now?" Martha asked indifferently.

Roberta nodded. "You think we could get Doctor Walker out here to see what's the matter with me? I really think I need a doctor."

Martha pushed her bowl away, sipped her coffee, and sat back in her chair. "Why? He jus' gon' tell you what I already know."

Roberta went to her bed, crawled into it, and pulled the blanket up to her chin. "It do me good to be offa my feet. You think I got the flu?"

"You ain't got no damn flu, chil'," Martha chuckled.

"Doctor Walker might be able to give me somethin'. Whatchu think?"

Laughter welled up inside Martha to the point that she thought she'd burst. Hadn't this girl paid any attention to the things she'd taught her these past few years? Martha had explained to her time and time again what signs to look for in a woman who was expecting. She'd drilled them into her head, and even went so far as to make Roberta repeat them back to her just to make sure the girl was paying attention. And now this fool had the nerve to lay up there and act as though she hadn't learned a damn thing.

Martha charged over to Roberta and yanked the blanket off her.

"Miss Martha?" Roberta shrieked.

"Getcho ass up outta that bed, heffa!" Martha demanded, laughing.

Roberta stared back with a pitiful expression on her face. "But I'm sick."

"You ass ain't sick, Roberta! Yo' ass gon' have a baby, but that ain't nowhere near bein' sick! Now, get yo' fas' behind up outta that bed!" Martha grabbed Roberta by the wrist and pulled until Roberta finally rose to her feet.

Roberta was stunned. "A baby? Naw, Miss Martha. I know I can't be havin' no—"

"Who is he, gal?" Martha stood defiantly, with her fists pressed into her hips. "Who the hell is he? Can't be that li'l sissy boy you been hangin' 'round with, 'cause he gon' . . . ain't he?"

Roberta timidly nodded her head. "Yes, ma'am. I mean . . . no, Miss Martha. I ain't done nothin'!"

"Who the hell is he? And I want the truth, gal! Or I swear I'm gon' take a switch to yo' ass and whip it outta you!"

Roberta swayed slightly back and forth and dramatically

pressed the back of her hand against her forehead. "I think I'm jus' sick. I tol' you, I think I got the flu!"

"Ain't no damn virus, gal! Ain't you learnt nothin' I done taught you? You had yo' menses?" Martha glared into Roberta's face. "Answer me!"

"I . . . I . . . well, yes," she lied.

"When? You got the only pussy that bleeds in this house, gal, and I ain't seen no sign of no menses in mo' than a month. So when you have it, Roberta?"

The girl shifted uncomfortably from one foot to the other, trying to remember the last time she'd had her period, then looked into Martha's angry face and shrugged her shoulders. Roberta had been so swept up in the whirlwind of Charles that she hadn't given much thought to anything else. And what if Martha's suspicions were true, and Roberta was pregnant with Charles's baby? An anxious feeling welled up inside her of fear mixed with elation that threatened to overtake her. Of course Martha was right. She was always right about things like this. And nothing could've made Roberta happier than she was at that moment. But nothing could've scared her more, either. She hadn't been with Charles in nearly two months, since right after Nadine's funeral. The few times she had seen him in town, he never even seemed to remember who she was, and when he did acknowledge her, he'd smile politely, nod his head in her direction, and keep on going.

Martha turned and marched over to her cupboard, removed a mason jar similar to the one she'd given Nadine, and poured part of its contents into a tin cup. Then she carried it back to Roberta and thrust it at her. "Drink it," she demanded. "It might not be too late to catch it."

Roberta was appalled and swatted the cup in her hand across

the room. "Ain't nobody catchin' nothin'!" Roberta shouted. "You stay away from me with that mess. You jus' wanna kill me like you killt Nadine!" she said venomously.

"I didn't kill that woman!" Martha screamed. "I ain't never killt none of 'em and I didn't start with that one!" Guilt still plagued Martha over Nadine Cooper's death. There were times when her instinct reassured her that she'd prepared the concoction the way she should've. And instinct sometimes caused her to glance suspiciously in Roberta's direction, but Martha could never prove anything.

"I ain't drinkin' that," Roberta said determinedly. It wasn't just the memory of Nadine's death from Martha's brew that kept her from drinking it, but also the revelation that a part of Charles grew inside her body. If she could, Roberta would keep it right where it was so that she would never again be apart from him. This child connected them in a way she'd never dreamed was even possible, more than marriage, life, or death.

Martha headed back into the kitchen to get another cup. "You will drink it, Roberta. You gon' drink it 'cause I said so."

Roberta followed her, insisting on berating her. "They say she had blood comin' from everywhere, Miss Martha, from her eyes, nose, mouth, even her ears. All 'cause she drank the tea you made fo' her." Roberta stood back and crossed her arms over her chest. "I ain't drinkin' that mess. I ain't lettin' you kill me too." And she wasn't about to kill Charles's child either. If he knew about it, then surely he'd want his baby as much as she did, and he'd want Roberta too, like he'd wanted her before.

Martha abruptly turned to Roberta and slapped her hard across the face.

"You ain't never 'preciate nothin' I ever do fo' yo' li'l ass! I took you in when that tramp of a momma of yo's laid up with that dead man, then put a bullet in her head!"

Roberta jumped up and screamed back at Martha. "Don't you ever let one word 'bout my momma come out of yo' big mouth again!"

Martha slapped her again and again. "I ain't takin' care of yo' bastard chil'! I ain't doin' it!"

Suddenly Roberta balled up her fist and punched Martha hard in the stomach. Martha's wide eyes locked onto Roberta as she slowly sank down to the floor on her knees, and for a moment there was silence.

Roberta was shocked by what she'd just done. There was no denying she'd wanted to do it a thousand times over the years, but there was no way she ever thought she could go through with it. After all, Miss Martha had taken her in and cared for her when nobody else would. But sometimes she'd go too far, and this was one of those times. "My chil' ain't no bastard! I know who the daddy is! You a bastard, Martha! You ain't nothin' but a bastard yo'self!"

Martha managed to crawl over to her rocking chair, pulled herself up into it, and eventually caught her breath. Roberta stood in the doorway, prepared to run if she had to. Martha stared wearily at the girl and rubbed her belly. Lord, she was too old for all this mess. She'd grown tired of Roberta, and she was too old to be taking care of another woman's child, especially a woman who hit her like Roberta had just done. "Who the daddy then, 'Berta? 'Cause he gon' have to be the one to take care of you from now on. I can't do it no mo'. I won't."

Roberta trailed behind Martha on the way to Charles's house. Martha knocked on the door and Miss Meryle answered. "Martha?" she smiled, looking surprised to see her. "How you doin'?"

Martha's expression was serious. "I'm lookin' fo' yo' boy, Meryle, Charles. He home?"

The woman looked over Martha's shoulder to Roberta, standing behind her with her head down. "He out back. Is everything alright?" she asked, concerned.

Martha shook her head. "No. No, it ain't."

Charles was working in the backyard, chopping up a tree that had fallen over during the last storm and piling up the wood to be used for fire once it started getting cold.

"Charles Brooks!" Martha called out.

Charles turned to see Miss Martha, followed by his mother and Roberta. His heart sank into his stomach.

"Yes, ma'am?" he said, wiping the sweat from his brow.

Martha reached out, grabbed Roberta by the wrist, and pulled her up next to her. Roberta's eyes never left the ground. "This here is Roberta Adams and she say you the daddy of the baby she gon' have. And I say, if that's the case, then you need to do right by her and marry her. 'Cause I can't take care of her no mo' and I sho' ain't takin' care of no baby that ain't mine."

Charles stood speechless, staring among the three women until his gaze finally rested on Roberta—sweet Roberta, soft to touch and kiss. Just by looking at the girl, he knew that there was no use arguing. He and Roberta had been together, and the small voice of reason lurking in the back of his mind reminded him that he should've left that girl alone.

But Charles had been a fool, choosing carelessness and his fondness for pretty thighs over common sense.

"Charles?" Miss Meryle looked confused. "You been with this girl like that?"

Charles ignored his mother's question and asked one of his own. "That true, Roberta? You havin' my baby?"

Her eyes slowly rose to meet his, and Roberta nodded her head.

Charles took a deep breath and put down his ax.

"Charles—" his mother started to fuss, but Charles put his hand up to stop her. This wasn't her problem to deal with, it was his.

"I'm gettin' too ol' to be lookin' afta this gal, anyhow," Miss Martha explained. "'Sides, she ain't no chil' no mo'. Ain't been one in quite some time. If she been with anybody else, they'd have married her off a long time ago, and the gal would have two, three chil'ren by now." She walked over to Charles, stood toe-to-toe with him, and stared up at him. "If that be yo' baby, Charles, then you need to be the one to look afta this gal. Not me."

Charles stared over Martha's head at Roberta planted behind her. She didn't need to say a word to him, because her expression said it all. He'd always figured on loving the woman he married. He wasn't in love with Roberta, but he'd crossed the line, all the time knowing he was the one who should've ended it before it ever had a chance to get started.

"Me and his daddy raised him right, Martha," Meryle interjected. "Ain't none of my boys ever run off from they responsibilities. Charles ain't no different. Ain't that right, son?"

He took a deep breath, looked over at his mother, and nodded. "No, ma'am. I ain't no different," he muttered grimly.

"Then you ain't got no choice but to do the right thing by this girl." Miss Merlye said firmly and then turned to leave, followed by Martha.

Roberta hesitated before following them back towards the house. "I'm sorry, Charles," her voice quivered. "But, I guess it's fo' the best." As she turned to walk away, Roberta took a deep breath and grinned from ear to ear. Her dream had come true and Charles Brooks was about to become her husband. "That man ain't never gonna marry you," Danny had told her. Danny was just too silly to know better about such things. That's all. The Lord sure did know how to work miracles, and all it had taken from her was faith, perseverance, and a a tablespoon of pinny ro' . . . all in the name of love and the Lord.

Oh Me, Oh My

Rock of ages, cleft for me
Let me hide myself in thee

Roberta sat proudly in church next to her husband, cradling their daughter Elizabeth Brooks in her arms and singing along with the rest of the congregation.

The Depression was over, so they said. Not that it mattered all that much to black folks in Bueller, Texas. None of them were any richer or poorer than they'd been before, with one exception; Edward Cooper had been hit hard. He'd carried on a charade for years, making it seem as if the Depression had taken mercy on him and spared him from the ruin it brought to so many others. But Nadine's death had brought the truth to light. Edward's fancy cars, land, and his big house all rose up like steam and evaporated into the air. Suddenly he was left looking like the old man he'd been all along, hidden behind a mountain of money. The thick hair on his head had turned white as snow and his once-regal frame quickly withered and shrank. Eventually Edward Cooper vanished without a trace. Folks said he just left town, without leaving a word to anybody as to where he'd gone. But some folks laid claim to the obvious and held on to it: Edward Cooper had vanished like all of his most prized possessions—his cars, his house, Nadine—as if by magic, and in the blink of an eye.

Roberta'd been Mrs. Charles James Brooks for more than a year now and felt perfectly contented and suited for the position. Folks had a way of staring at her, even after all this time, like she had no business whatsoever with Charles. Not that it mattered one way or another to Roberta what they thought or even what they said behind her back. The fact of the matter was, Charles was her man, and all those jealous women could rot in their own envy as far as she was concerned. As a matter of fact, Roberta often found herself pondering the notion and sometimes, while down on her knees, deep in prayer, she'd let slip a remark that she usually ended up repenting for. Something along the lines of, "Dear Lord, thank you fo' my husband, and my chil', and fo' puttin' food on the table. And Lord, did you see the way Mary Evans rolled her eyes at me today? It wasn't right, and you know it 'cause she did it fo' no other reason than to be spiteful. But fo' her punishment, Lord, I think you oughta make her find out that her husband, the good Reverend Evans, is layin' up with Johnnie May Carter on Friday evenin's on his way home from teachin' Bible study at the church. I know 'cause I overheard Miss Martha talkin' 'bout it to Evaline Johnson a while back." Naturally, the following morning she'd feel awful about repeating that kind of gossip to the Lord and would apologize a hundred times before supper.

Being married to Charles had been everything she'd dreamed it would be. Roberta woke up before dawn every morning, even before Charles, staring into his handsome face, relishing the fact that he was real and not a dream anymore. He was even more beautiful asleep than he was when he was awake, and on more than one occasion the sight of him sleeping soundly next to her took her breath away. Nothing else in the world moved her like thoughts of her husband. Charles was on her mind from sunup to sundown and all through the night when she was sound asleep.

He'd been a good man, a better husband, and a doting daddy to Elizabeth. That child couldn't even get a good cry going with Charles around. "Go see 'bout her, 'Berta," he'd say. And Roberta would shake her head and pick that child up before she drove her daddy out of his mind with worry. There was never anything wrong with her, though. Roberta knew it each and every time that girl cried. But Charles was a man, and men didn't know a thing about raising children.

Charles worked long hours. He'd put in a full day at the mill, and then put in time as a handyman to anybody who could pay him. Sometimes he wouldn't even come home until after dark, and when he did come home, he'd be too tired to do anything else but eat and go to bed—oftentimes even forgetting to kiss Roberta goodnight.

"You work too hard, honey," she'd tried telling him. "Ain't no need fo' you to work yo'self to death. Why don't you jus' quit one of them jobs and spend mo' time at home?"

Of course he didn't listen. Charles also had a tendency to brood. She'd never seen this side of him before they married, but concluded maybe he'd always been that way and she'd just never been around to see it before. Lately, grumblings of a war from the mouth of Roosevelt tugged at Charles, and he'd been talking more and more about registering with the Selective Service and joining the Army to help defend his country. And this wasn't just any war. Roberta had heard people talking about a world war, in which the men would have to leave Texas and go to someplace across the ocean and maybe even fight against people who had never even seen a black man before.

"They need men like me, 'Berta. They need young men who

ain't scared to fight." Charles wouldn't even look her in the eyes when he spoke about this war. He just stared straight ahead, looking right at it as if guns were being shot right in front of him and he was already there.

The last thing she needed was for her man to be off somewhere too far away, fighting a war. She hadn't had Charles long enough to let him go.

"Yo' country don't care spit 'bout you, Charles. You ain't nothin' but a niggah to them and they don't care 'bout you one way or 'nother. Let all them white fools go off and fight and die for this country. They the ones who probably started the war anyhow."

That's when he'd look at her and stare right into her eyes, as if she'd wounded him, without even meaning to. "This here my country, Roberta. And I deserve to fight fo' it too. Jus' like any other man," Charles would say defensively.

"But what 'bout me and 'Lizabeth? If you go off fightin' in some ol' war way 'cross the ocean, who gon' take care of us?"

"I can send you some money every month. You and 'Lizabeth won't have to worry 'bout nothin', and my momma can help with the baby," Charles reasoned. "Or you could go stay with Miss Martha."

"I can't stay with Miss Martha and you know it. She tol' me never to set foot in her house again. You 'member I tol' you 'bout that? And yo' momma . . . well, she ain't too fond of me, neither."

"My momma ain't got nothin' 'gainst you, girl. Now you bein' ridiculous."

"But Charles—"

That's when he'd get up from the chair and leave, walking slowly down the road in front of the house, back and forth, until Roberta could hardly keep her eyes open any longer and sleep won out over her will to wait for him.

Roberta swallowed hard at the thought of him leaving. She

wouldn't let him leave. That was something she didn't even need to think about. Charles was just talking right now. In time, he'd forget all about that war and realize he needed to stay home with her.

The more she argued, the more determined he became, and all she could do was pray that Roosevelt would decide that he had all the men he needed to fight his war and that Charles would just get in the way.

Martha had been sitting in the next pew over, cutting her eyes in Roberta's direction all through the service and watching her sitting prim and proper, acting as though she were too good to even acknowledge the midwife these days. Martha had been the one to pull that baby Roberta was clutching in her arms from between her legs, and she hadn't charged her a dime to do it. Ever since then Roberta hadn't even bothered to give her the time of day. It was sinful, the way she treated her. She'd been the one to make sure that Roberta always had a roof over her head, a warm bed to sleep in, and a hot meal on the table, and all she got in return was complete and total disregard from the girl. As angry as Martha was, she was more hurt than anything. Roberta had been like a daughter to her. She'd taken care of her when she was sick, and worried over her as if she'd given birth to that girl herself. The least she could do was visit Martha from time to time, or sit with her and let her hold her new granddaughter. Elizabeth Brooks was the closest thing Martha would ever have to a grandchild of her own, and Roberta could've at least brought her by so that Martha could see how pretty she was growing up to be.

"Least you could do is come see 'bout me," Martha whispered to Roberta at the end of service and on their way out of the church.

Roberta had seen Martha staring at her, and she'd hoped to be gone before the woman managed to catch up with her and

Charles. She rolled her eyes, then turned and stared into Martha's wounded expression.

"You told me not to come back, Miss Martha," Roberta replied indignantly. "You said, 'Get yo' fas' ass on outta my house and don't you never come back!'" Roberta mocked. "You 'member that?"

"Hmph!" Martha huffed impatiently.

Roberta shrugged. "So . . . I ain't comin' back."

"You ol' peculiar gal!" Martha spat. "You always was peculiar."

Roberta started to argue. "If I'm so *peculiar* why you want me to—"

Charles was having a conversation with his friend Grady Jones, and hadn't noticed Martha and Roberta talking.

"Afternoon, Miss Martha." Charles turned and smiled at Martha, then tipped his hat. "How you been doin'?"

"Like you care. Like either one of you care," she snapped, fighting back genuine tears and pushing past Charles. "I could be dead for all y'all care. Dead and rotten in the ground."

Charles and Roberta watched her march down the road back towards her house. "Maybe you ought to go see 'bout her, Roberta," he said.

Roberta shook her head. "She jus' want folks to feel sorry fo' her. That's all it is."

"Even so, it wouldn't hurt to stop by and sit with her a spell," he insisted.

Charles had dropped Roberta and the baby off at Martha's, promising to return within the hour. Roberta had made him swear to it.

Not surprisingly, the house hadn't changed much. Martha had taken out Roberta's old bed in the front room and replaced it with two smaller wire-back chairs with vinyl seats. Between them she'd placed a petite walnut table with a lace coverlet on top and a vase filled with fresh wildflowers.

Roberta sat down, daintily removed her hat and gloves, smoothed down her dress, and crossed her legs at the ankles like ladies were supposed to do. She'd read it in one of those fancy fashion magazines.

Martha cooed at the child she held lovingly in her arms and spoke softly in a language that made no sense at all.

"This here ganny muh's baby? Oh, she such a tweet tang, ganny muh's baby girl is a tweet tang. Tweet 'nuff to eat, she is."

Roberta shook her head and rolled her eyes. Martha had a way of acting ridiculous, sometimes to the point of being embarrassing, but she was too country to understand the kind of fool she was making of herself.

Roberta folded her hands in her lap and sighed. "Well . . . how you been Miss Martha?" she asked indifferently.

Martha sat back and began bouncing the baby gently up and down in her arms. She didn't appreciate Roberta's smart-aleck tone and desperately fought back the urge to smack her right across the mouth.

Roberta stared at her, then asked again, "You been alright, I take it?"

"Fine," Martha said quickly. "I'm jus' fine."

"I'm glad to hear that."

"Are you?" Martha asked, cutting her eyes at Roberta.

"Course I am," Roberta said sarcastically. "Why you gon' ask me that?"

"You don't act like you glad I'm fine. It been near three months, Roberta, and you ain't come out to see 'bout me even one time." Martha held up a crooked finger to help make her point.

Roberta rolled her eyes at Martha's overly dramatic outburst. "Oh, Martha," she chuckled, trying to sound sophisticated.

"Don't you 'oh Martha' me, heffa! I ain't too ol' to still put a lickin' on yo' uppidity behind!"

"You ain't puttin' a lickin' on nothin'!" Roberta snapped. "In case you don't remember, I got me a husband now, and ain't you or nobody whippin' on me. I'm a grown woman with my own chil'ren, in case you haven't noticed!"

Martha stared at her for a moment, then suddenly burst out laughing. "Grown? Havin' babies don't make you grown, gal. Pigs and cows have babies all the time, but they still ain't smart 'nuff to keep from endin' up on somebody's supper table." Martha fought to catch her breath. "And as fo' havin' that husband of yo's, hell, he only married you 'cause me and his momma made him. That man didn't give two hoots 'bout marryin' yo' silly ass. Think I'm lyin'? Go ask his momma. Tell the truth and shame the devil, Roberta. You jus' got lucky." Martha's eyes twinkled.

Rage rose up in Roberta, and if Martha hadn't been holding that child in her arms, Roberta would've jumped on top of her and stomped her into the ground. Martha was an idiot midwife who didn't know a thing about being a lady, a real lady, who had her own man and made her own babies.

"Oh, I'm grown alright, Miss Martha," Roberta said icily, suddenly feeling venomous. "I'm a woman now and Charles know it. He know I'm all woman. Wanna know what we be doin', Martha?"

"That's Miss Martha to you, gal!" Martha demanded. "I'm the one who raise you, and you gon' show me some r'spect or sit still while I put my hand 'cross yo' mouth."

Roberta ignored her threats. "Me and my husband, we be doin' it all the time."

Martha rolled her eyes and cooed down at the baby, ignoring Roberta's foolish antics. "I don't want to hear 'bout that, gal."

Roberta sat up straight and defiantly propped her fists on her hips. "We be doin' it mornin', noon, and all night long. He put his thang deep inside me and make me wanna throw my legs all up in the air and call out his name!"

"Roberta!" Martha snapped. "Don't you talkin' filthy in my house!"

Roberta smiled mischievously. "Oh, it's filthy alright. Me and my husband be makin' filthy all over each other, sweet and sticky like honey." Roberta licked her lips in exaggerated fashion, relishing the shocked expression on Martha's face.

"Charles's thang is long and he push it in and out of me real slow," she said, wrinkling her nose, "'cause that's how we both like to do it. Slow. Hard."

Roberta closed her eyes, threw herself back in the chair, and raised both her legs up in the air, forming the letter *V*. Martha's mouth fell wide open at the sight of the girl rotating her hips against nothing at all, and pressing her hand between her thighs.

"He push it in and outta me a hundred times, Martha! Over and over again 'til I scream, 'Charles! Oh, Charles! Yes! Yes! My lovin', lovin' man, Charles'." Roberta's hands roamed freely over her breasts and thighs. "'Baby! Oh baby!' he say to me. 'Give it to me, baby!' Then I say to him, 'Give it to me, Daddy!' He like for me to call him Daddy. 'Daddy!' I scream. 'Daddy! Take it! Aaaaah! Aaaaah! Aaaaah!'" Finally she collapsed in the aftermath of her feigned orgasm. Martha sat breathless in her chair, shocked at what she'd just seen. Roberta grinned slyly, slowly sat up, and carefully took her daughter from Martha's arms.

"Look at her." She smiled lovingly at Elizabeth. "Sleepin' jus' like an angel and lookin' like her daddy." Martha was too stunned to speak, but she slowly rose up from her seat and went out onto the porch. A few minutes later she returned, carrying her moonshine jug, and filled her teacup to the brim with the clear concoction she'd found so much comfort in over the years. Martha sipped quietly until finally Charles pulled up in front of the house to reclaim his family.

"I'm so glad you doin' well, Miss Martha," Roberta said sweetly, getting up to leave. She smiled, then leaned down and kissed Martha softly on the cheek. "I'll be back to check on you again real soon, now. Ya hear?"

Martha watched silently as Roberta and Charles drove away, hoping she'd never have to endure the pleasure of that girl's company ever again.

THE DEVIL DOWN BELOW

This Burden I Must Bear Alone

Ezra Tate trudged home in the heat of an East Texas summer, cursing under his breath about that old truck of his that had just broken down again. He was a big man, and a big man like him had no business walking four miles to get home in one of the hottest summers he could recall. Sweat poured down his face from beneath his old fedora and burned his eyes. Those boys of his should've been out of school by now and working in the fields. He'd gather up the oldest one, Josiah, and head back to see if they could get that truck running well enough to get it home.

Ezra stopped to take a breath at the foot of the steps leading up to the front door of the house he'd built when he was a much younger and thinner man. Back in those days walking four miles wouldn't have bothered him at all. He'd built it for his wife Dora as a wedding present, thirteen, maybe fourteen years ago. He smiled at the fond memories he still had of Dora. Ezra had never loved a woman the way he'd loved her. She was a pretty dark-skinned woman with long thick hair and soft brown eyes that made him weak to her every whim. Whatever Dora had wanted, Ezra had just about broken his neck to get it for her. Not that they'd ever had a lot, but all he'd ever wanted to do was make her happy. Until she'd died some years back, he figured he'd done a pretty good job of it, too.

Dora had taken ill all of a sudden, came down with a fever, and all the praying in the world hadn't been enough to keep her with him. When she died she'd taken a piece of him with her, and Ezra had never given much thought to finding another wife, despite having three children to raise by himself. He and Dora had had two boys, Josiah, fourteen, and Ezra Jr., twelve, before she'd died. And then there was Sara. Dora had come to him with Sara, who was only two at the time of their marriage. But that little girl had been the spitting image of her momma and Ezra had fallen in love with her too, even though she wasn't his daughter by blood. It didn't matter to him, though. He'd raised her as his own, and loved her just as much as either of his sons. Ever since her momma passed, Sara had taken on the responsibilities of the house—cooking, cleaning, tending to the garden, sewing. Dora had taught her well, because at eleven years old, when her momma passed, Sara stepped right in and took over where Dora had left off. She was a strong little girl, quiet as mouse most of the time, and shy. Dora had been shy too, which was one of the reasons he'd fallen in love with her. Nothing perturbed him more than loud, mouthy women, wearing too much makeup and strutting around in low-cut dresses. Dora had always been respectable and taught Sara how to be respectable, too.

Ezra climbed the stairs and slowly opened the front door. He'd opened it just enough to peek in, and the sight of her made him catch his breath in his chest. Sara stood naked in the large

wooden tub in the kitchen, humming to herself and bathing. She
hadn't seen him. Ezra started to turn away and close the door to
wait for her to finish taking her bath, but he couldn't bring himself to do it. The sight of his stepdaughter was breathtaking, and
he couldn't take his eyes off her. Sara had grown into a woman
and as much as he'd closed his mind to the fact, his eyes insisted
on revealing that truth to him. Sara rubbed the wet towel over her
full breasts and under her arms, then slid it down to the soft, fem-
inine round of her stomach to just above the black triangle
between her legs. Ezra blinked away a bead of sweat threatening
to drip into his eye and disrupt the vision of her. Her long smooth
back curved at the base into her round bottom that melted into
legs that looked just like her momma's. Dora had been beautiful
like that, he thought to himself. Ezra's heart began to ache.

Without thinking, Ezra reached down to his groin and
squeezed the erection pressing hard against his overalls. *Lord have
mercy!* he pleaded in his mind. All he wanted at that moment was
her, to gather her up into his arms, lay her tenderly down at his
feet, and ease himself inside her. He squeezed his eyes shut,
rebuking the vision that had just crossed his mind.

*She yo' baby girl, Ezra! You can't be thinkin' like that 'bout yo'
baby girl!*

Water glistened off her smooth black skin as she stepped out
of the tub and reached for her towel. Ezra quietly closed the door
and eased himself back down the stairs. He walked to the back of
the house and sat down on an old tree stump near the edge of the
woods with his back to the house, feeling himself growing hard in
his pants. Images of Sara standing naked in front of him formed
behind his eyes and burned into his mind. This wasn't the first
time he'd seen her. There were always glimpses of her womanhood convicting him, tempting him to love her in ways he knew
were forbidden.

"Lord, I never would hurt her," he whispered pitifully, glancing up at the pale blue sky. "She my baby girl, and I never would do nothin' to hurt her."

But he wanted her. Ezra wanted Sara in a way he hadn't wanted a woman in years. Every time she hugged him, kissed his cheek, brushed up against him, her Pappo, Ezra's body filled with a desire for that girl that threatened to make him lose his mind. Sometimes the devil wreaked havoc on him, especially late at night. Ezra would ease out of bed and go into her room, just to watch her sleep, he'd tell himself. After all, she looked so much like her momma. His Dora.

She ain't yo' real daughter, Ezra. She ain't yo's and ain't nothin' say you can't take that girl, and take her right now. You know she won't say nothin'. She love you too much to say somethin'.

Ezra would relieve himself with his hand while he sat across the room and watched her sleep. It was as close as he dared to ever get, because he suspected that the minute he ever touched her like that, he'd get lost in her, and he didn't know if he'd ever be able to find himself again. He might hurt her more than he ever intended. Sara had never been with a man before, he was sure of that. Folks made fun of him for not letting her out of his sight for long.

"She ol' 'nuff to court now, Ezra," the women at the church would tell him while he glared at some nappy-headed boy smiling in her face or staring at her. "She a young woman and you got to let her go sometime. Shoot! By the time I was her age, I was married and had my first chil', gettin' ready to have my second one. That ain't no girl no mo'. She a young woman now."

Sara was nearly seventeen and everything about her was a woman. He wasn't blind. But she was precious to him because she was all he had left of Dora.

"Hey, Pappo," Sara called out from behind him. The sound of her voice startled him and Ezra quickly adjusted his pants, being careful not to let her see him, and then slowly stood up from the stump. She was carrying an empty basket and started taking the clothes off the line.

"Hey, baby girl." Ezra blinked away tears before she could see them.

She smiled warmly at him. "I didn't know you was home. Why you here so early? You feelin' alright?"

"That ol' truck of mine done broke down again," he quickly explained.

Sara frowned. "Again? Where it break down at?"

"Over near Wilbert's place. Where yo' brothas?"

"They in the fields, I 'spect. You know how they is. They run in, grab 'em somethin' to eat, and run on out the do' without even sayin' hello." Young life twinkled in her bright eyes, and even that was a temptation for Ezra.

"Well, I'm gon' go see if I can round up Josiah to help me get that truck home." Ezra adjusted his hat and started to walk away.

"Well, supper ought to be ready by the time y'all get back, Pappo. We havin' red beans and cornbread."

"That's good, baby girl," Ezra said as he hurried away. That truck could wait awhile. Ezra needed to make another stop first. He reached into his pocket and found a wadded-up five-dollar bill and some change, then hurried off to where he knew he'd find some relief. Otherwise, he might break his promise to himself and do something he knew he had no business doing.

"Five dollars?" the prostitute said, frowning. "That all you got?"

Ezra stared at her. "It's all you need and you know it."

She rolled her eyes and left him standing in the doorway. "Well, c'mon," she said, sprawling out on the bed. "I ain't got fo'ever."

Ezra didn't bother taking off his clothes or even his hat, and plunged into her, indifferent to this woman altogether. He pumped furiously, in and out, angry at being driven to come here. He was angry with her, and angry with himself. He was angry with Sara for growing up like she had, and filling him with the kind of temptation he knew was wrong.

She ain't yo' real daughter, Ezra.

Put it in her! Put it in her hard and harder and over and over again!

Fuck her, Ezra!

You know how bad you want her! You know you do!

Can't help yo'self, man!

Harder!

Ezra looked down into the face of the woman, grimacing and grunting beneath him, and watched it turn into Sara's face. Sara's beautiful face with soft brown eyes, staring up at him, dismayed by what he was doing to her. Her lips moved, but no words came from them. Ezra pounded himself inside her, desperate to fill her up with every inch of him, and to make her his.

You can have her, Ezra! All you got to do is take her!

For God's sake! Do what you been wantin' to do!

She belong to you, Ezra!

Ezra growled, then collapsed on top of the woman, relieving himself. For a moment the two lay breathless in a heap on the bed.

"Get up offa me, niggah!" The woman pushed him with all her strength, trying to get him to get up. "You ain't fuckin' me no' mo'! I ain't got to take this!" Tears streamed down the sides of her face.

Slowly Ezra raised himself up and off the woman. He looked down at her and watched her scoot away from him to the head of the bed, trembling. What had he done?

"You get the fuck outta here and don't never come back! I don't want yo' goddamned money! Get the fuck out!" She threw his money at him, then buried her face in her pillow and cried.

Ezra closed the door quietly on his way out. He still needed to find Josiah to help him with the truck. But more importantly, he needed to talk to Dora's momma in Clarksville and see about sending Sara out there to stay with her for awhile.

It Surely Would Be Grand

Momma Harper got to be ninety, maybe even close to one hundred years old," Ezra explained to Sara, sitting next to him as he drove. "All them kids of hers is gone—moved north, I'm thinkin'. Anyhow, she ain't got nobody and she need lookin' after."

Sara hadn't seen Momma Harper since before her mother died. Clarksville seemed like a world away from Timber, and Pappo assured her that it was only about a hundred miles, but Clarksville was bigger than Timber. Sara tried to take in the whole town as Pappo slowly made his way down the main street, heading towards Momma Harper's house.

"You can see picture shows in there," he said, pointing to the theater. "I ain't never seen one, but I hear they even let coloreds in sometimes. Over yonder," he pointed across the street, "is where you get yo' food—salt pork, vegetables, cornmeal. All of this is what they call uptown. Momma Harper live up the road a piece, close 'nuff to walk here."

A few minutes later they turned onto Crow Street where Momma Harper lived. The small gray wooden house sat up on bricks, lifting it off the ground to help keep snakes out. Momma Harper had a whole acre of land to herself, and Sara could see where the garden had been years ago when she was a child and they'd come to visit. Nothing grew in that garden now but wild-flowers and weeds.

"Clarksville ain't but the size of a pea to the likes of Paris, which is where I was born," said Momma Harper. "Even back in them days, Paris was a big place that left a shadow on top of you if'n you didn't get out the way fas' 'nuff. We lived on a farm so big it fit all of Clarksville. My pappy moved us here when I was jus' a girl. Had to been back 'round the time they freed the slaves or shortly thereafter," she said, searching her memory. "Clarksville wasn't nothin' but a bit of a town back then, not much more than a few folks scattered here and there, tryin' to start over from bein' slaves all they lives. 'Course I never knowed much 'bout bein' one, since I was such a young gal. I 'spect that's what I was, though. I jus' didn't know it at the time. Bueller be right 'cross the river. It ain't much bigger than here, but it's close 'nuff to spit in, dependin' on where you standin'. Ever been to Bueller, honey?"

Sara shook her head, "No ma'am."

Momma Harper smiled radiantly. "Well, you ain't missed nothin'."

Right away Momma Harper seemed to welcome Sara's company, and talked to her for hours about how she'd grown up, and how she'd married her best friend from her childhood, Seth Harper, who'd taken good care of her until he'd died and who'd fathered all eleven of her children. Dora, Sara's mother, had been the youngest.

"I was in my fifties or maybe even older when I had that gal." Momma Harper laughed. "Lord know I wasn't thinkin' she was gon' come. I thought my time fo' havin' babies was through, but He saw fit to give me that last one. Her pappy spoilt her rotten, he did, 'cause he was too ol' and tired to know better. Why, we already had grandbabies when that gal come along. She was my sweetest one, though, sweet as pie she was." Momma Harper looked worried. "Can't say I know what her name was, though."

Sara laughed. "Her name was Dora, Momma Harper. Dora May," Sara reminded her.

Momma Harper smiled and warmly patted Sara's hand. "That sho' is a pretty name. But . . . that ain't yo' name, though?"

Sara shook her head. "No, ma'am. I'm Sara, her daughter. Remember?"

Sara's grandmother had a better memory for things that had been long ago. Significant things like when the Negros finally got word that they'd been set free and the Spanish-American War. She remembered the sweet things Seth would whisper to her after the children fell asleep, but she didn't always remember to get up and go to the bathroom when she needed to. She didn't remember her children's names, or her grandchildren's. Sometimes she didn't even remember to eat. And there were moments when she'd look at Sara, confused as to who this girl was and what she was doing in her house. Moments like those frightened Sara, but they frightened Momma Harper even more.

Clarksville wasn't a thing like Timber. It moved faster and always seemed to be awake. People rushed around like ants, in a hurry to get someplace. Shops were filled with everything from fruits and vegetables to tobacco to pretty dresses hanging in windows for everybody to see. Sara's arm was bruised from all the times she'd pinched herself, making sure she was awake and not in bed dreaming.

Pappo had always kept her close to home, too close, but she'd never complained. Sara had never been allowed to venture too far off, and as she grew older he seemed to become even more protective. But in Clarksville Sara enjoyed the freedom of being a young woman for the first time in her life. After she'd put Momma Harper down for a nap, she'd put on her hat and walk from one end of Clarksville to the other.

"You one of Miss Harper's grandbabies?" Momma Harper's neighbor Mrs. Robinson squealed at the sight of her.

Sara smiled, "Yes, ma'am."

"Well, she need somebody over here to look after her. She ain't got no chillen 'round to speak of. They done all died off, or moved up North and left her sittin' here all by her lonesome. Ain't that a shame?" Mrs. Robinson said sadly.

"Yes, ma'am," Sara agreed. "It's a real shame."

"Dora May yo' momma? My, my, don't you look jus' like her. Sho' was a pretty li'l girl, and you the spittin' image of her. Why, if I didn't know no better, I'd say you was her. She here too?"

"No, ma'am. She passed on a few years back," she explained sadly.

"It's a shame, I tell you, a cryin' shame. But sometimes it's jus' the Lord's will, chil'. And can't none of us question God's will."

"No, ma'am," Sara whispered.

"How many chillen you got?" she asked.

"Oh, I don't have any. I ain't even married yet."

Mrs. Robinson looked surprised. "Is that right? Well, girl! You better get to workin' on it. You look plenty ol' 'nuff to have yo'self a man and some chillen. How old is you?"

"I'll be seventeen next month." Sara said proudly.

"Seventeen? Chil', if you don't hurry, you gon' be a ol' woman 'fo it's all said and done. Men 'round here don't want no ol' woman. And you a pretty girl. You ain't got no business not havin' a husband. And don't be too particular, neither. A hard-workin' man is the best kinda' man. You mark my words. Some of these young girls sittin' 'round holdin' out fo' one of them high-yella boys to come down from the North to sweep 'em up and take 'em back to Harlem or even Detroit. But them boys don't know nothin' 'bout a honest day's work, or takin' care of nobody 'sides themselves. But don't you worry," Miss Robinson winked. "Them boys 'round here gon' get a whiff of you sooner or later."

Pappo had never allowed Sara to even talk to boys. *Them hardheads is only after one thing and they ain't gettin' it from no daughter of mine,*" he'd fuss.

Sara never argued because Pappo knew best. But Pappo was a one hundred miles away in Timber and he couldn't fuss at her from all the way down there.

Men smiled and tipped their hats at her while she walked down the street in Clarksville, and Sara would say hello and smile politely, but she never stopped long enough to talk.

"Hello, Miss," they'd say, with their eyes twinkling like stars.

Hers twinkled back.

Handsome young men buzzed around her in all shapes, sizes, and shades of brown. Sara found herself smiling all the time, mostly on the inside, until she couldn't hold it in anymore and a warm flush rose up in her face.

She had an idea of the kind of man she wanted to marry—a man like Pappo—strong and hard on the outside, but soft and warm on the inside. One who treated her the way Pappo treated her mother. He'd treated Dora like she was a flower that he didn't want to crush.

Sara's mother had had a strubborn streak in her, though, and would insist that he not coddle her the way he did, but Pappo always argued, *"Coddlin' ain't what I'm doin', Dora May. I'm takin' care with my wife, 'cause that's what a man is s'posed to do."*

"But you treat me like I'm gon' break, Ezra Tate, and I ain't made of glass," Dora would complain, but Sara could always see a smile hidden behind eyes that pretended to be angry. *"You needs my help out there in them fields, and I'm yo' wife, and that's what a wife is s'posed to do. She s'posed to be there fo' her man when he need her."*

Ezra would walk over and kiss the tip of her nose, then rest his hat on top of his head before leaving, knowing that the last word belonged to him. *"I do needs you, honey. I needs you here when I come home, waitin' on me with a warm meal, and some of that sugah that taste so sweet on you."* He'd wink, then head out the door.

Sara always laughed whenever Ezra acted like that. Dora would glare at her and fuss. *"Ain't nothin' at all funny 'bout that daddy of yo's, li'l girl. He ain't nothin' but a mess, and stubborn as a mule."* But soon a smile would spread across Dora's face, too. Ezra Tate was a charmer. That's what he'd always been, and that's the kind of man Sara wanted for her own husband. A charming man, but practical, too.

Baby, Won't You Please Come Home

Being Mrs. Charles Brooks was more than a notion, Roberta thought, staring out the kitchen window at the memory of him driving down the road while she washed dishes left over from breakfast.

"When you gon' get tired, Roberta?" she muttered the question to herself. Roberta and Charles had been married for three years and she loved him more now than ever. She wondered if she'd ever lose the strength to love him so much but knew she wouldn't. Charles had been a bittersweet prize she'd won. She'd always known that he'd married her out of obligation. For Charles, loving Roberta had nothing to do with marrying her, but Roberta always figured it would come when it was supposed to. Charles would wake up one morning, turn to her lying in bed next to him, tell her how much he loved her, and Roberta would sigh and curl up against him, knowing it was true and that everything was fine. Years later that moment still hadn't come, but she couldn't lose hope. And when it did come, she could finally rest from the burden of carrying all the love for both of them.

Roberta sang absently to herself, "*Jaybird said to the peckerwood, I like to peck like a pecker should, But give me some, yes, give me some, I'm crazy 'bout them worms . . . you gotta give me some.*" She laughed, thinking of how she craved Charles the way that jaybird in the song craved her worm.

His friend Grady had asked Charles to drive to Clarksville in his place to repair a roof for his aunt, because something had come up and he couldn't get the time away to do it himself. It was a paying job, so Charles jumped at the opportunity, but Roberta hadn't been happy about it at all.

"Grady should be the one out there fixin' that ol' woman's roof hisself," she said out loud, scrubbing cooked egg from the cast-iron skillet. The sound of Charles Jr.'s crying trampled her thoughts. Roberta glanced, annoyed, in the direction of her son in the other room who'd been crying for well over an hour. It was times like this when she hated that boy. Roberta cringed, and then she looked over at Elizabeth, nearly four years old now, sitting quietly in the corner playing with the baby doll Granny Meryle had made for her. Elizabeth's dark wide eyes stared accusingly at Roberta.

Roberta turned her attention back to finishing the dishes and shrugged. "Sometime you jus' gotta let 'em cry," she mumbled weakly, more to herself than to the little girl. "He jus' want to be held, that's all," she said, more convincingly this time. "He always want to be held. Everybody 'round here got that boy spoiled."

Charles had him spoiled, insisting he be picked up every time he so much as opened his mouth to yawn. He had both of the children spoiled, especially Elizabeth. But the children were worrisome when he wasn't around. Elizabeth watched her constantly, waiting for her to do something wicked that would stay in her memory until she was old enough to tell her daddy about it, and CJ cried all the time. Elizabeth could be especially worrisome whenever Charles came home from work. He'd be so tired he could hardly walk in the door before the child hurled herself up into his lap and wrapped her arms tight enough around him to strangle the man.

"Get offa yo' daddy, gal!" Roberta would end up scolding her.

But Charles would protectively snuggle her close to him and kiss her cheek, almost as if he were doing it to spite Roberta. "She fine, 'Berta. She jus' givin' her daddy some of that sweet lovin', that's all."

It was moments like that when Charles seemed to want to show Roberta that he was capable of giving love to everyone but her. He'd break her heart, but she would never give up on him. Roberta ignored his indifference to her and pulled his affection from him like she pulled thread from a seam. She'd learned to do that from the beginning with Charles when he was pining over Nadine Cooper. But he'd made love to Roberta. She'd even ignored the moments when he'd called out Nadine's name instead of hers, knowing and relishing in the fact that Nadine was gone for good, and Roberta was all he had left.

How could a woman be jealous of her own child? Roberta wondered, staring woefully at Elizabeth playing quietly in the corner. But that's what she was, jealous of any woman, no matter how young or old, getting too close to him, threatening to push her off the rope she balanced on over his heart. After three years he'd never told her he loved her, but he said it to Elizabeth all the time, and to Miss Meryle, too. But the words had never escaped his mouth for Roberta's sake.

Roberta finished washing the last of the dishes and wiped her hands on her apron.

"What else? What else I got to do? What—"

There was plenty to do around that house. Things always needed cleaning, or fixing, or—Lord! Why didn't that boy just shut up? Reluctantly she walked over to the room where CJ was still crying. The seven-month-old infant sat up in his bed and looked at Roberta, staring desperately through red swollen eyes. He reached out to her, hiccupping through tears, but Roberta was devoid of the instinct to mother him. She reflexively cupped her hands over her ears as his wailing seemed to grow even louder, until his crying sounded more like screams digging into her skull like an ice pick.

She felt a slight tug at the hem of her skirt and looked down into the face of her daughter.

"Can I have a drink?" Elizabeth asked in her small voice. "Please, momma?"

"Go sit down!" Roberta snapped. The girl hesitated and then looked at her brother in his crib, as if her attempt to rescue him had failed.

"She gotta a ol' spirit. Some chillen jus' born with a ol' spirit already in 'em," Martha had told her not long after Elizabeth had been born. Roberta saw it too sometimes, wisdom of the ages behind Elizabeth's dark eyes, and it frightened her if she let it. Roberta leaned down and turned the girl in the opposite direction, then swatted her backside. "Go sit down, now! 'Fo I tan yo' hide!"

Elizabeth did as she was told and reluctantly found her place in the corner of the room.

Roberta turned her attention back to the baby. "Be quiet, CJ!" The dark shadow of contempt washed over her face. "You heard me, boy! I know you did! Now—"

CJ's screams filled the room and echoed in Roberta's ears. She was so tired of this boy crying all the damn time. She was so sick of holding him and rocking him and coddling him every second of the day. It seemed like all she did was give in to him. Just to shut him up. Just to keep him quiet.

Roberta stormed into the room, grabbed the baby, held him up in the air, and screamed into his face. "Hush! You hear me? Hush, CJ! Quiet!" His crying pierced through the air. She knew what he wanted. Roberta quickly unbuttoned her blouse, then slumped down on the bed and resentfully filled his mouth with her breast. His small hand grabbed desperately at her as he sucked hungrily on her nipple.

Roberta rocked back and forth, loathing every minute of his suckling. She'd always hated it, even more with Elizabeth, but nobody had to know. Nobody but the children, and she knew they'd never tell, because children held all the secrets about their mommas sacred. Which was as it should've been.

Makes Me Weak Way Down in My Knees

The shortest route between Bueller and Clarksville was to drive through town, and he'd have come right out of one and landed into the other in no time. He'd been asked by his best friend Grady to do some repair work for him at his great-aunt's house in Clarksville, and in the same breath he warned Charles to stay far away from his cousin Sara, who was staying with the old woman.

"She my baby cousin, man, and I know how you are. You lay one finger on her, Charles, and I'll beat yo' black ass, man—I swear!"

Charles just shook his head. He and Grady were just alike when it came to women. Both of them had always had more than their share, and neither one of them could ever get enough. They were greedy men with no bottom to them. Since he'd gotten married, though, Charles's insatiable appetite had pretty much been left hungry. Once word got out that he was marrying Roberta, cold shoulders greeted him in place of warm kisses. Besides that, Charles found himself working twelve-, sixteen-hour days with his and Grady's repair business. He felt like he'd aged a hundred years in no time at all, and Charles hardly had the time or energy he'd once had for women.

Charles drove leisurely, gazing out at the road still ahead of him, wondering who'd had the good sense to put this road back here in the first place. Charles smiled, then inhaled the cool morning air, knowing that the man who'd carved out this particular stretch of road must've been like him. He'd been in no hurry to reach his destination either, or maybe he'd just been in no real hurry to get home.

He'd always loved long drives and if he didn't have to stop, he never would've. Temptation rode in that truck with him, whispering in his ear, *Man, why don't you jus' keep on goin' and don't stop till you get to the other side of the world?* It took all the will power he had to squash it, but every now and then, like now, he listened to it and let his mind roam barefoot in all the places he'd like to go, like California. Charles didn't know a damn thing about California, except that he liked the name. It sounded like a woman's name, and he imagined her waiting for him, big and stretched out, smiling as she welcomed him with her arms open and her eyes shining. He'd heard she rested next to the ocean, and Charles had always wanted to see it. In the back of his mind he'd imagined himself wading knee-deep in it, with his pants rolled up and his hands buried in his pockets while he watched the sun sink down inside it. That was where he wanted to be.

He scratched his head, awed by how quickly life had changed directions on him. It seemed like just the other day he was a cocky sonofabitch, flitting around like a bee from one flower to another, sampling damn near any woman who'd let him. Nadine's nectar had been the sweetest, though, he thought fondly. Every now and then the essence of her still tingled the tip of his tongue and Charles found himself missing her, regretting that he never did do the one thing he should've—just loaded her into his truck and drove off with her, all the way to California. He chuckled at the thought. That old man of hers would've come running after them, but his legs would've given out long before he ever made it that far.

Charles's thoughts inevitably drifted back to Roberta and the children he'd left at home early that morning. A wife and two kids separated him from California or anywhere else other than Bueller, for that matter. He loved his children, Elizabeth and Charles Jr. Loving Roberta, however, was a different issue altogether. Lord, that woman worked his nerves. Charles had done the right thing where Roberta was concerned. He'd owned up to his responsibilities and to his mistakes and married her. Most of the time he'd even go so far as to believe he'd been a good husband, as good as he knew how to be. Four years ago Roberta had a been a young girl, desperately in love with him. She hadn't changed and neither had he.

Where you been, Charles?

Whatchu need, Charles?

Where you going, Charles?

I love you, Charles.

I can't live without you, Charles.

He'd never counted on being that girl's reason for living, and he sure as hell never wanted it. But Charles had played the game of fools and gotten caught up in encounters too brief to change his life the way they had. At least, he'd believed they were brief at the time. Now he knew better.

"How you gon' love me when you don't even know me, Roberta?" He'd asked her that question all the time in the beginning. Roberta would stare back at him with wide eyes, as if she couldn't believe he didn't know the answer. She tugged at him all the time, trying to pull something out of him that just wasn't in him, and without even trying Charles hurt her feelings, hoping she'd finally say the one thing he wanted to hear more than anything; "I can't take this no mo', Charles, and I want you gone."

He'd be a fish blessed by the gods if she ever said that, and then Charles would swim away as fast as he could, happier than he'd been in years because she'd finally let him off that hook of her own free will.

Charles hesitated before disturbing the old woman napping in a chair on the porch of the old house. Must be Aunt Josephine, he thought to himself. He cleared his throat and removed his hat before calling out to her, "Miss Harper?"

Miss Harper bobbed her head and muttered something to herself, but she didn't wake up so Charles called out a little louder, "'Scuse me, Miss Harper."

The old woman snorted and woke up with a start. Charles was worried that he might've scared her. "Miss Harper," he said quickly, "How you doin'? My name is Charles and Grady sent me over to—"

"Grady?" she asked, staring confused at Charles. "You Grady?"

"Naw, ma'am. I ain't Grady, I'm Charles." He took a few steps closer so that she could get a better look at him. "Grady sent me over to see 'bout yo' roof that need fixin'."

Miss Harper took a deep breath and sunk back into her chair. "Boy, don't be goin' round tippin' up on folk like that. If'n I'd'a had my gun, you be leavin' up outta here with a bullet in ya."

Charles couldn't help but laugh. That old woman couldn't see him well enough to shoot him. "Yes, ma'am. I do apologize."

Miss Harper patted herself gently on the chest and then turned her attention to the young man standing at the foot of her porch. "Sho' is warm for October, ain't it?"

"Yes, ma'am. I s'pect it's gon' get cold soon 'nuff, though."

She frowned. "I don't too much care fo' the cold. The older I gets, the colder it seem to get," she said, laughing. She studied Charles intently, "Now who you say you was again?"

"My name is Charles, Miss Harper, Charles Brooks."

She thought for a moment. "Brooks. I don't reckon I know anyone named Brooks. Yo' people here in Clarksville?"

"No, my people live in Bueller by way of Oklahoma. They come out of Alabama and Tennessee, I believe."

"I see. You kin to any Trimbles? I know some Trimbles outta Oklahoma."

Impatience began to creep in, but he held it at bay, knowing how old people tended to carry on. "No, ma'am. Don't know no Trimbles."

Charles glanced at the window in time to see a young woman peep at him from behind the curtain. Just then Sara opened the screen door and stepped outside.

"Hello? Is there somethin' we can do fo' you?"

Baby cousin, he thought, staring up at this pretty dark-skinned girl on the porch. Grady was no fool. He knew that the moment Charles laid eyes on this girl, he'd trip over his own feet to get to her if he could. For a moment she reminded him of Nadine, but softer around the edges. She was the kind of girl Nadine might've been had Edward Cooper not gotten hold of her and wrapped her up in dollar bills.

"My name is Charles," he said, smiling.

"He a Brooks out of Bueller, 'cross the way, but he ain't no kin to them Trimbles outta Oklahoma," Miss Harper interjected.

"I come by to fix the roof. Yo' cousin Grady sent me."

"Oh, yes. Well—"

Miss Harper interrupted, "Sara, why don't you take him 'round back and show him where that hole is?"

"Yes, ma'am." Sara obediently led Charles to the back of the house.

Baby Cousin had a fine figure on her, Charles thought, admiring her from behind. Grady had given him the blues about this girl, and for good reason.

"The hole is right over here," she explained, pointing up to the corner of the house. "Thank goodness we ain't gettin' a lot of rain and that it ain't been too cold. But if you ask me, I think the whole thing might be rotted out. Don't it look rotted out to you?"

Charles peeled his eyes off Sara long enough to examine the area she pointed to. "From here it don't look too good. Might have to replace a good part of it."

"We can't afford to fix all of it. Maybe if you could just patch it up good, that would last us awhile."

Charles shrugged. "Well, I can patch up the hole, all right, but it wouldn't be long fo' you gon' have to get somebody out here to fix it again." Charles caught a glimpse of disappointment, but this girl was too pretty for him to let that happen. "Tell you what . . . I'm gon' do my best to fix the whole thing and I won't charge you a penny mo'."

Sara hesitated at his offer. "I can't ask you to do that."

"You didn't ask me. I made the offer, and if you as smart as I think you are, then you'll take it."

Sara smiled and set Charles on fire from the inside out. "That's fine, Mr.—"

He reached out to shake her hand. "Call me Charles."

"Charles. That's fine, Charles, and thank you. Thank you so much." She walked past him back towards the front of the house, "Well, I'm gon' leave and let you get to work. I've got plenty of my own inside."

Charles watched her leave, then mumbled to himself, "Damn girl!" He shook his head, remembering quickly how pretty girls always managed to get him into trouble, or rather, his love of pretty girls. Sara disappeared around the corner and into the house, and Charles shook off the effect she'd had on him and started unloaded his tools to get down to the business of fixing Miss Harper's roof.

From time to time Sara caught a glimpse of Charles from the kitchen window while he worked, careful not to let him see her. His offer not to charge them any extra money had come as such a surprise. Momma Harper didn't have much money, just what she and Seth had saved over the years in mason jars hidden under loose floorboards in the kitchen pantry. From what Sara had seen, it had been quite a bit of money, mostly pennies, dimes, nickels, silver dollars. Momma Harper had been living off that money for years, though, and she'd told Sara quite a few times that there also was money outside in back of the house that Seth had buried years ago, but she had never been able to remember where.

Sara was rolling dough for chicken and dumplings when she heard a tap on the window. She turned in time to see Charles, wiping sweat from his head with the back of his hand.

Sara opened the window. "Yes?"

"Don't mean to trouble you, Miss—"

"Sara." She smiled.

He smiled back and stared into her soft brown eyes. "Sara. I was wonderin' if I could trouble you fo' some water?"

She filled a glass with cool water and handed it to him. Charles drank it all in one gulp, then handed the glass back to her. "Thank you, kindly."

"No trouble." She blushed.

Charles put on his hat and went back to work. She hadn't noticed before, but he had dimples. Sara hadn't seen too many men with dimples, but on him they looked good. Her neighbor Mrs. Robinson had warned her about men like him, the pretty ones, slick as ice and just as cold was how she'd explained them.

"*They quick to tell you all kinda sweet things, but don't you believe 'em, girl. Don't be no fool over no man, 'cause all they wanna do is crawl up yo' skirt, get what he want and leave you standin' there with a baby that look jus' like him, hangin' on yo' hip. Ain't nothin' worse than havin' a take care of a baby that look jus' like the niggah' who broke yo' heart. They make some pretty chil'ren, though.*"

Sara laughed. Everybody always seemed to go out of their way to make sure she knew how bad men were. Not too many people seemed to have anything good to say about men, not even Pappo. Sara watched Charles rummage through his box of tools. She'd only just met the man today, and he hadn't been anything less than kind and generous. He'd worked hard from the moment he'd come by, stopping long enough to take a drink or get a quick bite to eat. And on top of all that, he was about the most handsome man she'd ever laid eyes on. Sara shrugged and went back to her dumplings.

I've Been Saving It Up

She lay wide awake in bed that night while Momma Harper lay in the bed across the room, snoring faintly, having been asleep for hours. Sara had been living with Momma Harper for several months now, and the longer she stayed away from Timber, the harder she knew it would be for her ever to go back. She missed Pappo and the boys, though, much more than she'd ever let on. If he knew how much he'd probably make her come home, so Sara always assured him that she was fine and enjoying her new home and her new life in Clarksville more than she ever thought possible. She knew him well enough to sense loneliness in him, too. She'd always been close to him, even closer than she was to the boys, and the bond between them went beyond that of father and daughter. Sara believed it was even soul deep.

Before he'd brought her here, he'd made her promise to be a sensible girl, one who thought with her head and not with her heart.

"Young girls can be kinda silly sometimes," he'd warned her. "Fallin' fo' any kind of fool to come 'long who know how to say what he know y'all like to hear."

"But I ain't like that, Pappo. You know I—"

He put his hand up to stop her like he always did when he didn't want to be interrupted. "Me and yo' momma . . . maybe we sheltered you too much sometimes. I know we did, 'specially me." Pappo looked off into the distance across the field, but Sara could see tears glistening out of the corners of his eyes. "That's 'cause I always wanted the best fo' you, baby girl, and I never want no daughter of mine to end up with some fool who can't take care of her or treat her right."

Sara softly placed her hand on top of his. "I know, Pappo," she whispered.

"Clarksville is a big place. Things out there move faster than they do down here. Folks move fast too." He stared lovingly at her, hoping he was doing the right thing in sending her away, knowing he had no choice. "I want you to take care of yo' grandmomma and be a good girl." Ezra smiled and then corrected himself. "Be a good woman, Sara. 'Cause that's what you is now. A woman."

Sara sighed at her memories of the last time they were together. She was a woman now, and she had no idea what had changed in the moment he'd confessed that to her and the breath before, when he'd called her his "baby girl." Had the right of passage from girlhood to womanhood always been so simple? Once Pappo declared it to be so, then was it so? She was Sara Tate, the same Sara Tate she'd always been, but suddenly she'd been thrust into a new town, a new house, and womanhood, and Sara wondered if she'd ever be able to catch up with it all.

Pappo had warned her about falling in love with fools, but

he'd never told her what a fool would look like. For all she knew, she might trip and fall right on top of one and never even know it. Maybe this Charles Brooks was a fool. He'd worked hard, though.

Sara squeezed her eyes shut and rolled over on her side, facing the window. She'd cracked it just enough to let the stuffiness of the house escape into the night air. The breeze was a welcomed relief, though, and she inhaled deeply, hoping it would be enough to clear her mind so that she could finally doze off to sleep. Why did she even concern herself with Charles, anyway? He would only be around the house another day or two until he'd finished the work he'd started, and then she'd never see him again. That man probably had more women chasing after him in Bueller than he knew what to do with. She'd always imagined that the man she'd fall in love with and marry would chase after her and court her like Pappo had courted her mother. Before she died, Sara's mother used to go on about how he would bring her flowers and even how he asked her daddy for her hand in marriage. Charles didn't strike her as that kind of man. Maybe Mrs. Robinson had been right, and pretty men like him were selfish and conniving. The only thing he'd done all day was hammer on the house and drink up most of her water. Maybe tomorrow she'd charge him a penny a glass. After all, cool glass of water wasn't always so easy to come by.

To Get a Little Joy from Life

Her mind wasn't as sharp as it used to be, but Miss Harper was no fool. She watched the young man finish loading his tools into the back of his truck. He'd fixed her roof and was getting ready to leave. That young girl, as usual, was off somewhere doing chores that didn't need to be done, trying to look busier than she really was. She'd dusted so much the past few days Miss Harper swore the girl had taken the shine clean off her good table. She couldn't so much as put a spoon to her mouth before she appeared like a ghost out of nowhere, coaxed it out of her hand, and ran back into the kitchen to wash it right along with a sink full of dishes that weren't even dirty.

The girl wasn't fooling anybody but herself. She'd been eyeing that boy on the sly since he'd come by two days ago, and he'd catch a glimpse of her whenever and whereever he could, too. Miss Harper had seen all this during times when they both thought she was napping. What most folks didn't know was that old folks didn't really sleep as much as people thought. They only pretended to doze off so that they could eavesdrop on everybody else and find out what they were really thinking. The ones that liked her never said one mean word about her, even when they believed she was asleep. And the others, well, that's when they'd start whispering and carrying on about how she was too old and senile and not worth a damn anymore to a soul. Those were the people she stopped letting into her house. They thought she was crazy and had forgotten them, but Miss Harper remembered her enemies even better than she did her friends.

Charles put the last of his tools in the truck and walked over to the porch where Miss Harper was sitting, pretending to nod off. He removed his hat and cleared his throat before calling out to her. "Miss Harper?"

Miss Harper bobbed her head and then slowly opened her eyes. "Whatchu want with me, boy?"

"Well, I'm gettin' ready to go now."

"You leavin' already?"

Charles smiled. "Yes, ma'am. I'm all done, and I'm gon' be gettin' on back down the road. I done cleaned up 'round back and I don't 'xpect you should have anymo' problems with that roof of yours."

Miss Harper slowly rose from where she was sitting and walked over to the edge of the porch. He sure was a fine young man and would certainly make some woman a good husband, she thought, smiling. She hadn't noticed a ring on his finger, and figured this one had been slick enough to avoid falling for any fast little thing to come along. Smart and good-looking? Fine marriage material, she concluded.

"Who you say sent you here?" she asked.

Charles chuckled. "Grady, ma'am. Grady Davis. Yo' great-nephew over in Bueller."

Miss Harper shrugged her shoulders indifferently. "I 'spect I gotta lot of great-nephews all over kingdom come. Don't recall no Grady, though. Don't recall none of 'em, to be truthful."

"Yes, ma'am. I understand," he said warmly.

Miss Harper looked at him as if he'd said something ridiculous. "Naw, son. You too young to understand what it is to be as ol' as me. But I 'preciate you tryin'."

He laughed. "I best be gettin' on now."

Just then Sara, who'd been inside the doorway listening, hurried out onto the porch, then quickly tried to compose herself. Miss Harper had known the girl was there all along and smiled. Dumb as a cow, that's all that girl was, Miss Harper surmised.

Sara looked anxiously at her grandmother and then down at Charles. "You leavin'?"

"Yes, ma'am, I'm leavin'." Sara missed the hint of regret in his tone of voice, but Miss Harper didn't.

Charles turned to leave when Miss Harper stopped him. "Young man, "I was wonderin' if you might be available to do some mo' work fo' me 'round this here ol' place."

"Momma Harper?" Sara asked, concerned.

Miss Harper waved her hand in Sara's direction to hush the girl before she said something foolish. "I got a ol' outhouse close to my new one out back that I want taken down 'cause it's full of snakes, and I don't much care fo' snakes. They get into my house and scare the mess outta me."

A slow grin spread across Charles's face and he listened attentively. "I understand."

"And some of my flo'boards is loose. I'm 'fraid this gal gon' trip and fall and break her neck one of these days." She winked.

Embarrassment washed over Sara's face. "That ain't true, Mo—"

Charles looked at Sara. "We wouldn't want her to break her neck, Miss Harper. That would certainly be a shame."

Sara finally gathered her good sense and decided to put her foot down before her grandmother talked herself into business dealings she couldn't afford. "Momma Harper, I think you need to go inside now."

Sara's grandmother looked at her and frowned. "Why? Can't you see I'm talkin' business, li'l girl?"

"Yes, ma'am," she said condescendingly. "But you talkin' 'bout a awful lot of work, and probably entirely too much money." She glared at Charles, who was still standing and grinning at the foot of the porch.

"It's my money, and if I want to spend it on fixin' up my house, why can't I?"

"We can get Pappo and the boys to come up and do all that work for nothin'."

Miss Harper rolled her eyes and shooed Sara's protests away. "Why I gotta wait on somebody else when I got this nice young man right here in my yard who can do it fo' me?" She smiled sweetly at Charles, who nodded his confirmation.

"Momma Harper, you can't afford all that work. You needs to save yo' money, and—"

Sara's grandmother propped her hand up on her hip, tilted her head to one side, and glared at the girl so hard, Sara shrank in her shoes. "Jus' who you think you talkin' to, chil'? And how you gon' be stingy with my money, li'l girl?" *What is that child's name?* Miss Harper wondered to herself. She had been calling her little girl for the last week because she couldn't remember her name to save her life. Sweet girl, too.

Charles looked up admiringly at the old woman. "I assure you, Miss Harper. I can fix mos' anything that's broken, and I can give you a good price on it, too. I ain't no thief and I ain't got no intention of takin' all yo' money."

Miss Harper laughed. "Well that's right nice of you, young

man, and I thank you fo' not tryin' to steal from me." "I 'xpect to see you here in the mornin'?" she asked, turning to Charles one last time before going inside while Sara held the door open for her.

"Bright and early, Miss Harper. Bright and early." Charles caught Sara's glance one last time before she followed Miss Harper into the house, and he smiled brilliantly at her.

Sara shook her head and let the screen door slam behind her.

"You better watch how you let that do' slam, li'l girl! I don't take kindly to no do' slammin' round here!" He heard Miss Harper fuss as he walked back to the truck.

"I'm sorry, Momma Harper," he heard Sara say apprehensively.

Charles whistled the whole way home. That Miss Harper was a sly one, that was for sure. He'd seen right through her ploy to keep him coming back out to the house. Sara had missed it, but he'd caught on pretty quick.

"Whatchu doin', Charles, man?" he asked himself on the drive to Bueller, back to his wife and children. Hell, he was taking advantage of a paying job, that's all he was doing. He was helping an old woman make some repairs around her house. That's what he was doing. And he was looking forward to seeing that pretty granddaughter of hers . . . bright and early. That's all he was doing.

Gotta Have a Kiss and a Sweet

Charles had spent much of the morning tearing down Miss Harper's old outhouse. He'd chopped the wood from it and stacked it next to the house for her to use when winter came. All that was left was to finish filling the hole left behind where the outhouse had been. Miss Harper had managed to keep him working for nearly two weeks since he'd first come by to repair the roof. Sometimes when he'd pull up she seemed to have no idea who he was, or even who she was for that matter. Sara would usually intercede and comfort the old woman, while Charles went on about the business of working.

Charles finished shoveling just in time to hear his stomach growl.

"You ought to be good and hungry by now," Sara said, smiling and coming towards Charles, cradling a bowl in her hands. He told her every day that he'd brought plenty to eat, but every day she'd surprise him with a bowl or plate of something good and hot.

The aroma made its way to him before she did, and Charles inhaled it. "You must've read my mind, Miss Sara," he grinned. "Or heard my stomach makin' all that racket all the way inside the house."

She laughed. "I heard it, all right, and it said to me, 'Girl! you betta get that man somethin' to eat fo' he fall over from starvin' to death.' So here I am."

"Mmmm," he moaned, shoving red beans and cornbread into his mouth.

"Don't you wanna sit down and eat?" Sara motioned to the stoop on the side of the house.

Charles nodded, followed her without saying a word, and sat down.

"Oh!" Sara hurried back inside. "I forgot somethin'." She returned a few minutes later with a glass of lemonade.

Charles gulped it down in one swallow. "Thank you kindly," he belched.

Sara laughed. "You want some mo'?"

He wiped his mouth with the back of his hand. "If you don't mind."

Minutes later Charles was scraping the bottom of the bowl of the last bite of his meal. "That sho' was good, girl. I really 'preciate yo' hospitality."

"Well, it's no problem. I always end up makin' mo' than me and Momma Harper can eat, anyway. It usually jus' go bad 'fo we get to it. There jus' ain't no way to make a little bit of beans."

"Naw. I guess it ain't."

The way he stared at her sometimes still made her uncomfortable, and Sara felt her face flush with warmth. Charles liked to gaze into her eyes and didn't seem to think much of it, or of the effect it could have on a girl. He'd hypnotize her for moments at a time until she came to her good senses and turned away, only to feel him still watching her. He had the kind of eyes that could burn a hole into whatever held them, deep and penetrating, to the point of being intrusive at times. But they were beautiful eyes and she'd grown fond of them the past few weeks.

"This house need so much work on it. Momma Harper been in it by herself fo' more than fifteen years 'fo I come along, and she ain't been able to do much to it. Her chil'ren have moved North, mostly—or died." Sara thought about her own mother Dora. "If you hadn't come 'long when you did, the place woulda probably fallen to the ground pretty soon."

"Yeah, it need a lot of work."

"I know we ain't payin' you properly," she said apologetically. "Momma Harper ain't got much money, and—"

"It ain't no problem, Miss Sara."

"Oh, but I know it is. You practically doin' all this work fo' nothin' and, I jus' want you to know we grateful. That's all."

Charles patted his full stomach and let out a quiet belch. "And I'm 'preciatin' all this good cookin' and these fine meals of yo's too."

"You think you gon' be gettin' anymo' work done today, or do you need to go lay out under one of them trees to get yo' nap?" she teased.

"You might need to let me doze off fo' a minute or two, 'cause right at the moment I ain't much good fo' nothin'," He winked.

Sara shook her head. "You better not let Momma Harper hear you say that, or else she might come runnin' out here with a switch and chase you all 'round the yard. I'll bet that'll put a fire under you."

"Naw, I don't think I wanna be chased down by Miss Harper. As full as I am, she liable to catch me."

"She jus' might, or shoot you in the leg first and then whip you. I hear she ain't above such things." Sara gathered up the dishes and headed back inside.

It had been a long time since he'd felt this way about a woman. Charles could hardly take his eyes off Sara when she was close. He hadn't loved a woman since Nadine Cooper, and even that hadn't been right. Charles had been young and in love with the idea of that woman more than he'd been in love with Nadine. He'd figured that out a long time ago. Charles had accepted the fact that he'd never truly loved any woman other than his own momma. Sara threatened to touch a chord in him that hadn't ever been tugged on. It wasn't anything particular that she did, he concluded. She was a sweet girl, pretty and easy to talk to when he wasn't staring into her eyes. He liked being around her, is all. That was something he couldn't say about Roberta. Charles welcomed an audience with Sara and dreaded every minute he had to spend with his wife. Maybe that was all the difference.

Sara came back a few minutes later carrying a small saucer. Charles's eyes lit up at the sight of her as she sat back down next to him.

"I almost forgot 'bout dessert." She beamed. "I hope you ain't too full fo' cobbler."

Of course he liked cobbler, even more because she'd made it and thought enough of him to bring him some. Charles never said a word, but he felt himself leaning in close to her, holding her gaze with his and doing the one thing he'd hoped he'd do the first time he'd laid eyes on her. Her lips were as warm as that cobbler she'd brought him. She'd never been kissed. Every instinct in him told him that, and so Charles was careful. He had to be or else she'd run away and leave him wishing he'd never done it. She quivered a bit, but he held her where she was, willing her to stay put just for a minute, and she did. Sara tasted sweet, and there was nothing else in the world that he wanted more than her.

*   *   *

Charles drove home with Sara burned into his mind. She hadn't run away from him like he thought she would after he kissed her. But she hadn't known what to do with it, either. That was fine because Charles knew full well what to do with it, and in time maybe he'd finish what he'd started with that girl. A picture of Roberta and the kids tried to squeeze their way into his thoughts, too, but Charles shook them off. Thoughts like that didn't fit well with Sara. Not at all.

And Left His Mama Standing Here

Roberta had been staring at him nearly all night. Charles lay sleeping next to her and even now, with his eyes closed and in that faraway place in his dreams, she could see that he was different. She couldn't really explain it, and she couldn't even call it by name. It was something that a woman just recognized, that was all, an innate fear that warned her of changes occurring in her man's world that did not include her.

Charles had been driving back and forth religiously to Clarksville for nearly three weeks. He was like a man who couldn't help himself as determination rose up in him like the sun and hurried him out the door every morning before dawn. Reluctantly it dragged him home every evening, too tired to eat, play with his children, or make love to his wife. And there was an odor coming from him that wasn't familiar. At first her mind tried convincing her that the smell on him was that of some other woman. Her perfume. Her love. Roberta quickly dismissed that nonsense.

The aroma of another woman would've been tart like unripened fruit and stale from his long drive home. This was something else that fueled anxiety way down deep in her soul. When she looked into his eyes, she could almost see the image of this thing that was taking over her man. But just before she could finally see it clearly, it faded quickly into the black inkwells of Charles's eyes.

He gettin' restless now.

Roberta sat straight up in bed and quickly scanned the darkness for the person who'd said that. Years ago she'd have dismissed it as belonging to BettAnn. Sometimes it sounded like Danny's voice. She looked over to Charles to see if he'd heard it, too, but he lay sound asleep. She'd heard someone, she could've sworn . . . but there was no one there. Roberta slowly eased back down onto her pillow. The sound of BettAnn's and Danny's voices had disappeared into the recesses of her memory. This new voice wasn't familiar. It scared her.

Her mind played tricks on her sometimes, especially when she was tired and worried. She looked at Charles and envied the peaceful expression he slept behind. Lord, he was fine, finer than any man in town, and he lay in her bed every night making babies with her, Roberta thought proudly. She'd lay down her life for him if he'd just ask.

Sleep finally started to weigh down on her, and Roberta's eyelids slowly fanned themselves closed. Everything would be fine in the morning, she thought to herself. Roberta would see to it.

Don't you let him go.

The warmth of the whisper lighted softly over her ear. She heard it just before drifting off to sleep, but this time it didn't panic her. Roberta embraced the warning in her heart and smiled.

"No," she whispered back. "I won't."

* * *

Wearing her nightgown and carrying both her children, Roberta rushed past Charles and frantically jumped into the passenger side of his truck before he knew what was happening.

"You ain't goin' to Clarksville without us, Charles!" she screamed from inside the truck. Both of the children were crying.

Charles glared at her from outside the truck, shaking his head, angry at how foolish she was acting.

"You look like a wild woman, Roberta!" he shouted. "And you makin' a fool of yo'self! Get on outta that truck so I can go get some work done!" Charles marched over to where she sat and yanked open the door. "I ain't got time fo' yo' nonsense, Roberta!" He reached over her and took CJ from her arms. "I got to go! Now get outta the truck and go back in the house!"

Roberta grabbed Elizabeth and clutched her tightly to her chest. "And you can go, but you takin' us with you, Charles! I ain't gettin' out of this truck! So give me back my baby and let's go!" Roberta reached out her hand and roughly grabbed CJ by the nightshirt.

"Daddeeee!" Elizabeth shouted, reaching out her arm to Charles. Roberta ignored the little girl's protests and held her face against her breast.

"Let go of the baby, Roberta!" Charles demanded. He ripped her hand from the baby's shirt.

"Daddeeee!" Elizabeth fought to get free from Roberta's grasp.

"Look at whatchu doin', Roberta!" Charles yelled, trying to pry her hand off Elizabeth. "Let go! Let her go!"

Roberta's eyes burned fire red at Charles. "You let go, Charles!" she growled. "And you get in this truck and take us all to Clarksville, or ain't none of us goin'!"

Charles had had enough. He hurried back into the house and put CJ in his crib where he knew the boy would be safe, then rushed back out the car, pulled Elizabeth from Roberta's clutches, and then lifted Roberta from the seat.

Roberta kicked and screamed at the top of her lungs. "You ain't leavin' me! You ain't leavin'—"

Charles dumped her in front of the house and started to walk away, but not before Roberta jumped to her feet and ran after him. She jumped onto his back and held on with all her strength.

"Roberta!" Charles shouted, trying to shake her off him.

"I'm goin' too, Charles! I'm goin' or ain't none of us goin'!"

Somehow he managed to pull her arms from around his neck, and Roberta fell hard to the ground.

Charles glared down at her. "I'm goin' to work, Roberta," he said, clenching his jaws and out of breath. "Them kids need you to look after 'em and to stop actin' like a fool. 'Cause that's what you doin', woman. You makin' a fool outta yo'self, and I ain't puttin' up with that shit!"

Roberta slowly rose to her feet and dusted off the back of her gown, suddenly looking like a stunned child who'd been scolded for being bad. "You get yo' ass back in that house and fix them kids somethin' to eat! I'm gon' be home later on."

She dried her face with the hem of her gown and nodded her head. Roberta hadn't meant to make him so angry, but she was afraid all of a sudden and didn't know why. If she could've explained it to Charles so that he would understand, maybe he wouldn't be so upset and maybe he'd take her and the kids to Clarksville with him. But from the expression on his face, she could tell he wasn't in the mood to hear anything she had to say.

Roberta watched Charles speed off in the truck until it disappeared in the distance. He thought she was a fool. But Roberta was no fool. She was just lost in him, and there was nothing foolish about that. If he'd just sit still for a minute, he'd realize it too. But Charles was always moving and going and doing whatever he could to be away from home—away from her. She'd never been blind to the fact that he didn't love her, but there was always that small hope burning inside her that one day he would. Roberta would hold on to that hope until the day she died. What other choice did she have?

Elizabeth stood on the porch, watching her mother sway in the wind like a branch on a tree, tears streaming down Roberta's cheeks, long after Charles had left. "CJ hungry momma, and me too. I'm hungry, too."

The faint sound of the girl's voice was like an echo coming from a faraway place. "Go get you a biscuit, baby. Get you a biscuit out the kitchen."

Just Like a Flower

Charles drove the nails deep into the pine boards of Miss Harper's bedroom floor. He'd worked steadily all day, refusing to stop even to eat. Goddamned Roberta had lost her mind all over him that morning, and he still couldn't get past it. There never seemed to be middle ground with Roberta. She pushed too hard, and pulled on him so tight she hardly left him room to think. Charles ran away from home every day because whenever he was around her, she choked him with the way she needed for him to be in her face all damn day. One thought had plagued him since he'd left home, and it bothered him, while it filled him with a sense of relief and a hope of being free all over again, to do whatever the hell he wanted. Charles pounded another nail into the floor, and for a split second he imagined his hammer coming down hard on Roberta's head. Guilt pushed that thought away. Roberta had pissed him off, but Charles had been the one who lost his senses at the sight of that girl standing naked in front of him in that barn. He'd known better than to ever lay a hand on Roberta and had gone so far as to break his own damn rule of not messing around with girls her age. Now here he was, married to her crazy ass with two kids to look after. All of a sudden Charles saw his hammer coming down on top of his own hand.

"Awww, shhhhiiiit!" he yelled out. Charles's thumb throbbed as blood spurted out from the tip.

Sara rushed into the room, "Charles you—oh my goodness!" She hurried to the drawer and pulled out a rag, tore a strip off it, and helped Charles to a seat on the bed. Sara quickly wrapped the material around his thumb to help stop the bleeding.

"Damn!"

"I think it look worse than it is," she said, concerned. "Is that too tight?"

Charles shook his head and tried not to look as embarrassed as he was.

"Hold this tight," she said, getting up and hurrying towards the kitchen, "I'll be right back."

The pain in his hand was excruciating and seemed to find its way from his toes to the top of his head. Charles closed his eyes and held on tight to his thumb. Sara came back a few minutes later with a basin filled with ice and water and a clean towel. She sat back down next to Charles. "Lemme see." She carefully unwrapped the material from his hand. "It ain't bleedin' as much." Sara carefully placed his hand in the basin. "This'll help."

"That's what I get fo' not payin' attention to what I'm doin'." He grimaced. Just then his stomach growled.

Sara laughed. "No, that's what you get fo' not stoppin' to eat. Yo' mind wasn't on hammerin', it was probably on food. I know I can get kinda crazy myself when I don't eat."

He saw her lips moving as she rambled on and on about something he could care less about. Sara looked up at him, smiling, laughing, and consoling him all at once, and suddenly he realized what it was he'd been missing out on all this time. Sara had no expectations of him like Roberta had, and she had no preconceived notions of him the way Nadine had. To her, she was just Charles. She was easy to be with, and he could sit next to her all day long and be nothing more or less than who he was. He'd stretched himself as thin as a rubber band trying to exceed Nadine's expectations of him, and he held on tight to himself, trying to keep Roberta from pulling him apart. Sara's voice calmed him, and her touch soothed him on the inside.

"It's gon' swell, and you probably gon' loose that nail, but I think you should be fine." She smiled.

All she needed to do was smile at him and it was enough to set a fire in him he'd been holding back since he'd first laid eyes on her. Charles slowly raised his uninjured hand to her face, remembering the last time he'd kissed her, and giving in to the urge to feel her lips against his again.

"Momma Harper's gon' be back soon. She at the deaconess meetin' at the church. Did I tell you that already?" she explained nervously.

Charles sighed at the relief he felt as his lips pressed against hers. *This one right here,* he found himself thinking, *she should've been the one.* Someone like her would suit him so much better than Roberta or even Nadine, for that matter.

Charles lay Sara down on her back and lowered himself on top of her. Her bewildered expression questioned him, but there was nothing he could say. Charles stared into her eyes, hoping she'd stare back into his and see the man he wanted to be. His lips met hers, and he knew that there would be no turning back. Not for him. Not now.

"We can't do this, Charles," Sara said, worried. "It ain't right. Please—please get off me." Sara tried pushing him away, but Charles wouldn't budge.

"Naw," he said, gently taking one of her hands in his and kissing it. Charles gazed adoringly into her eyes and smiled. He could see in her eyes that she thought he'd hurt her, but that was the farthest thing from his mind. He traced his finger around the outline of her lips, then softly kissed them. Her heart beat fast like a rabbit's, against his chest, letting him know that she was afraid. Charles waited a moment, listening intently for that small voice of reason to warn him to get up and move on without laying a hand on this girl, but it never came. "What if I was to tell you I love you, Sara?" He smiled at her, hoping that she'd believe him and that it would be enough, because at the moment he meant it. If he could just have this, he thought, just this once, it would fuel him for a lifetime. He needed some light in his darkness, and there was no other place to get it but from her.

"You love me? But . . . how can you say somethin' like that, Charles? It ain't right and it certainly can't be true."

To hell with righteousness or truth. Charles hadn't sought out either since he'd first met Sara. She was all he wanted. Charles knew that, and Sara needed to know it too. "You think entirely too much, Miss Sara." He playfully tapped his finger against the tip of her nose and kissed her again. " 'Course I love you, girl. I knowed that the minute I saw you. And if you think 'bout it, you probably love me too."

Sara opened her mouth to speak but the words wouldn't come. Charles tenderly ran his hand over her hair and planted kisses on her forehead and cheeks. His fingers found the top button to her blouse and slowly began unbuttoning it. This one time . . . that's all he wanted. That's all he needed, and Charles would be on his way.

"Tell me you love me too, Sara." He whispered, kissing down her neck and across her chest. "I need to hear you say it, honey. I need to hear you say you love me."

She closed her eyes and whispered, "I don't know, Charles."

"Yes you do, honey. You know like I know ain't nothin' wrong with this, Sara. Ain't nothin' wrong with you and me."

Charles felt like he'd been set free from the inside out. He raised himself up over her, knowing that this time he'd never regret one moment with this woman. "I jus' need to hear you say it, sweetheart 'cause it would mean everything to me to know you feel the same way I do."

Sara swallowed hard and reached up to touch his face, thinking that maybe it was love all along that had been tickling her insides everytime she saw him, or even thought of seeing him.

Charles saw past the hesitation in her eyes deep down to what he wanted to see, and realized that she didn't need to say a word.

Charles drove home with the essence of her all over him, and in his heart. He'd stayed late to finish laying the floor in the parlor, kissed her goodbye before he left, and never told her he wasn't coming back. He swallowed hard at the thought.

The smell of supper cooking invited him into the house. Roberta and the children sat at the kitchen table, dressed up like it was Sunday, smiling at the sight of him coming through the door.

Roberta practically leaped up from her chair and kissed him on the cheek. "Hi, honey," she said enthusiastically.

"Hi, daddy." Roberta had tied a bow on Elizabeth's head big enough to throw her off balance if she tilted it too far in any direction.

"You go wash up fo' supper, baby," she said, motioning Charles to the basin. When he came back, Roberta carefully placed his plate down in front of him. Charles stared down at a meal fit for a king—fried chicken, butter beans, cornbread, greens.

Roberta sat down across from him, staring admirably at the children, then back to him. "And we havin' sweet potato pie for dessert," she announced proudly.

Charles sat speechless for a moment. "What's the occasion?"

"Well . . . I jus' thought it would be nice, 'specially after we had that fallin' out this mornin'," Roberta said apologetically.

"We didn't have no fallin' out this mornin', Roberta," he said unemotionally. "You did."

Roberta ignored his comment and smiled. "Y'all eat yo' food 'fo it get cold," she said to the children.

Charles still seemed a little angry to her, but Roberta knew that after he tasted her sweet potato pie he'd be just fine.

Wonder What Will Become of Poor Me

Grady took off his hat and headed straight for the bar in Claudine's juke joint.

"Claudine, my queen," he sang, leaning in to the woman behind the counter. Grady managed to steal a kiss before she snatched away.

"I told you 'bout kissin' on me, boy!" she snapped. "Do it again and I'm gon' put my whole fist in yo' mouth!"

He laughed, "Aw now, why you got to be so mean? Every time I come up in here you got yo' face all frowned up."

She rolled her eyes and poured him a drink. "Yeah but I'm grinnin' from ear to ear 'fo you walk through my door. That oughta tell you somethin', Grady Thompson."

"It don't tell me nothin' 'cept yo' ass is ornery as a rattlesnake." Grady turned up his drink and finished it in one gulp, then put his glass back down for her to fill again.

Claudine propped her hand on her hip and laughed, "I'm

ornery as hell and too much woman fo' you, boy! Now, get yo' ass away from me 'fo I hurt yo' feelin'."

"You scared. That's all it is," Grady fussed at Claudine over his shoulder as he headed to where Charles sat.

Charles laughed. "Better be careful with that woman, man. One of these days she might snatch you right up and I bet my last five dollars that say she'd break yo' boney ass in two."

"Ain't no such thing as too much woman fo' a man like me, son," Grady said loud enough for Claudine to hear. "Like I said, she scared to death that once I get started, she ain't gon' be able to get her fill of my kinda lovin'."

"Keep on, chil'," Claudine hollered from across the room. "And I'll give you a ass whuppin' to the likes that you ain't never had an ass whuppin' befo' in yo' life."

"Jus' tell me when and where, sweetheart. I'll be waitin'."

Charles shook his head and laughed. "You plum crazy, man."

"That's a fine woman, though. You can't tell me she ain't. Old as she is, she sho' is fine."

"Fine and mean as hell. I hear she got a pistol under that skirt and don't mind takin' aim and pullin' that trigger, neither."

"I like 'em mean. A mean woman can take a man to town in bed. Ride him like he a buckin' bull—hard and strong and she ain't lettin' go 'cause she wanna tame his buckin' ass. That's the kinda woman I like." Grady looked in Claudine's direction, smiled, and lifted his glass to her. "Speakin' of mean—how's yo' woman doin'?"

Charles shook his head and sipped from his glass, not bothering to answer the question.

"Oh, I'm sorry, man. Roberta ain't mean, she jus' crazy as hell."

"Yeah well, crazy or not, that's my wife you talkin' 'bout, man." Charles tried to sound offended, but he wasn't.

"She still talk to herself?"

Charles tried not to laugh. "She don't talk to herself, Grady."

"'Course she do. She jus' do it when you ain't there is all. I hear she talk to herself all the damn time, walkin' down the street mumblin' and fussin' to somebody who ain't nowhere but in her mind."

"You heard wrong, then. Roberta don't talk to herself no mo' than anybody else, and that's what I know."

"All right. Then maybe she talkin' to ghosts. Is that it? She talk to ghosts?"

Charles slammed his glass down on the table, "You got a beatin' comin', Grady. You mouth is too smart sometime and fo' that, I need to beat yo' skinny ass."

"You can't do nothin' with this skinny ass, son. How many times I got to tell you that?"

"Every time I whup yo' skinny ass—that's how many times, which is damn near all the time. I been beatin' yo' ass since we was kids, man. Jus' poundin' on yo' big head every time I got the itchin' fo' it," Charles teased.

Grady cut his eyes at Charles. "Go to hell, man."

"Save me a seat, son."

"Hey, you know Aunt Josie passed," Grady said solemnly.

"Aunt Josie?"

Charles's memory drifted back to the last time he'd been to Clarksville, months ago. He hadn't forgotten Miss Harper, and especially Sara. That girl had left a mark on him that he couldn't wash away, no matter how hard he'd tried. It was like she'd burned a permanent hole in him and there was nothing he could do to close it up. He hadn't expected Sara's impression to linger so long on him. He hadn't expected to miss her or to be tempted on more than one occasion to drive back over to that house just to see how she was doing or hold her and kiss her one last time.

He hadn't mistreated Sara, but he'd lied to her, made her believe in something that wasn't quite true—him. Charles had no excuse for his deception. He'd been a greedy man caught up in his craving for Sara, never mind what she'd wanted. He imagined her standing on that porch day after day, looking for him to come driving towards the house, bringing flowers and a marriage proposal. He'd imagined the disappointment that shadowed her face at dusk when she gave into the realization that he wasn't coming after all.

"Miss Harper, man. Don't tell me you don't remember my Aunt Josie over in Clarksville? Hell, you took damn near all her money."

"Naw, Grady. I didn't know she passed. Sorry to hear that."

"She was a old woman. Damn near a hundred, I think."

"When she die?"

"Few weeks back. Sho' was sweet, but she never could remember my name. I don't think she knew anybody's name, to tell the truth."

"So, what happened to yo' cousin? The one stayin' with her?" Charles asked hesitantly.

Grady shook his head in disgust. "Fool girl got herself in trouble. Sittin' up in church at the funeral tryin' to hide it."

"Hide what?"

"She gon' have a baby, man. Got herself in trouble by some fool who ain't even man enough to marry that dumb-ass girl."

Charles nearly choked on his drink. "How you know she gon' have a baby?"

"I got fo' kids my damn self, man. 'Course I know a pregnant belly when I see one. Shoulda kept her ass in them sticks where she come from."

"She didn't go back?"

"Naw. She still in the house. Didn't nobody else want it so the girl stayed even after her daddy come up to get her. Left without her fast behind, too. Can't say that I blame him."

Oh Daddy, Look at What You Doin'

I don't always 'member yo' name li'l girl. I used to know it. I'm sho' I did. I know it's buried inside me somewhere too deep fo' me to dig it up. When a woman get ol' like me, somethin' start tellin' her to keep the precious things hidden so nobody can take 'em from you. I 'spect that's where yo' name is. And I know it must be precious to me 'cause I hid it so good I can't even find it myself. You keep yo' precious things hidden too when you get ol' like me. That way, when it's yo' time, you can take 'em with you to heaven and keep 'em always."

Momma Harper had told her many things before she'd died. Some of what she said made no sense at all to Sara, but other things were treasures that she swore she'd keep forever. Sara had been afraid and excited all at the same time when she'd left Timber. More than anything else, she'd been eager to become the woman

Pappo had told her she was on the drive to Clarksville. He never told her, though, that being a woman would mean that her whole world would turn over on its side and leave her scratching her head, wondering what could possibly happen next. After he'd heard about Momma Harper dying, Pappo rushed up in that old truck of his to gather her up and take her back to Timber, but she refused to go. By then Sara knew about the child she was carrying and that she'd have to figure out a way to take care of herself. Pappo had been angrier at her then she'd ever seen him, and he even threatened to pick her up and put her in that truck himself if she didn't listen to reason. His reason. Not hers. For the first time in her life she defied him, stood her ground, and told him to his face, "I ain't goin' back with you, Pappo. I'm a grown woman and I'm stayin' right here."

Her words cut him. His disappointment of her, cut back and Sara watched him drive away, wishing she could change her mind and knowing it was too late. For nearly a year she'd taken care of Momma Harper all by herself. Sara had lived a whole lifetime in Clarksville in a matter of months, and going back to Timber wasn't an option that suited her. She'd been foolish enough to fall for the first man to come along and she'd been left with a child of her own to have to take care of. Her lessons had been hard and hurtful, but they'd been lessons, and Sara wouldn't run from them. Pappo wanted to protect her from life and what it had to teach her. But Pappo couldn't protect her anymore. Timber was the glass jar he wanted to keep her in, and Sara knew she would never be able to breathe again with him watching over her the way he tended to do.

She found a job shortly after Momma Harper died, as a housekeeper and cook for a white family on the other side of Clarksville.

It was a long walk and Sara had to leave the house before dawn to get there in time to make breakfast, and she didn't get home again until after sunset, but she made enough money to take care of herself and even put some away for when the baby came.

Sara couldn't remember the moment she'd given up waiting for him. It just happened one day that she didn't glance out the kitchen window, expecting to see him climb out of his truck, and she stopped anticipating that every knock on the door was his. Her heart didn't break, really. It seemed to melt into the realization that she was left alone by a man who never really cared for her in the first place. Miss Robinson had warned her about men like Charles, and every chance she got, her neighbor turned up her nose and smirked at this silly girl who hadn't listened to her good reason, dumb and pregnant with that pretty man's child.

Eventually, she settled in to her life as it was, more scared than she could ever give in to. Sara had to learn what it was to make do and get by the best way she could. And that's when he showed up. Charles didn't even look real, standing on the porch, fumbling that old grey fedora of his in his hands, searching for the right words to say. Sara knew even before he opened his mouth, that there was nothing he could say to make a difference anymore. Charles had been her hardest lesson of all, one she'd promised herself she'd never have to learn again.

"How you doin', Miss Sara?" he asked hesitantly, glancing down at the small round outline beneath her blouse.

What an odd question to ask, she thought, staring at him from the other side of the screen door. And then she realized he'd only asked it because he couldn't think of anything meaningful to say.

Charles shifted in his shoes. Her silence was unnerving and

the last response he'd hoped to get. He cleared his throat. "I'm, uh—I heard 'bout Miss Harper, and I'm sorry fo' yo' loss."

She studied him for a moment, searching for a glimmer of anything that looked like sincerity. He seemed to mean what he said. Perhaps, Sara concluded, this was the most honest and sincere thing Charles had ever told her.

"Thank you," she replied quietly, and with that she closed the door between them.

Charles stood dumbfounded for a moment, halfway expecting her to open the door and scream "gotcha!" But the door didn't open, so he knocked again.

"Sara, I need to—I need to talk to you, honey," he called out.

When she didn't answer, he knocked again.

All of a sudden the door flew open and Sara glared at him. "Godamnit, Charles! I said thank you, now get the hell off my porch!"

Charles swung open the screen door and wedged his foot in the doorway before she had a chance to close it again, but Sara slammed the heavy wooden door hard against his shoe.

"Aw shiiiit!" Charles screamed, hopping around on one foot.

Sara quickly bolted the door and hurried over to the window, and peeped out. Served him right, she thought. No one deserved a broken foot more than Charles, and she prayed he'd hobble on it for the rest of his life. Maybe she'd broken it so badly that it would get infected and need to be cut off altogether.

"Damn!" he muttered, limping over to the chair Miss Harper used to nap in. "I hope you happy now, girl!" he shouted. "I think you broke my foot!"

Sara cracked open the window. "I hope I did. And if you don't get outta here, I'm gon' break some other things too."

Charles rubbed his throbbing big toe and laughed, preparing himself to wait out the rest of the afternoon for her if necessary.

*   *   *

He'd been sitting there for almost an hour. Sara watched Charles from the window, sitting leisurely out front like he had all the time in the world. Out of the corner of his eye he saw the curtain move.

"I ain't got nowhere in particular to go, Miss Sara," he called out to her. "You wanna be stubborn, I can be stubborn too. I got all day."

A few minutes later Sara opened the door, stepped out onto the porch, and glared at him. "If you don't leave, I'm callin' the sheriff. He'll make you get off my porch."

"Aw, now, I know you don't wanna call no sheriff. You know what they liable to do to a black man trespassin'?" Charles sighed. "I heard they hang 'em. But don't hol' me to it."

"What would I care 'bout them hangin' you?" Tears stung her eyes. "If you ask me, I think hangin' is too good fo' a man like you. 'Specially after what—"

Charles hadn't missed the hurtful sound in her voice. "You probably right 'bout that," he said solemnly.

Sara sniffed. "I know I'm right. I don't need you to tell me how right I am."

Charles sat quietly for a moment. "You never did answer my question. How you doin', Miss Sara?"

Sara blotted her eyes dry with the collar of her blouse. "I'm doin' fine without you if that's what you wonderin'. That make you feel better—ease yo' worries?"

Charles shook his head. "Naw, it don't 'cause I got a feelin' it ain't the truth."

Sara shrugged. "Oh, it's the truth all right. And you can get back in that truck of yours and go back to wherever it is you run off to, 'cause don't nobody need you 'round here."

Charles studied her for a moment before asking, "I'm the daddy?"

Sara's angry gaze cut into him. "You ain't no kind of daddy to my baby," she said callously. "So if that's all you come down here fo' was to find out, then you need to go back to Bueller, 'cause I ain't got the time or interest in you at all! I'm gon' be the one to take care of my own chil' and I don't need no sorry man like you to call hisself the daddy of my baby!"

Charles stood up slowly and took a cautious step in her direction. "Why don't you lemme come inside, honey, so we can talk 'bout this?"

"You ain't got nothin' to say that I wanna hear!" Sara hurried inside, with Charles close behind her.

"Not even I'm sorry?" he said, grabbing the door before she had a chance to slam it in his face.

The painful expression on her face threatened to break him in two. "It's too late to be sorry." Tears streamed down her cheeks, and instinctively he reached out and wiped them away.

She'd wasted too much time on him—missing him, worrying over him, hating him. But still, buried beneath all of those emotions, Sara loved him. His touch had been enough to remind her of that.

Charles motioned down to the swelling beneath her blouse and grinned. "I um . . . sho' am happy 'bout bein' a daddy."

Sara rolled her eyes. "I tol' you, Charles, you ain't the daddy."

Charles raised his eyebrows. "Oh I ain't? You been layin' up with some other man 'sides me, Miss Sara?"

"Even if I was, that ain't none of yo' business." Sara folded her arms defensively over her chest.

"I think I am the daddy and if I am, then it is my business."

"Well it ain't gon' be none of yo' business when I move back to Timber 'cause Pappo ain't gon' let you anywhere near me or this baby," she snapped.

"Grady say Pappo has already come and gone, honey, and he left you here by yo'self. I don't think Grady was lyin'."

"Why did you even bother comin' here?"

"I tol' you, girl. To see 'bout you."

"Well, you seen me. Now you need to get on, 'cause I don't ever want to see you again as long as I'm walkin' on this earth!"

Charles slowly walked towards her and backed her away from the door, then closed it behind him.

Sara started to protest. "Charles Brooks, if you don't get outta my house—"

Charles raised his hand and gently pressed his palm against her stomach. "And whose baby you say this is? 'Cause he sho' feel like he mine." He smiled.

Sara was too busy being angry to notice him slowly backing her towards the bedroom where they'd first made love.

"Well, he ain't!" She sniffed, pushing his hand away. "And what make you think it's a boy anyhow? I know it's a girl! And she ain't yo's neither!"

"Naw, darlin'. That's my son, all right. He know it and I do too. If you'd stop fussin' long 'nuff and pay attention, you'd know it too."

Sara felt the edge of the bed pressed against the back of her knees and suddenly realized where she was. "Don't you even think 'bout touchin' me, Charles!" Tears filled her eyes. "You ain't gon' touch me again, 'cause I ain't so foolish as I was back then!"

Charles gently cradled her face between his hands, closed his eyes, and softly pressed his lips against hers. "You ain't never been no fool, Miss Sara," he whispered. "But I damn sho' was fo' lettin' you go."

He carefully leaned her back on the bed and kissed a trail from her lips down to the rise of her stomach. Charles closed his eyes and inhaled deeply, relishing the familiar scent of her that he'd feared he'd forgotten. And inside her was a portion of him, left behind for safekeeping. Charles sat up on the edge of the bed and carefully maneuvered Sara onto his lap, straddling him. "He mine alright, Miss Sara," he said between kisses. "And you mine too. I'm the one that's got to make this work. That's all there is to it."

Charles freed himself from his pants, pushed aside her panties, and slowly entered her, taking extra care not to hurt her. Sara clung to him, wrapping her arms tightly around his neck, she closed her eyes and let Charles start all over with new promises, trusting that this time he'd keep them. He'd have to.

"Don't leave me again, Charles," she begged softly. "Please."

Charles thrust in and out of her, affirming his role in her life, branding images of himself that would last forever. "I ain't never leavin' you again, sweetheart. I mean that."

Oh, the Best of Friends

B rooks!" Grady called out.

Charles turned around in time for Grady to bury his fist hard into his chin.

"Why her, man?" Grady roared. Charles stumbled and clutched his face. "Why you hafta mess with that girl? She kin to me, man!" Grady loomed over Charles, "She family, niggah!"

Charles caught his balance against the wooden post of the fence he'd been hired to put up at the Clemmons place and glared at Grady like he'd lost his damn mind. The taste of blood filled his mouth.

"What the hell—" he started to ask, but before he could, Grady lowered his shoulders and lunged into Charles knocking him to the ground. Charles struggled to catch his breath as Grady straddled him and grabbed him by the collar. "Why you mess with that girl, Brooks? I trusted you, man! I trusted you with my family and you got to go fuck with 'em!"

Grady raised his fist to hit Charles again, but Charles caught it before he could and in one motion rolled Grady over on his back and forced his own fist into Grady's stomach.

"Umph!" Grady moaned, drawing his knees to his chest. Charles slowly stood up and spit blood from his mouth.

Grady twisted on the ground until he could breathe again, then used the fence for leverage to pull himself up. "She kin, man!" he grunted, gulping for air. "Did you think I wasn't gon' find out? You was wrong fo' that, Charles. You know you was wrong, and I ain't got no choice but to whoop yo' black ass!" Grady gasped for air. "Jus' lemme catch my breath."

Charles put the pieces of the puzzle together in his mind. He knew what Grady was talking about, just like he knew that Grady had every right to be pissed. Hell, if it were him, he'd have probably snuck up and sucker punched some fool for messing around with his cousin, too. Especially if he knew the sonofabitch had a wife and kids waiting for him at home.

Charles shook his head and shrugged. "I'm sorry, Grady. I never meant to—"

It was obvious from the look in Grady's eyes that he wasn't interested in apologies. "I wish to hell I could whoop yo' ass, niggah! I wish—jus' one time—"

"I didn't go there intendin' fo' it to happen, Grady. You gotta believe me, man. It jus'—I ain't never meant to hurt that girl."

Grady's Aunt Helen had asked him to drive to Clarksville to check on the house and to find out how long Sara was planning on staying in it. Sara had answered the door, too far along to hide her round belly.

"Who's the daddy, girl?" Grady demanded.

Sara sat across from him, unable to look him in the eyes. "He's somebody 'round here. Somebody you don't know."

Grady paced back and forth. "He gon' marry you?"

Sara wrung her hands together in her lap and never answered.

"What's his name?" Grady asked angrily. "I'ma go straighten this shit out, Sara. If he any kind of man at all, he'll do what he s'posed to do and marry you. Yo' daddy know?"

She shook her head.

"Tell me who it is?"

"This ain't yo' business, Grady," she said. "I don't need you startin' no trouble that ain't yours."

"I don't give a damn 'bout what you think I need to be doin', girl. I know what I need to do, and that sonofabitch is gon' do what he need to do, too, by the time I finish with him. Now, who the hell is he?"

Sara never said his name and Grady finally left the house, mad as hell and determined to find the man she'd been fooling with.

"What's yo' name, boy?" Miss Robinson called from behind her screen door.

Grady turned and answered, "Ma'am?"

"You kin to Miss Harper and that gal livin' here?"

"Yes, ma'am," he sighed. "My name is Grady and I live over in Bueller."

Miss Robinson stepped outside onto her porch and motioned for him to come closer. "Miss Harper was a good friend of mine."

Grady shifted impatiently. "Yes, ma'am. I know."

"She had such a good heart to her and never turned her back on anybody in need."

"She was a good woman, Miss—?"

"That gal took good care of her 'fo she passed. You kin to her too?"

"Yes, ma'am. We cousins."

Miss Robinson shook her head. "Sho' is too bad what kind of predicament that gal got herself into."

"Ma'am?" Grady asked, interested now.

"You know the boy she been foolin' with? He live over in Bueller too."

Grady stopped in his tracks. "Naw. She said he was somebody from 'round here."

Miss Harper smirked. "Ain't no other man been 'round that house the whole time she been there 'cept one, and I think I heard him say he was from Bueller. You know, he ain't been back here since 'fo Miss Harper passed. Left that gal with a baby in her and ain't been back." She smacked her lips. "It's a damn shame, I tell you. I seen him, though, sneakin' and kissin' on he and her lettin' him. Of course, Miss Harper didn't know."

The old woman hadn't said the man's name, but Grady had in his mind, and just as quickly pushed it aside. "You sho' he wasn't somebody from 'round here? She said he—"

"He came out a while back to fix the roof, then stayed around to help out with other things. I guess one of 'em was that girl. Said his name was Charles, I believe. You know somebody named Charles in Bueller?"

"If all you wanted was a woman, man, you coulda had you a woman. Hell! Got plenty of women right here in town that'll oblige yo' goddamned ass anytime you want it. Why the hell you gotta go after that one? That girl don't know shit. Ain't never been with nobody from what I know and—" Grady straightened up and looked Charles in the eyes. "She coulda gotten married, man. She coulda found herself a husband, somebody to to look after her. Somebody who cared 'bout her. What the hell can you do fo' her?"

Charles hung his head and rested against the post.

"Not a damn thing, Charles. 'Cause yo' ass got a woman and kids and ain't shit you can do fo' her."

"It ain't like you think it is, Grady," Charles explained. "I care 'bout Sara."

"Yeah, well carin' 'bout her ain't worth a damn now, is it? She stuck havin' yo' baby by herself, fool. And carin' 'bout her ain't gonna put food on the table fo' that baby. Sara got to do that, and she got to do it by her damn self."

Charles shook his head in frustration. "You think you know, man, but you don't. Like I said, it ain't like you think it is."

Grady picked up his hat and slapped it against his thigh to dust it off. "You ain't got to try and explain nothin' to me, man. It ain't like I don't know. Hell, she a nice-lookin' girl," he said callously. "You and me—we always been the same. We get us a li'l bit and move on. Go back home to the wife like nothin' happen. Ain't that right?" Grady stepped closer to Charles and pointed in his face. "But we don't mess with family."

"I'm in love with that girl, man," Charles muttered.

"What did you say?"

Charles cleared his throat and said it again, "You heard me. I'm in love with Sara, Grady."

Grady studied Charles for a moment, then suddenly burst out laughing. "Man! What the hell you talkin' 'bout? Whatchu mean you love her? How you—" Charles wasn't laughing. "You serious, man?"

"More serious than I ever been. I love that girl and I ain't got no intention of leavin' her to take care of my chil' alone."

"Oh? You gon' bring her and the baby to live with you and

Roberta? I don't think yo' wife gon' care too much for that arrangement, man. Call me crazy, but—"

"I'm tellin' you that I'm gon' take care of her. That's what I'm sayin'."

"And how you gon' do that? How you gon' take care of all them women and all them damn kids?"

"I jus' am, Grady, that's all there is to it," Charles said, frustrated.

"Do Sara know you married? She don't. Do she?"

"Naw, not yet. Right now, she don't need to."

"Aw, niggah! What the hell kind of shit is that? That girl got it in her mind that y'all gon' get married. You tell her that? I figured you was jus' bullshittin' her, but—tell me you didn't tell that girl you was marryin' her."

"Look, I don't know what I'm gon' do. I'm still tryin' to work it all out in my head."

"Fool! You shoulda been workin' it out with yo' dick 'stead of that big head of yours. Whatchu gon' do? You can't have two wives. Last I heard that was against the law," he said sarcastically.

"I ain't leavin' her, Grady. And somehow I'll make this work. I'm gon' have to, that's all. I'm jus' gon' have to."

Grady scratched his head and stumbled back towards his truck. "I got a pistol man, and it got a bullet in it with yo' name on it." Grady opened the door and climbed into his truck. "I don't know what the hell you gon' do or how you plan on doin' it."

"I said, I'd take care of it," Charles insisted.

Grady nodded. "I can't fight you and win, Charles," he said coldly. "But I always been a better shot than you. If you say you gon' take care of that girl, then you take care of her." Grady started up his truck. "Else, I'll put a bullet on yo' ass. And you know I will."

Charles watched as Grady's truck disappeared down the road. He knew well enough that Grady would shoot him, all right, but that's not what bothered him. What Charles couldn't figure out was when he'd convinced himself that he loved Sara so much. He couldn't remember the time or the place when it had happened, and what surprised him most was that he didn't seem to care. All he knew was that she was a part of his life now as much as anybody, and his mind was consumed with thoughts of how to include her and keep her separate at the same time. How could he keep from losing Sara? Charles was wading in murky waters again. Sometimes he treaded where he didn't want to tread but went anyway, usually after a woman, right into a whole lot of trouble he didn't see coming.

Charles went back to work, hoping to finish before sunset and get home before Roberta worked herself into a frenzy waiting for him.

Don't Broadcast It on Nobody's Radio

Gossip wasn't gossip unless somebody told it to somebody else. Until then it was only a bittersweet flavor tickling the back of her throat, daring her not to repeat it. Martha heard it from her good friend Arlene Robinson from across the river.

"Sho' is a shame, I tell you," Arlene said, shaking her head. "That chil' come up here to take care of Mrs. Harper, her grandmomma, fo' she died. 'Member, Mrs. Harper been my neighbor fo' years."

"Oh yes, I 'member her. Nice woman."

Mrs. Robinson rolled her eyes. "She was a silly woman. Silly as they come and jus' got sillier the older she got."

Martha looked stunned, but she really wasn't all that surprised. Arlene never did mind talking bad about folks, especially dead folks.

"That young man been creepin' 'round fo' months now. He came out to fix on the house, and even after Mrs. Harper passed, he kept comin'. Next thing I know, that girl's belly starts swellin' round and big as a watermelon."

"He didn't marry her?"

"Hmpf!"

"You think he married already?"

"My guess is that he is. Or he could jus' be up to no good with a whole slew of women and chil'ren from here to Alabama. The girl keep sayin' he proposed. Say he gon' marry her soon as he get up the money to take care of her properly, but he give her a little money here and there to help buy food and keep the lights on. Sometimes he come by and fix on somethin' 'round the house. But I say, if he was gon' marry her, he'd have done it by now. That chil' been here goin' on three months now and that fool girl still waitin' on that man to carry her off to some church or judge to marry her. I don't ever think he will. You might know him, Martha. He from Bueller. Handsome fella. His name is Charles. Charles Brooks, I think it is."

Martha's heart stopped beating the moment she heard his name. The news filled her with anticipation and apprehension all at once, ballooning inside her until it became too big to keep to herself. But there was only one person she wanted to share her news with, who needed to know, and who deserved to know, though the news would crush her. Martha laughed impulsively at the thought, then felt guilty for relishing the secret she was carrying to that child. Lord knows, the last thing she ever wanted was to hurt the girl. But didn't she deserve it sometimes? After all, over the years Roberta had blossomed into nothing less than a monster, an insolent beast who insisted on turning up her nose at Martha and prancing around like a queen, bragging, always bragging about the big fine fish she'd hooked.

"Look like the fish done jiggle his worm in front of another fish and caught one fo' hisself," Martha said out loud, laughing. She hadn't been this tickled in years.

Roberta's house loomed in front of her, inching its way towards her with every step she took, as if it were as anxious to hear the news as she was to share it. If her knees weren't so bad, she'd have skipped the rest of the way, knowing that every second counted. She hoped nobody else had gotten to Roberta before she had. Martha wanted to be the one who told and she quickened her pace, racing against no one at all, just in case they might sneak up behind her and speed off towards the house.

Martha had dreamed of a moment like this, ever since Roberta had married that man and thought she was better than everybody else perched on the branch of a big elm tree she was like a fancy red robin, sticking out her chest and singing at the top of her lungs and looking down on Martha as if she were no consequence. Martha deserved better. The only time Roberta had anything to do with her was when she wanted her to look after her children.

"Me and Charles need some time alone together. We gon' go have a picnic down by the river, which is where we first met. Maybe we'll even make another baby. You know, he wants a big family." Martha always agreed so that she could see her grandchildren. They were precious to her, in a way that Roberta had never been.

She walked slowly up the steps of Roberta's house and knocked on the door. Of course Charles was out working, which was fine. This wasn't news for him. It was news for Roberta.

Roberta answered the door with a vacant look at her eyes, as if she didn't even recognize Martha.

"Hello Roberta," Martha said sweetly, "I hope I didn't catch you at a bad time."

Obviously she had. It was nearly noon, Roberta was still wearing her nightclothes, and her hair was wild all over her head. The sound of CJ crying came from the back room, and Elizabeth stood in the doorway next to her mother, still wearing her nightgown too.

"Hi, Granny Muh," Elizabeth said sweetly.

"Hey, baby, how you doin'?" The little girl shrugged and her gaze fell to the ground.

Something concerned Martha about the whole scene, but she couldn't put her finger on it. Roberta's absent stare was disturbing. Martha had never recalled seeing it before, and she worried that maybe somebody had already brought her the news.

She cleared her throat. "Well, you gon' keep me standin' out here all day, gal, or you gon' invite me in?"

Roberta hesitated for a moment before stepping to the side and letting Martha in the house.

"The baby alright?" Martha asked, sounding concerned. She started to walk to the back room where CJ lay in his crib, but Roberta pushed past her and closed the door before she could even look in on the boy.

"He just sleepy," she said.

"You sho' he ain't hungry? Sound like a hungry chil' to me."

"Whatchu doin' here, Miss Martha?" Roberta asked.

Martha tried to smile, ignoring the harsh tone of Roberta's question. "I jus' came to see 'bout y'all, that's all."

"We fine."

CJ wailed from the bedroom. "You sho' you don't want me to look in on the baby, Roberta? He might be ailin'." Not that Roberta would've given two cents about whether or not that boy was sick. Martha had seen straight through the act Roberta put on in front of just about everybody, doting on those children and making a fuss all over them that just wasn't natural whenever she thought somebody was watching. But Martha was always watching and had seen the sly pinches Roberta gave to Elizabeth when the girl wouldn't sit still. And that boy of hers cried all the time except when his daddy was home. Martha had strolled passed the house, sometimes in the mornings or even in the afternoons, only to hear that child screaming from the back room from the top of his lungs.

Roberta folded her arms defensively over her chest. "Charles ain't home."

"Well, I didn't come to see Charles, honey. I come to see you and the chil'ren. Y'all feelin' alright?"

"We fine, Miss Martha," she said indifferently.

As fine as she always was, stuck up in the house with a holler-ing child, she thought. As fine as she could be, dodging the accu-sations of Elizabeth's gaze. As fine as she could be, with a husband who was gone all the time. *"Honey, I got to go to work."*

"Tell them people you need to stay home sometimes, Charles."

"But Roberta, I got to go to work."

"It's late, Charles. You need to be gettin' on home now, 'cause I'm lonesome without you. I'm sick of this boy cryin' all the time. And why that girl keep lookin' at me like she see somethin'? In me? 'Round me? On me?"

"I got to go to work."

"You hear me, Roberta? I say, I sho' would like somethin' col' to drink. I'm a bit parched after my walk over here."

Roberta opened up the cabinet and pulled out a glass, then filled it with water from the pitcher sitting on the table. It wasn't cold but she didn't care. She held out the glass, Martha took a sip, wrinkled her nose, and sat the glass down on the table.

She cleared her throat. "I s'pose yo' icebox aint workin'?"

"I was 'bout to lay down and take a nap, Miss Martha."

"Oh, so you ain't feelin' good. That's what I thought. From the looks of you, gal, the first thing I thought when I saw you was that you was feelin' poorly." Martha stood up and pressed her hand against Roberta's forehead. "Don't feel warm. Maybe you jus' tired," she said condescendingly.

Roberta pushed her hand away, annoyed. "If you don't mind," she said, walking towards the door. "I needs to get some rest 'fo' Charles get home. I got to be gettin' supper on shortly."

Martha smiled and then sat back down. "Speakin' of Charles—he workin'?"

Roberta stared at her, surprised that Martha would ask the question. "Of course he is. He always workin'."

Martha smiled radiantly. "Well, you know what they say? A hard-workin' man is the best kinda man, 'cause you always know what he up to."

Roberta shook her head at the nonsense spewing from Martha's mouth. "I got to get that boy quiet, and—"

"If you ain't feelin' good, honey, I can see 'bout him," Martha said, starting to get up from her seat.

"No!" Roberta said, though she wasn't sure why. She wanted the boy quiet but didn't want to be the one to quiet him, and Martha could've been such a help at the moment, but . . . no. She didn't want her to go near him, because . . . because . . . "I think he might be hungry after all." All of a sudden her nerves rose up in her like fire and she clenched her hands into fists, hoping to fight back the trembling she knew would come, then sat down on the divan, took a deep breath, and held it.

"Roberta?" Martha asked, looking concerned. "You alright?"

Suddenly the crying stopped. Roberta and Martha looked at

each other, and then Martha got up, quietly opened the door, and peeped in on the child who lay sleeping and out of breath in his crib. She pulled the door shut, and put her finger to her lips.

"He musta been sleepy after all," she whispered.

Martha sat back down and gulped down the last of her water. Out of the corner of her eye she felt Roberta's eyes burning a hole in her, willing her to leave, but Martha wasn't about to. Not until she'd done what she'd come there to do.

"So you say Charles is workin'?"

"That's what I said." Roberta didn't bother to hide her annoyance.

"You sho'?" Martha asked casually.

Martha was up to something. Roberta had studied the woman for years and knew there was something burning the tip of her tongue that she was dying to say.

"My husband is workin', Martha, like he always workin'." If she let her sit there long enough, the floodgates of Martha would open up and spill everything inside her all over the floor.

Martha leaned forward and stared intently at Roberta. No, the girl didn't know a thing, because whatever state of mind she was trapped in kept her from knowing what her man was doing behind her back. Martha had no choice but to be the one to enlighten this girl. It was her duty.

"Yo' man might be workin', gal," she said icily, "or he might be laid up with that other woman I hear he got on the side." A sinister smile spread across her lips. Roberta's face showed no emotion, no expression whatsoever. But Martha knew the spark had been set, and it was only a matter of time before the flicker turned into a flame, into a fire, into a roaring blaze.

"Do you hear me? He ain't workin' all the time. He fuckin' and makin' babies with some woman who ain't you. And I come out here to tell you that, 'cause don't nobody else in this town give shit 'bout you to tell you the truth but me."

Roberta didn't move or blink and seemed to be holding her breath. "My good friend Arlene Robinson tol' me all about it," Martha went on. "She say she seen him all the time at Mrs. Harper's house. Mrs. Harper passed away awhile back. Did you know that, Roberta? I used to take you to Arlene's house in Clarksville and you used to play with her grandchildren. Why, you even help me to deliver one of them babies. Cute li'l girl with curly hair. It wasn't that long ago. Surely you know where Arlene lives. The girl is her neighbor, and she livin' in Mrs. Harper's house. Charles been fixin' it up fo' her. Did he tell you that, Roberta? Charles done fix it up fo' her real nice, and from what I hear, he got a boy by her too. Betcha didn't know . . . did you, 'Berta? Betcha didn't know a thing."

Martha stood out on Roberta's porch and inhaled a breath of liberation, smiled, and adjusted her hat before beginning her long walk home. It sure felt good to get all that mess off her chest. Carrying that kind of news around was certainly a burden and Martha never cared much for burdens. Now she'd handed it off to its rightful owner and it was up to Roberta to carry it. Martha strutted back down the road, her chest stuck out and head held high, the way she'd seen Roberta do it.

"Pride cometh 'fo' the fall," she muttered to herself, smiling. Roberta had no reason to be so proud. She'd tricked a handsome young man into marrying her, a handsome young man that all the other girls in town wanted, because Roberta had spread her legs for him and trapped them both in this mess. Adultry was a sin for Charles, but at that very moment Martha knew Roberta was paying the price for it. Lord help that man, she repeated in her mind, because he'd pay the price for it later. Roberta's wrath could wreak hell on earth in that house. She'd seen signs of it over the years. That girl had a mean streak in her.

Charles would be home soon, Roberta thought as she hurried around the kitchen. She'd bathed the children and dressed them nicely, the way he liked to see them looking.

"We got some pretty babies, Roberta. I like to see 'em dressed up, even if we ain't goin' to church."

Roberta had brushed through her hair, braided it down the back of her head, and pinned it up at the nape of her neck. She'd put on her burgundy dress with the small yellow roses. Charles always said that was his favorite. The inviting scent of cornbread saturated the house. She was making his favorite—red beans with ham hocks, and cornbread. Roberta pulled the hot pan from the oven and spread thick, creamy butter across the top.

"He fuckin' and makin' babies with some woman who ain't you."

Martha was too silly for words sometimes. But then, that's how old women were—silly and full of the kind of nonsense folks let slip in one ear and out of the other. Just because a man worked hard didn't mean he was with another woman. Most women felt that way, though, because that's probably what their men were doing. But Charles was different. He worked from sunup to sundown, making money to take care of his family. They had more money than people realized, because he didn't believe in flaunting it all the time. Charles could've bought them a big house right in the middle of town if he wanted to, but he didn't care to show off what he had.

"I'm puttin' my money 'side fo' my kids so they can go off to one of them colleges if they want to, or buy they own house."

"Yo' man got hisself a woman on the side—"

Roberta glanced out the window, expecting to see his truck

pulling up outside. It was about time for him to be home. The sun had set an hour ago, and Charles knew she liked for him to be home by sunset.

The children sat propped at the table like dolls. They stared wide-eyed at the food Roberta placed on the table and their mouths watered in anticipation as this was the first meal they'd had all day. Roberta hadn't meant to let the day slip by without feeding the children, but sometimes . . . it happened. Then they'd eat like pigs at dinner, filling their stomachs so fast and so full they'd make themselves sick. Roberta stared at them salivating at the sight set before them at the table, knowing they were starving, and daring them to touch just one morsel so that she could slap their small hands.

"We got to wait on daddy, y'all."

Thirty minutes later Charles's truck pulled up in front of the house. He walked in, grunted hello, kissed each of them on the cheeks, and went to wash up before sitting down at the table.

Why would Martha say such a thing? Roberta wondered, watching him eat and chatter with the children. Maybe because she was jealous. Martha had never had a man like Charles and she was too ridiculous to hide her jealous nature. Besides, when would he have time for another woman? Working all the time, where would he find the energy? After dinner Charles would march right into that room, peel his clothes off, and collapse in bed, just so he could get up before sunrise and start all over again.

Roberta felt relief creep into her body. Martha was just jealous, she concluded, trying to make trouble where there was none, all for the sake of giving herself a twisted sense of satisfaction that she'd somehow bested Roberta.

"I'm tired." Charles groaned as he stretched his arms high over his head. "I'm gon' turn in fo' the night."

Roberta made sure to kiss him warmly on his cheek before he

left the table. " 'Night, honey. And you have sweet dreams." She smiled and hugged him.

Charles closed the door behind him to the bedroom. Roberta reminded herself to pay Miss Martha a visit real soon and tell her to keep her trifling lies to herself. If she chose to believe silly rumors, then that was her business, but there was no reason for her to bring her petty gossip all the way out here to Roberta. Her family was fine, and Charles was home and in their bed where he belonged.

I Caught Him with a Trifling Jane

Charles had made promises to Sara. Some he'd kept and others he dangled in front of her, close enough to see but not close enough to touch, and she was beginning to wonder if he really would marry her. Charles had said he would, but not until he'd taken care of some business he had back in Bueller. "I got some ol' debts to take care of," he'd told her. "And I can't get married 'til I pay 'em off."

"What debts, Charles? And what difference do that make where you and me are concerned?"

"I ain't goin' into all that with you, Sara. You jus' take care of this boy of ours and let me worry 'bout the rest," he assured her. "But I'll tend to it, you'll see, and when I do," Charles gathered her up in his arms, "you, me, and my boy is goin' to finally be together like a family. I'm gon' stake my life on it."

He'd leave it at that, thinking he'd appeased Sara and put her at ease. But when she was alone her doubts plagued her. Charles had always been vague in his explanations, which left too much room for her to draw conclusions of her own that made her twist uncomfortably in a chair or try and shake them from her head. She'd heard that maybe he was already married. Mrs. Robinson had implied it more than once, and others had whispered it when they didn't think she could hear them. Sara fought with herself, telling herself that she needed to have faith in the man she loved, to believe in the father of her child. Otherwise, she'd be forced to concede to the fool laughing at her, mocking her, staring back at her from the mirror.

"This boy look jus' like me," Charles said proudly, holding Adam in his arms.

Sara smiled, "You the only one he look like."

"He act like you, though. He a good boy. I can tell it already."

Adam had fallen asleep. Sara gently took him from Charles and laid him in his crib. She came back to Charles and sat on his lap.

"We gon' live in Bueller when we get married?"

Charles didn't answer. He just smiled and kissed her chin.

"I think that's where I want to live, jus' so we can be close to yo' momma. Don't you think that would be best?"

"I think that's a fine idea," he smiled. "As a matter of fact, I got a surprise fo' you. I got a house there that belonged to my grandaddy I been workin' on fo' us. It's small, but I'm addin' another room to it, maybe even two, and after we married, it'll be plenty big enough fo' all of us."

Sara's eyes twinkled. "Oh, that would be wonderful, Charles. Can you take me to see it? I'd love to see what it looks like."

"Now hold on, girl. That ol' shack ain't been lived in fo' a long time and it need a whole lotta work 'fo it's presentable to my bride. I ain't ready to show it to you jus' yet."

"But I don't care. I can look past that and see a nice home, Charles. Our home. I jus'—" Sara looked disappointed. "I need to know it's really gon' happen, we really gon' get married and be together."

"Ain't I been tellin' you that, Miss Sara?" Charles put his hand under her chin and raised her lips to his. "Course we gon' get married."

"I need to know when, Charles."

"When I get things in order, honey. I tol' you I got to work some things out first, and I got to work on that house too. That's gon' take time, and you have to be patient. I keep tellin' you it's gon' happen, honey, but I'm not gon' do it less I can do it right. That's jus' how I am."

Sara did what she always did before he left—she let Charles have the last word and choked back questions and suspicions until the next time she saw him. Only next time never seemed to make its way back to her and Charles would leave her again, standing knee-deep in assurances and love for him.

You sit still and watch yo' brotha like a good girl. Momma be back in a bit.

Clarksville was close enough to see clear as day if you opened your eyes wide enough and faced north on a sunny day. How many times had she and Danny run away to Clarksville, vowing never to return to Bueller, only to be home in time for supper? How many times had they promised each other that the next time they went would be the time that they stayed, married each other, and lived on the edge of the woods behind that kind old lady's house next door to Mrs. Robinson's? What was her name? She'd let them pick pears off her tree in the backyard and had given them licorice for helping her to stack the wood on the side of the house. Miss Josephine, that was her name. Miss Josephine had given them a spot of land big enough to build their own house if it's what they wanted, because she thought they were in love and she knew they were children and would probably fall out of love long before they ever finished that house. Roberta had been so young back then, no more than ten or eleven. Danny was the first boy she'd ever kissed on the mouth, and she'd wiped it right off as soon as they'd finished. They snuck off to that place until each of them decided that they'd much rather marry someone else—so yes, she knew where Clarksville was.

A grey pickup truck was parked in front of the house.

That ain't his, she told herself. His truck is a different shade of grey. It look a lot like it, but it ain't his.

It's his, all right. It's the same one he pulled off in this mornin', girl. You know better.

Roberta walked across the open field until she came to the oak tree that kissed the sky. She stood behind the tree, staring at the truck that looked so much like her husband's, wishing that it belonged to some other man. She leaned against that tree, picking off pieces of its bark until she'd cleared away a section the size of her hand. Roberta had lost track of time. How long she'd been standing there wondering about the man inside that house, wondering if it was Charles or someone who looked like him.

Miss Robinson came out of her house wearing white gloves and a pale pink hat. She waited for a few minutes, adjusted her gloves, and picked a few weeds from the potted plant on her porch before leaving out the front gate and heading down the road. She stopped abruptly, then turned to look back in the direction where Roberta hid behind the tree. Roberta ducked down quickly to avoid being seen until Miss Robinson disappeared from sight.

Them kids are hungry, but you don't give a damn. You never do give a damn.

Roberta shook her head, trying to shake loose the vile voice accusing her of being wrong. "They fine. They always fine. And I'll be home soon."

Slowly the door to Miss Josephine's house opened and Roberta stared, unblinking and transfixed, as Charles stepped out onto the porch, still wearing the worn faded pants and grey-blue shirt he'd left the house in that morning. Charles said something that Roberta couldn't hear, then he turned to the dark-skinned woman who appeared in the doorway behind him as if by magic. He pulled her close to him, then kissed her long and passionately the way Roberta wanted him to kiss her. He lingered for a moment, staring into the woman's eyes, smiling warmly at her as if she mattered. The woman watched him leave the way Roberta had watched him leave the house every day, waving as he vanished down the dirt road.

He said it. Did you hear him, Roberta? He said it to her, and not to you. How come he don't say it to you?

Roberta's feet had planted themselves in the ground like the roots of that old tree, deep and permanent. She stayed where she was long after Charles drove away and long after that woman closed the door behind her. The sun wouldn't set for another couple of hours and Charles never came home before sunset.

"I love you too, sweetheart!" he'd called out to that woman before driving off.

He said it to her, and not to you. How come he don't say it to you?

All of a sudden Roberta realized she'd forgotten to take a breath, and when she did, the world spun around in circles so fast that Roberta had to wrap her arms around the trunk of the tree to keep from falling. A few minutes later she composed herself and headed in the direction of home. She had a chicken baking in the oven and still hadn't bathed. She needed to comb Elizabeth's hair and wash the morning dishes before Charles made it home.

What a lovely day it was, she thought, strolling through the field of wildflowers and savoring the aroma of spring. Roberta walked through the open meadow, enchanted by blackfoot daisies, bluebonnets, and firewheels sweeping against her calves. The sun warmed her back and she turned to where it hung in the sky, closed her eyes, and let it kiss her face. Roberta smiled through rivers of tears streaming down her cheeks, and the lyrics of a song resonated through her mind.

Lovin' is the thing I crave
For your love I'll be your slave
You gotta give me some, yes, give me some
Can't you hear me pleading? You gotta give me some

Lord have mercy! All she wanted to do was die.

It's Rainin' and It's Stormin' on the Sea

Charles's routine never skipped a beat. The next day Roberta stood as usual in front of the house, watching Charles's truck disappear and fade away into the road. Dark sunken crescent moons under her eyes had begged him to ask the question, "You ain't sleepin' again, Roberta?" before he'd left.

Naw, Charles, she said to herself. *I ain't been able to sleep fo' worryin' over you.*

Roberta saw movement out of the corner of her eye and turned in time to see Elizabeth watching her from the doorway.

"You sad?" Roberta asked her.

Elizabeth nodded. "Yes, ma'am," she said, sounding small.

Elizabeth always looked sad when her daddy left the house. She missed him as much as Roberta did. The look in her daughter's eyes reminded Roberta of her own longing and sense of loss. Elizabeth was just a child, though. What did she know about loving a man hard enough to make her bones ache? What did she know about losing him to another woman?

Roberta turned to look back down the road, still haunted by the image of her husband speeding away . . . speeding away . . . to . . .

"Me, too," she nearly whispered. The road blurred behind the tears forming in her eyes.

From the moment she'd confessed to God and the angels that she loved him, he filled her completely, leaving little room for anything else. Even herself.

Got a good man? He ain't so good. He ain't so good at all.

The voice had no form, no face, no scent, but sometimes he taunted her, tortured her with words that plagued her spirit, and she couldn't shut him up, no matter how hard she tried. The best she could ever do was to pretend she didn't hear him. Or had it been a woman's voice she heard? Roberta wasn't always sure. But she paid no attention to it, most times, dismissing it and keeping busy doing things that kept her mind off the whispers bombarding her all the time.

Lick yo' fingers, Roberta. He still there. Taste him? He still there.

And he was. The faceless, formless voice never lied. In all the years of listening she'd try to catch it lying to her, but everything it said always proved to be the truth.

He'll cry you crazy 'fo you let him starve to death. You better feed him. Try again tomorrow.

It hadn't lied about that. CJ's cries had outlasted her sanity every single day.

That gal got eyes like dead men. They see everything and nothing all together. She see everything and nothin' in you.

It hadn't lied about that either. Elizabeth had a way of looking through Roberta like she was a ghost and right into her heart, like it was a mirror.

She'd hated it, the faceless, formless voice. She'd come to depend on it when she was all rolled up and twisted in her confusion, but wished she were strong enough to wad it up like paper and toss it into the fireplace to watch it burn.

That bitch got him now. (Laughter) You gon' let her? Huh? You gon' let her?

She'd known all the shortcuts. That's how she'd spent her summers, finding shortcuts, through groves of trees, wading through streams, running over hills, chasing destinations and hideaways. Roberta tramped over weeds, rocks, and shrubbery to where that woman was. To where Charles probably was too, spreading himself all over her . . . the bitch! Her legs burned from the force she put into moving them forward . . . forward . . . always forward. Roberta gulped pockets of air, trying to inhale, knowing she was suffocating the whole time. When was the last time she'd had air? She couldn't remember. Twigs and small branches cut into her arms, legs, and face, pulled on her hair, trying to stop her, but Roberta was determined to face that woman. She'd face Charles too, if she had to, and remind him of who the hell he was fuckin' with. No one knew what kind of woman she was, not really, or what she was capable of. Not really. But some people did.

Dead folk know you. Eula. Nadine. Mr. Bobby . . . dead men with black eyes. Dead folk know you.

The faceless, formless voice reminded her.

I know you tooooooooo.

Eula. Nadine. Dead men with . . . Nadine. She'd been the last one to try and take Roberta's man, to get in the way of what she'd wanted more than living. And look at what happened to her. Roberta laughed, muttering a childish rhyme she'd never had the courage to sing out loud before.

Squaw Root and Pinny Ro'
Catch her, catch her
By the toe
If she holla
Don't let her go
Squaw Root and Pinny Ro'

She and Danny used to make up rhymes together all the time. Silly ones that made them fall to the ground, rolling back and forth clutching their bellies, and laughing until tears ran down their cheeks.

She stopped suddenly and stared off into the distance. There it was, the house where Charles spent his time and his love. And there she was, too. Roberta's heart jumped in her chest at the sight of the woman on the side of the house, tending to a small garden. Roberta maneuvered closer to get a better look, finally crouching down behind an old tree stump big enough to hide behind.

She looked young to Roberta, not so young that she wasn't a woman, but not quite old enough to call a woman either. And she was darker than Roberta, the color of molasses. She wore blue jeans, belted around her waist with a piece of rope, and an old shirt that looked big enough to belong to—Roberta swallowed hard, then closed her eyes and strained to listen for the sound coming from this girl. She was humming. It was a warm sound, and welcoming, like it wanted you to come on in, just to sit and listen and feel better when it was over. But she couldn't make out the melody. How come she couldn't make out the melody?

Because her man love her and your's don't!

The voice bit into her thoughts. It did that sometimes, trying to get her attention off something nice and onto something ugly.

A woman don't hum that tune less she got a man who love her! Stop actin' silly!

What a horrible thing to say! Roberta wanted to scream, but held her tongue. And it was horrible, but then, wasn't it always?

Nadine Cooper got in the way too.

Sure she had, but she'd taken good care of Nadine years ago and won Charles in the end. She'd only done what was necessary, that's all. Nadine didn't want that baby, and now she didn't have to have it and she didn't have Charles, either.

Squaw Root and Pinny Ro'
Catch her, catch her
By the toe
If she holla
Don't let her go
Squaw Root and Pinny Ro'

Roberta crept closer to the house. She crouched down beneath one of the windows and then happened to peek inside. The child lay quietly in its crib.

Squaw Root and Pinny Ro'
Catch her, catch her
By the toe
If she holla
Don't let her go
Squaw Root and Pinny Ro'

The child and the momma. One went with the other. Didn't they go together? Of course they did. One with the other.

That boy crazy 'bout his chil'ren. I ain't never seen a man love his chil'ren as much as Charles do.

Everyone who'd ever seen Charles with his kids said it, thought it, felt it.

"Love you, 'Lisbeth. Daddy love you with his heart, baby."

Nadine didn't have the child, Charles's child, and she didn't have Charles either. Charles was only with this girl because of this baby. Roberta closed her eyes and sighed deeply at her revelation. It was simple, really. The woman in the garden never noticed or heard Roberta slowly open the front door and close it quietly behind her.

The child and the momma went together. They were one, and when one died, the other died too. She'd learned that from Nadine Cooper. And she'd learned it from Eula May Adams.

Roberta only thought of her mother in her dreams. Beautiful Eula May, running as fast as she could after the man ahead of her. Running past Roberta and pushing her aside to get to him. The man didn't seem to be moving at all to Roberta. He almost seemed to be standing still, but Eula May could never catch up with him. She ran so fast that she exhausted herself until finally she fell dead to the ground. In Roberta's dreams, Eula always fell dead. It wasn't until she died that he noticed her. He sniffed hard like he could smell the blood seeping from her ears, and he always turned around in time to see Roberta crouched over her mother, crying and trying desperately to shake her awake. His black, lifeless eyes would burn holes into Roberta, and she'd look up at him through her tears and grief into the black pools of his eyes. Blacker than midnight or hate or hopelessness. All of a sudden he marched towards her with heavy footsteps that shook the ground, with eyes that drilled into the core of her and with hands curled into fists bigger than her head, screaming words she couldn't hear, but he blamed her for what had happened to Eula and to him. Roberta trembled when he stopped and stood over her and she begged him to leave her alone. Slowly he reached down to grab her by the throat, but before he touched her, she'd wake up

in her own bed, a grown woman with a husband and children of
her own.

Roberta stood over the child who looked so much like Charles
it was like looking at Charles himself. He lay awake and quiet,
staring up innocently at Roberta like he knew who she was. Her
heart fluttered in her chest and she knew she'd fallen in love with
him, Charles, all over again. He never had a chance to cry. Roberta
pressed the pillow against his face, ignoring the kicking of his legs
and the flailing of his arms.

> *Squaw Root and Pinny Ro'*
> *Catch her, catch her*
> *By the toe*
> *If she holla*
> *Don't let her go*
> *Squaw Root and Pinny Ro'*

He was so small, she didn't have to press down hard, and she
didn't, so as not hurt him. Ooowee! That boy looked just like that
man, didn't he? "Yes, Lord," she whispered, smiling. "He sho' do,"
she said, warmly, proudly, like she'd given birth to him herself.

She hadn't noticed that his arms and legs had finally gone
limp, lost in the euphoria of doing what she knew was the right
thing to do, if she wanted to keep her man. The momma and the
baby went together. Didn't they?

Roberta carefully placed the pillow back on the bed where
she'd found it. Then, like she'd been nothing more than spirit,
she crept out of the house and back towards the meadow in the
distance.

*   *   *

Sara had been working in the garden ever since she'd put Adam down for his nap. She stood up, stretched her back, and realized from the position of the sun that he should be awake by now, and hungry too. She laughed at the thought. That boy not only looked like his daddy but he had his appetite too. Sara turned in time to see a female figure standing in the open field across from the house. The woman wore a floral peach-colored dress with an apron tied around her waist.

"Hello?" she called out, thinking that maybe she was a neighbor, but the woman just stood there, staring at her. She dusted off her blue jeans and walked towards the front of the house. "Who in the world—"

The woman smiled strangely and turned to walk away. *How odd,* Sara thought, watching the woman disappear into a wooded area. Sara shrugged her shoulders and went into the house to check on Adam.

"Noooo! Oh, Lord, noooo!"

Roberta heard Sara's cries from as far away as she was and it nearly broke her heart, but not quite.

Squaw Root and Pinny Ro'
Catch her, catch her
By the toe
If she holla
Don't let her go
Squaw Root and Pinny Ro'

Send Me to the 'Lectric Chair

He made love to her with a passion that had been absent in their marriage from the beginning. Charles thrust his love into her, his heart and soul, in a way she always hoped he would. Roberta smiled beneath him, staring up at the ceiling and holding him close. This was the way it should've been between a husband and a wife. Like Adam and Eve, there was no one else in the garden but the two of them, naked and joined together by God.

They'd argued earlier. Roberta slung accusations at him before he'd even closed the door behind him about the woman and the child who looked so much like him. Naturally he denied it, but Roberta was no fool. She'd seen him with her own eyes, kissing that woman in the doorway of that old house, and she'd waited outside for hours until he finally emerged, grinning at all the secrets he held dear locked behind that door.

That chil' look mo' like him than the kids he got with you. He look jus'—

She squeezed her eyes shut and shooed away the whispers in her mind that insisted on reminding her of the dead child she'd left that afternoon. None of that mattered now. Roberta had done what was her right to do. She'd fought for her man. She'd eliminated the one thing capable of taking him from her, and promised herself that she'd wipe it clean from her memories and forget it ever happened.

The momma and the baby go together.

And they did and now he was free to belong to her.

Desperation crept up on Charles in a way he hadn't expected. He'd been a fool to think she'd never find out. But then, he had been foolish about a lot of things in his life. Roberta knew about him and Sara, and everything that mattered to him was suddenly at risk. Charles had cooked up his own pot of trouble and if he didn't do something about it soon, he'd drown in it.

He hadn't gotten a chance to stop by the house and see Sara that day, but he would get by there first thing in the morning to check on her. She couldn't stay in that house, not now that Roberta knew. But where could she go? he wondered, fighting back panic. Back to Timber? Maybe for the time being, just until he could find someplace else for her and the baby, it would be best. He'd take her himself, though. First thing in the morning, he'd go by the house, get her packed up into his truck, and take her home. And what would he tell Roberta? Timber was more than two hundred miles away. If he left early enough, he could make it there and be back sometime tomorrow night. Sara wouldn't be happy about it, and Lord knew he wasn't looking forward to it, either. But it was all he could think to do.

"I love you, Charles. I love you so much," Roberta whispered in his ear.

Of course she did, he thought to himself. And maybe that would be enough to buy him the time he needed to straighten out the mess he'd gotten himself into.

Eventually Charles's release left him limp and lightly snoring on the bed, holding Roberta close to his chest.

Look at that full pretty moon tonight, Roberta thought, staring out the window. She had prayed to it—worshipped it—just to get him. One night, years ago, when she was a girl, it had heard her and answered her and placed him in the palm of her hand. That night the moon was hallowed, full, and ready to rain down blessings on whoever called on it, which was what she'd done. And now he lay next to her, more beautiful than he'd been even back then, but not as beautiful as he'd be tomorrow.

A lump welled in the back of her throat and tears began to fill her eyes. That boy had been beautiful too, just like his daddy. He'd looked so much like Charles, it was scary, but she'd done what needed to be done. And once that child had faded away, that woman would have no choice but to fade away with him, like old memories. Maybe she already had. And maybe that's why Charles had made tender love to her until she couldn't help but cry. He did love her, even though he'd never come out and said it. Even if he never would say it. Roberta knew in her heart that somewhere in his was buried the kind of love for her that she had for him, and there wasn't a woman in the world who could take that from her.

Charles's heart beat gently in his chest while he slept, dreaming. Dreaming of . . . of . . .

That boy looked just like him. Didn't he? He looked like he knew how much his daddy loved him.

Charles lay dreaming. Was he dreaming of her? Of who? Roberta? Or the woman in the garden, humming the sweet kind of melody that sounded like she was in love and loved.

His eyes had been dark orbs like Charles's eyes, deep, penetrating eyes that seemed to look past the flesh and straight into the soul where love lived. Darkness lived there too, sometimes, the kind that didn't make much sense at all. The kind that left Roberta breathless for no reason. Had he seen that in her before she . . . He had eyes like his daddy. The black eyes. Dark eyes. Black . . . cold . . . eyes. Like Charles's eyes. Like Mr. Bobby's . . .

"Momma say monsters ain't even real," she whispered, then squeezed her eyes shut and wrapped her arms tightly around Charles.

Charles moaned sleepily and then pulled her closer to him. "I'm here, honey. I'm . . . right. Sara." Her name rose up in a billowy cloud from his lips and hovered above his head.

Sara. Roberta watched it. She heard it. She felt it. *Sara.*

Warning compelled him to open his eyes. The moment he did, he knew he was about to die. Charles felt as light as air and heavy as lead at the same time. He slowly raised his hand to his neck. Roberta stood over him and stared hard at him, holding a butcher knife dripping with something dark that ran down her arm. He held up his own hand in front of his face and saw blood. His own?

"Sara," Roberta said indifferently. "That the bitch's name?"

"Yes," he tried to say, but the words wouldn't come.

And then she struck again. The last thing Charles saw was Roberta, but the last person he thought of was Sara.

*   *   *

Roberta sometimes believed the voices were real, but she couldn't be sure. It was hard to tell sometimes if she'd really heard them, or if she'd just imagined hearing them.

"She did it, alright," the husky male voice said. Was he speaking to her or to someone else? "Got his blood all over her."

"Where the kids?"

"His momma got 'em. They out front."

"She say why she did it?"

"She ain't said much of nothin'. Jus' stood there and laughed, then pissed on herself. She crazy if you ask me. Anybody who'd cut a man like that—damn near cut his head clean off."

"Yeah well, you know how violent niggers are. All of 'em got a mean streak in 'em like that, like animals. Take her down to the jailhouse. We figure out what to do with her there."

"She probably gon' get the chair."

"Or the crazy house. Watch it, man! She gon' piss all over yo' leg." They laughed. Roberta laughed too.

DEVIL'S GONNA GIT YOU

And Long to Kiss Me

1962

Some things were so pretty to look at, Adam wished he could stare at them without ever having to blink. Mattie was that pretty. Every time he saw her, his gaze rested there and he tried with all his might not to blink her away, even for a second. Adam peered at Mattie King from behind the bushes in her backyard, crouching down low so that she couldn't see him. She sat on the old swing hanging from that big tree behind her house, digging her toes into the dirt and twisting the ropes together, raising the seat of the swing off the ground until she could barely touch it anymore. The ropes would unwind, twirling Mattie around in circles until she was free to start over.

She a big girl, he thought. *She too big fo' swings.* He'd been told that he was too big for swings a long time ago, and she wasn't much smaller than he was, so Adam figured she was too big for swings, too. But it was all right with him if she liked swings, even if she was too big. He still liked swings too. It was a secret, though, that nobody knew but him.

Every time she twirled back to the ground her red-and-black pleated skirt floated up in the air, and Mattie would lean her head as far back as she could, straighten out our legs and arms, close her eyes, and hold on tight until she landed. The ribbons in her hair flapped around her head and she reminded him of a bird, free and flying in the wind. Adam's heart beat hard and fast just looking at her. It raced when she flew like a bird and when she stood still like a tree. It raced when she smiled or when she cursed out the other girls he'd seen her with on her way home from school. And it raced inside him once, when he saw her looking at him.

Adam wished for the courage to ask her if he could take her picture. That way, he could carry it around with him all day long and look at it whenever he wanted, even in the middle of the night. He didn't have a camera, though, and he didn't have the courage to ask her to pose for him, or even to say one word to her. Not that he wanted anything more than to look at her. In fact, he preferred not talking to her. Adam didn't really have anything to say to the girl, and he wasn't so sure she'd have anything to say to him that he wanted to hear. He just wanted her to stand still long enough for him to drink her up with his eyes and swallow the vision of her deep down inside him.

Then to his shock he saw Mattie climb down from her swing, walk over to his hiding place, and stand directly in front of him.

"I know it's you," she said, peering through the leaves at him.

He wanted to jump up and run away, but his legs had fallen asleep. How'd she know he was here? How'd she know it was him?

Mattie pushed aside some of the branches. "I see you in there. You can't hide."

"Come on outta there, now!" she demanded. Mattie folded her

arms in front of her, "I mean it! You come outta them bushes and talk to me, right this minute, or else—"

Or else—what? He wondered. Adam took a deep breath and slowly rose to his feet, bracing himself against a tree to steady himself while the blood rushed back down into his legs.

Mattie glared at him. "I knew it was you. It's always you, ain't it?"

He pushed all his strength into his legs, enough to keep from stumbling, and made his way past the shrubbery. For a moment their eyes met, but Adam blinked first and stared down at his wobbly legs, ashamed that he'd been caught.

"Why you hiding in my bushes all the time, watching me? And why you always staring and following me around? Don't you know it's rude to stare? And it's even more rude to follow people. Don't you know that?" she scolded.

"When somebody asks you a question, Adam, the polite thing to do is to answer them. It's the right thing to do," his mother had taught him. He'd already forgotten Mattie's question but knew he had to say something.

"M . . . my birthday is comin'. My b-birth . . . day be here next week—I think. I'm gon' b-be nineteen."

Mattie rolled her eyes. "Like I care about your birthday. If you that old, then surely you know better than to be staring at people."

He nodded, "Oh, I . . . I know a lot of things. I do. I know a-a lot."

She snickered and then caught herself. "My name is Mattie King, in case you didn't know," she said smartly.

Adam shifted from one foot to the other. A million needles were sticking into his legs, letting him know that he could run away now if he wanted to. "I-I-I know yo' name is Mattie. I d-didn't know it was K-King too."

"Well it is," she said impatiently. "And now that you know what it is, you need to leave me alone before I tell on you because I know your name too—Fool! And if you don't stop looking at me all the time, I'm going to tell and you're going to get in all kinds of trouble. Is that what you want?"

Adam shook his head and stared wide eyed into Mattie's face, "No! I-I don't want no tr-tr-trouble. I jus'-jus'—"

"Just—what?"

He swallowed hard before answering. As much as he tried to avoid trouble, it always seemed to find him. If Mattie told, then Adam knew somebody would get mad at him, even though he hadn't done anything but stare at her. To him, staring at Mattie was like looking at Miss Faith's flowerbed or a piece of chocolate cake. He never got in trouble for looking at those things, but somehow he knew he'd get in trouble for looking at her.

"I jus' l . . . like—I-I think you pretty is all," he tried to explain. "I . . . I think y-you pretty and—I like l-ookin' at you. But that's all. I-I can't h-help it." Tears were starting to fill his eyes.

Mattie saw them and frowned. "It just ain't good manners to spy on people, Fool."

"A-Adam."

"What?"

"My n-name is Adam. That's m-m-my real name. F-Fool is jus' what they c-call me."

Mattie fought back a smile, "Well, Adam, it ain't good manners to stare at people. You worry folks when you do things like that, and make 'em nervous," she explained patiently. "Like me. I know you get my nerves all wrapped up like barbed wire. My momma says that about me all the time, and now I know what she means."

He nodded, "Okay, M-Mattie."

"My friend Doris say you got a crush on me." He blinked. "She say I should tell somebody 'bout you watchin' me the way you do because you might drag me off in the woods one day and rip off my draws and make me do it with you. You know . . . sex?"

Adam frowned and glanced quickly at her, then back down to his feet.

"Is that true? 'Cause if you plannin' on doin' somethin' like that then I'm gon' have to tell my momma and—"

"I-I ain't never gon' don-nothing like . . . that! I . . . wouldn't n-never do nothin' bad to y-you!"

Mattie smiled mischevously. "So . . . you do have a crush on me?"

Adam shrugged again, not sure of what kind of crush she was talking about. The only time he'd heard that word was when his brother Moses put him in a headlock and told him he was going to crush him. Somehow, he didn't think that was what she meant, but he couldn't be sure, so he thought it was best not to say anything.

Mattie keyed in on his confusion. "That mean you love me?"

Adam stared at her, shocked that Mattie had found out. How in the world did she know he loved her? His mouth fell open, and Mattie reached out her hand and pushed his chin up to close it.

She laughed. "You better be careful, boy, before a junebug fly up in there and choke you. You must love me, then," she said casually. "I think that's how a man look when he's in love with a woman. My daddy probably looked like that when he figured out he loved my momma." Adam blushed. "Ain't nothing wrong with it, though," she said, trying to reassure him. "I figured you did, otherwise why else would you be staring at me all the time and sneaking up on me?"

Mattie smiled and then turned to go back inside the house. She had to check on supper and put the cornbread in the oven. Adam watched her walk away. Mattie turned around one last time. "You gonna be here tomorrow?"

He let his gaze fall to the ground and shrugged.

She smacked her lips impatiently. "Just tell me, so I'll know to come out here. Otherwise I might stop by Doris's on the way home or stay inside and watch TV or something."

He timidly nodded his head. Mattie thought for a moment before leaving and then asked, "You want me to bring you a sandwich tomorrow? We got bologna."

Fool fought back a smile and nodded again.

Mattie turned to leave. "See you tomorrow, then."

She stared out the window in the living room and watched him run down the road. Fool—Adam was harmless. Even though he was older than she was, he was just a boy, a cute one, too shy for his own good. She'd heard that he was "retarded," which meant he was different from everybody else. Mattie supposed that maybe that was why she decided to go ahead and like him. Maybe he'd have something interesting to say once he got past being so shy around her. Anything was better than talking to old boring Doris all the time. There was something sweet about him, sweet enough for her to hope he did come back by tomorrow.

Just a Room and a Empty Bed

G rady knocked on her door early in the morning, looking disheveled and out of breath, like he'd been running. Sara was surprised to see him so late at night, but she'd been up, watching and worrying over Adam who'd she'd found the day before lying limp and nearly dead in his crib.

"Grady?" she asked.

Grady's eyes were red and swollen, like he'd been crying, and the stunned look in his face fed the panic starting to rise up inside her. He came inside and sat down at the table. Sara sat across from him. "He dead, Sara. He dead—" Grady put his head down on the table and cried.

Tears welled up in her eyes. Grady wouldn't be out here this early in the morning with news like this unless it was about someone she loved. She hesitated before asking the question, afraid to hear the answer. "Who, Grady? Who dead?"

Grady rocked his head back and forth, choking on his grief. "He dead . . . he gon', Sara." He raised his head and saw that she was cry-ing too, but Sara still didn't know who Grady was talking about.

"Charles," he whispered. Sara began to shake uncontrollably, and Grady hurried over to where she sat and held her. "He gon', honey. He gon'."

Sometimes her memories were cruel, especially since she found out that Roberta was coming home. Sara had overheard that the other day in the store.

"I heard they lettin' Roberta Brooks outta that crazy house she been locked up in all this time. I hear she comin' back here to take up in Martha's ol' house."

"Mmm, mmm. That's a shame. Youd'a thought they woulda give her the 'lectric chair for that one, cuttin' her husband's throat like she did."

Sara had been such a child back then. Charles had promised to marry her, but in the back of her mind she had known he was already married. Enough people had implied it and he did, too, in all his excuses and vague explanations. Sara had gone out of her way to believe otherwise, hoping that her suspicions were just nervous jitters and that the rumors were wrong. It wasn't until he'd been killed that she had to face the truth, and she'd faced it every day for nearly twenty years.

Ever since she heard of Roberta coming home, Sara had been reliving the events of the day he died over and over again in her mind. She had known Charles wouldn't be coming over because he had a job to do in a neighboring county, but he'd promised to come by bright and early the next day. Sara had just put Adam down for his nap and had gone outside to tend to the small gar-den she'd planted on the side of the house. She had been proud of her garden, filled with onions, mustard greens, and tomatoes. Sara hadn't grown anything since then.

Sara had been on her way inside expecting that Adam would

be awake and ready to be fed. She looked across the road and saw a young woman standing there, watching her. She wore a floral-print dress with an apron tied around her waist, and she had smiled at Sara. But her smile hadn't been friendly. It was a knowing smile, taunting Sara with some secret that Sara might like to know. And in an instant the woman turned, walked away, and then ran across the open field on the other side of the road.

Then she went inside to feed Adam, and found him lying limp in his crib with his eyes half-closed, looking at nothing. Unexplainable fear rose up in her from her stomach to her throat, where Sara gave birth to it in the form of her own screams. None of her memories were clear to her after that, and she sometimes had trouble deciphering between nightmares and actual events. She remembered holding the boy in her arms. She remembered rubbing him from head to toe, kneading him like dough. Did she turn him over on his stomach and massage his back? She couldn't be sure. Did she hold him upside down by his ankles and let him fall to the floor? No, she didn't think she'd have done that. Did she beg God to let her child live, and to take her instead? Yes, she believed she'd done that. And God had taken mercy on her, and Adam let out a cry. It had been the most beautiful sound in the world.

She remembered nursing him, and noticing there was something absent in his eyes that had been there before, but she'd been too overjoyed in having him back to pay much attention. Gradually things came to light, though. Adam didn't start walking when he should've. He didn't talk right away, and when he did, most of the time he had difficulty pronouncing the words. She'd sent him to school but they sent him home, claiming he was slow; and didn't understand the things children his age should've understood. None of that mattered to her, though. Adam grew into his father more and more every day, and she loved him and was grateful for the handsome gift Charles had left behind, even if he was damaged. But even in that, he was just like his daddy.

The dividing line between Clarksville and Bueller had been erased seventeen years before when a politician running for mayor of Bueller discovered that the two had been one all along. Sara had told Charles she wanted to live in Bueller, and he'd promised her she would. At least Charles had been right about that.

Momma Harper's house burned down in 1947. She and Adam barely escaped and Sara lost everything she owned. Miss Robinson took them in until Grady came down after them.

"Why don't you go back to Timber, girl? Ain't nothin' fo' you up here. Go on back to yo' daddy."

Timber tugged at her sometimes, but not hard enough to make her want to go back. Pappo threatened all the time to come up and get her and the baby and drag her back, kicking and screaming, if he had to. But Sara insisted on staying because she'd outgrown Timber, and even Pappo.

"I'm a grown woman now, Pappo, and I can take care of myself jus' fine," she'd insisted. Pappo never followed through on his threats, and she knew how much it hurt him that she didn't want to come home. Sometimes it hurt her, too.

Grady ended up taking her and the baby in for awhile until Sara found a job and a place of her own, the old Wilson house less than five miles away from Grady and his wife. Back then there wasn't much to it, but with Grady's help the house suited Sara and her family just fine.

Sara paced back and forth on the corner of Wilson and Birch, waiting for her son Moses to pick her up. She'd just left her job at the Coswell house, where she'd been working as the housekeeper for nearly fifteen years. Finally Moses pulled up in his pale yellow pickup and Sara climbed in. He'd worked hard for the money to buy that truck. Sara had been angry about it in the beginning, but now she was glad he'd bought it. He'd promised to drop her off and pick her up every day from work if she let him keep it, so she did. Sara was disappointed that he'd dropped out of school in exchange for a job at the lumberyard. She'd always wanted her boys to finish school because she never did. But Adam couldn't go, and Moses didn't want to.

"Hey, Momma." Moses leaned over and kissed her cheek.

"Hey, baby." Sara sighed. "How was work?"

Moses shrugged. "It was all right."

He was a big, strong boy, solid as a brick wall, and stood well over six feet tall. Men around town teased him, calling him John Henry because of the way he carried that lumber up on his shoulders and effortlessly hoisted it onto the backs of trailers. His daddy had been a big man, too, strong as an ox. But Sara could already see that Moses was outgrowing his father. The boy was intimidating enough in size, but it was his temper that worried Sara most. Moses was like a firecracker, always ready to explode. He'd never exploded on her, but she'd seen him set it loose on Adam. Like the time Adam accidentally spilled his glass of milk all over the kitchen table and into Moses's lap. They were only children then, but Moses jumped up and punched Adam hard in the chest, knocking him backward and onto the floor before Sara had turned back around from getting the dish towel to wipe it up. She'd seen him slap Adam across the face before he realized that it was her coming around the corner, carrying groceries. She'd gotten off from work early because she hadn't been feeling well.

"Moses! What do you think you're doin'?" she screamed at

him, coming up the steps. Adam was trying not to cry, but she knew he was in pain.

"I told him to get in the house and he wouldn't do it!" Moses said in his defense.

"So you had to hit him?"

Moses's eyes darted to Adam, who never said a word to condemn him. "He wouldn't do like I told him!"

His father had had a temper, too, but not enough of one to rival his son's.

Sara hadn't married Simon Crenshaw, partly because he hadn't asked her and partly because she knew she could never love him. He'd been a tall, intimidating man, loud and obnoxious most of the time, because he could get away with it. He'd seen Sara coming out of the beauty shop one day, snuck up behind her, and said the silliest thing. "Did you leave some of that pretty fo' the other ladies in that place? Or did you jus' take it all witchu?"

She shook her head and kept walking. Simon kept walking too, until eventually he'd talked her into having a drink with him at Floyd's bar and grill. Sara had a taste of her first beer that night. She even danced to a song she didn't remember the words to because Simon had held her close, and all she could hear was the beating of his strong heart, and it reminded her that she was lonesome.

At first she believed he could be enough. As big as he was, surely he was more than enough man for any woman. Sara wanted to recapture the love she'd lost when she'd lost Charles. She missed being in a man's arms and looked to Simon to fill the void Charles had left behind. But he wasn't Charles. Simon was the one who said good-bye.

"Don't no man wanna be second to no other man," he told her, sitting on the side of the bed and slipping into his boots. "They's too many women out there who give they las' breath to be with me. 'Till you get him offa yo' mind, baby, you don't need no other man in yo' bed."

Sara didn't know it when he left, but she was pregnant with Moses. His words rang through her like chimes, though. Years later Sara still hadn't been able to let go of Charles's memory, and in time she resolved herself to the fact that she never would.

A broad smile spread across his lips at the sight of the truck pulling up to the house, and Adam leapt off the porch and ran down to it, opening the door for Sara to get out. The ritual was the same every day, but it never failed to catch her by surprise. Adam wrapped his arms around his mother's waist, lifted her in the air, and swung her around in a circle.

"Hey, Momma!" he yelled into her shoulder.

"Put me down, boy!" Sara said, laughing and holding on tight to her hat.

Adam sat her down gently and kissed her on the lips. "I'm glad you home, Momma," he said excitedly.

She had a different kind of feeling for Adam than she did for Moses. He'd figured that out a long time ago. Adam was the good one, always smiling and helping and too quick to kiss everybody's ass because he'd been too dumb to know better.

"Stop pickin' her up all the time, dummy!" Moses commanded.

Sara looked at him. "What I tell you bout callin' him that? You don't talk to yo' brotha like that, Moses."

Moses glared at Adam, who grinned sheepishly back at him. Sometimes Moses could see that Adam wasn't the fool everybody mistook him for. Only Moses could see it. Sara Tate refused to see anything else but that sweet boy of hers, shining like a star for her.

"He need to be careful, Momma," Moses retorted.

"Well, he don't mean no harm."

Her words faded into the air like all the other words she'd used to come to Adam's defense where Moses was concerned.

Moses was as far removed from his brother as fire was from water, and he preferred it that way.

"I-I-I look l-l-like my daddy, M-M-Momma?"

"Oh yes, Adam. And you're just as handsome as he was too."

"You l-l-loved my d-d-daddy?"

"Almost as much as I love you."

Moses had been a kid back then, when he'd heard them talking late one night together. They must've had that same conversation a dozen times through the years, leaving Moses on the outside to listen when they thought he was asleep or not paying attention. Funny how she never told him about how much she'd been in love with his daddy—or him. Not the same way she'd told Adam. But Moses had put it behind him. He was nearly eighteen now, and saw no more reason to care than he thought to piss in the wind.

"Be easy on him, Moses," Sara would tell him. "He ain't like you."

No. He wasn't a thing like Moses. Adam was like a rug that everybody felt they could wipe their feet on. His mind moved slow, like a snail, leaving a trail of snot in its path. Adam was that sweet boy everybody always thought he should be more like. Moses wasn't any of those things and he never wanted to be.

Moses stood outside the reunion, watching, and squashed the familiar twinge of jealousy that churned inside him. The bond between their mother and Adam had always been something he'd felt separated from. Sara would explain that Adam needed more attention, and maybe he did, but it didn't mean he didn't wish he needed her more, too.

Finally Moses walked over to his brother, half a foot shorter than he was, and grabbed him in a headlock.

"Who yo' daddy?" Moses taunted, forcing Adam to bend over.

"Get off-fa me, boy!" Adam shouted.

Sara shook her head and headed into the house. Out of the corner of her eye she watched Moses, making sure he never got too rough with his brother. Simon used to accuse her of being overprotective of Adam, a claim she never denied, because she knew how true it was.

"Who yo' daddy, I said?" Moses smiled roguishly, knowing that Adam wasn't strong enough to break free of his grip.

Adam balled up his fist and started punching Moses in the stomach, but Moses held fast to his wrestling hold. "I'm g-g-gon' kill you!" Adam shouted. "I'm . . . gon' . . . Get offa . . . me!"

Finally Moses let go and jumped back quickly, dodging the wild swing Adam took at him. His brother was livid.

Moses laughed. "I'm yo' daddy, boy!" he teased. "I gotchu good!"

The boys had been asleep for hours, but Sara sat up in the chair by the window in her room, staring out at the darkness.

I heard they lettin' Roberta Brooks outta that crazy house . . .

Lord, Sara thought, tears welling up in her eyes. What if Roberta Brooks really was coming home? Theirs had been a relationship of trespassings. Sara had been at fault for having an affair with Charles, and Roberta had killed the man. Sara suspected she'd tried to kill Adam, too, but that was something she could never be sure of. She'd never knowingly seen Roberta. If she had been at her house that day, Sara could never prove it. Grady had described Roberta to Sara once, after Charles's death, but she couldn't be sure that it was Roberta she'd seen that day Adam nearly died.

"Maybe I shoulda jus' gone back home," she whispered. Charles would be alive, and Adam would've grown into a normal man, strong like his father.

Her thoughts drifted to Pappo. He'd been dead almost six years and had never known his grandsons. She'd been so determined to stay away, for reasons that were foreign to her now. Back then it had seemed so important not to go back to Timber, but now—

"Young people can be so silly sometimes," Sara said out loud.

Somebody Has Shipwrecked Poor Me

The Greyhound bus cradled her like a baby and rocked her into a restless sleep riddled with dreams and reality that blended together, encapsulating the last twenty years of her life. Roberta woke with a start and stared out the window at rows of cotton planted in the wide-open fields. The sun was just starting to set and she knew she'd be home soon. She opened her bag and pulled out one of the peanut-butter-and-jelly sandwiches they'd given her before she left, unwrapped it, and took a bite. That was good of them to give her something to eat, she thought. Too bad they hadn't given her any milk to go along with it. She'd have loved the taste of a cool glass of milk. The bus passed a sign that read WELCOME TO ROLLERSON, TEXAS. That she'd been there would be something she could tell everybody about when she got home.

"Hey y'all! Guess what? I been to Rollerson. Barely big enough to piss in, but nice. I think I might go back one of these days."

Roberta chuckled to herself at the thought. The woman sitting next to her shifted uncomfortably and leaned out towards the aisle.

Nearly twenty years had passed, Roberta thought, gazing out the window, and it didn't seem that much had changed at all except her. Cotton and corn grew rampant, the sun still rose and set where it always did, and Rollerson, Texas, had probably been there since the dawn of time. Roberta, on the other hand, had grey hair on her temples. She'd gotten fat, too, almost as fat as Miss Martha had been. Martha had probably put a curse on her before she died. She'd willed her house and her weight on Roberta just to spite her, though she'd probably never be able to prove it.

She leaned back in her seat and tried to remember the dreams she'd had while sleeping. Over the years the business of remembering dreams had become a priority. God spoke to her in her dreams, sending her messages to help her make it through hard times. She'd come to depend on them, relish them. But it wasn't always easy picking out God's messages from the nonsense. Sometimes it would take her days, even weeks, to decipher her dreams and figure out what He was telling her. Sometimes she might've thought she was dreaming, but in reality she had been awake all along.

She closed her eyes and tried to remember what she could.

"I don't care if she killed the President of the United States!" Roberta remembered a woman with yellow hair, wearing a gray suit and sitting behind a table, cutting her eyes at the man in a black suit sitting next to her. "The government is discontinuing funding of this institution and insisting that black inmates be transferred to the state facility with white inmates!"

"But she's been diagnosed as criminally insane. You sayin' you want to let her back out in society?" The man was bald on top of his head, and he had combed a long strip of hair from all the way on the other side across the top, then spread out the few strands to cover as much scalp as he could. Roberta fought back laughter. He looked ridiculous.

"According to her records, she hasn't had an incident in over twelve years. Is that correct?"

"She tried to stab a staff member in the cafeteria. I'd say that was a pretty substantial incident."

"With a spoon?"

"It don't matter what she tried to stab him with. The point is, she tried to kill him!"

"But that was twelve years ago. She's been exemplary ever since."

Of course she'd tried to stab that fool. Mr. Leo, he'd insisted she call him—alabaster complexion, fiery red hair, pink lips. He'd walked past the table where she was eating and put his hand down the front of her dress and grabbed a handful of a titty he had no business touching. Hell yes! She'd have killed him if she could've. He was fortunate that all she had was a spoon. But Roberta was sure, if folks would've left her alone, she'd have gotten her point across with that spoon just fine.

"The bottom line is, there is no money. The state facility has no room for her. The woman has had no negative incidences documented in her record for years." The woman slammed the file in front of her shut and stamped something on the cover. Roberta was going home.

She tried not to think about what that meant. Roberta knew she was leaving one hell for another, because everything she'd held dear in Bueller was gone now—Charles, the kids. Especially Charles. The memory of him had been what had helped her survive all these years. Embers left behind of her love for him had been enough to get her up in the morning and get her through the long days of living in the asylum. In the beginning the other patients there had been terrifying. Roberta cowered away from them, slipping in and out of corners to avoid them, hoping they were too insane to see her. Eventually, she came to realize it wasn't the patients she needed to be afraid of, but the staff.

"This here is one fine nigger woman. Gonna have a good time with this one."

They kept their word too, and had a fine time at Roberta's expense. But it was all penance in her mind. Eventually other girls came along, brand new girls who'd lose their youth soon enough, she suspected. By the time they arrived Roberta wasn't so pretty anymore, and she faded into the walls with other women who'd at one time been young, pretty, and new.

Not surprisingly, no one met her at the bus depot. Roberta walked to Martha's old house, counting steps and retracing them from years ago. It didn't seem like much had changed at all. Every now and then someone would pass her, staring quizzically like she was someone they remembered, someone they'd grown up with. But Roberta didn't know these people, and they didn't know her. Not anymore.

She didn't waste a moment once she was inside the house. Roberta filled a bucket with hot soapy water, grabbed a scrub brush, and began scouring the house, ridding it of the residue left behind by Martha's ghost. The old midwife had had the good sense to have indoor plumbing put into the house, much to Roberta's relief. She scrubbed it with bleach until it sparkled like crystals. Martha also had added another room to the back of the house. Roberta wasn't sure what it had been used for, but she'd find something to do with it. Martha's closet was still filled with her clothes, and Roberta gathered them together, piled them in an old tin barrel in back of the house, doused them with kerosene, and lit the match, burning them to ashes.

Ashes to ashes. Dust to dust.

She'd cleaned all night and when she was done, Roberta stood up and looked out the window in time to see the sun rising up through the trees.

It was a new day, all right, one that held too many questions she didn't know the answers to, but at the moment she was too tired to care. Roberta ran water for her bath and unpacked her gown and a clean pair of panties to get ready for bed.

She'd sleep better than she had in years. That was about the only thing she knew, and the only thing that mattered.

Get It, Bring It, and Put It Right Here

Mattie stood with her hand propped on her hip, waiting impatiently for Adam as he walked tentatively towards the back door to her house. "Hurry up, boy!"

He wasn't sure about this. Mattie had invited him inside the house while her mother was working. Sara had always told him never to go inside the house unless the Mr. or Mrs. invited him in personally, and as far as he could tell, Mattie wasn't either of those things.

"Adam? I got a sandwich and some milk sittin' here on the table waitin' on you. You better hurry before it get spoiled," Sara teased.

He'd been by every day for the past week, meeting her in back of the house, eating her sandwiches, and pushing her in the swing. He said funny things without trying, like the time she braided a ring of daisies together and put them on his head.

She smiled and told him he looked just like Julius Ceaser. Adam frowned and scratched his head. "He live here in Bueller?" Mattie grabbed her side and almost fell over laughing. Adam tried to laugh too, but she knew he didn't get it, and she knew she'd hurt his feelings a little bit too. After that she made sure she was careful with him, because hurting his feelings wasn't hard to do.

Adam finally came inside and sat down timidly at the table.

"Oh no!" she said, disapprovingly.

Adam quickly stood up and looked terrified at her.

She walked across the room and opened the bathroom door. "Go wash your hands before you sit down and eat at my table," Mattie relished the upper hand she had over him.

Adam obediently did as he was told, then returned to the table, sat down, and looked to her for approval before he started eating.

She watched attentively while he ate, smiling the whole time. "Wipe your mouth," she said, handing him a napkin.

Where Adam was concerned, Mattie relished being the one in charge. She looked after him like he was a child . . . like he was a man who needed looking after. That's all he was; a grown child who needed looking after. He was strong, though, strong enough to pick her up off the ground and twirl her around until she laughed and screamed for him to stop. Adam had soft eyes, dark and warm, that embraced her everytime he let them linger on hers for any length of time, which wasn't often. His shyness made sure of that. But he was getting better at it. Now, when she wanted him to look at her, she'd put her hand gently beneath his chin and raise his face to hers, and if she smiled at him fast enough, he was less likely to look away. She loved his eyes.

Adam ate quickly so that he could get back outside before her mother came home. This girl was too fast for him sometimes. She'd insisted he come inside to eat, because *"Decent folks eat at the table, not outside under bushes."* The thing was, he wasn't even hungry. The sandwiches had been her idea, not his, but she always seemed so happy to see him eat them, and he made sure to eat every crumb and even lick his fingers after he'd finished.

Mattie had stopped calling him Fool when he'd told her his real name. She liked Adam better anyway. Fool was the kind of name you gave a person when you didn't know anything about them, or didn't care about them. She liked Adam. Maybe if other people sat down and talked to him awhile, they'd like him too and change his name to what it really was.

"You ever kiss a girl, Adam?"

Adam nearly choked on his milk. *What kind of question is that?* he wanted to ask, but instead he shook his head and went back to eating his sandwich.

Mattie chuckled. She'd shaken him up again, which wasn't hard to do, either. Adam was blushing but trying to pretend he wasn't. "I kissed Jerry K. in the third grade," she said casually. "I don't remember what the *K* stood for. Him and his family moved to Tulsa after school was over." She frowned. "I didn't like it, though. He tried to tongue kiss me. I thought, boy! You crazy? And punched him in the stomach." Mattie sat back, and looked off into the distance, carefully contemplating the rest of her conversation. "Back then I was too young to be tongue kissin', but I don't think I'm too young now."

Adam glanced at her quickly, then dropped his eyes back to his plate. "C-c-can I have . . . some mo' . . . milk?" He slid his glass towards her, knowing full well he didn't really want any milk. Adam just wanted Mattie to take her mind off kissing and think about other things, like the fact that he needed to get back outside before her mother came home to push her a few more times in the swing.

She poured him another glass, but Adam wasn't as smart as she was and she knew it. He knew it too. "You ever think about kissing me?" she asked, leaning close to him.

Adam gulped down his milk, feeling like he would bust, and stared at her for a moment. "Y-you ought not be t-t-talkin' 'bout things like that, M-M-Mattie. Me and you and kissin'—"

"'Cause you don't want to kiss me?" she asked, sounding disappointed.

Adam shook his head. "Naw! 'C-cause we ain't m-married!"

Mattie rolled her eyes and sighed. "I'm talking 'bout kissing, Adam. And you ain't got to be married to kiss somebody."

Adam wiped his mouth, stood, and quickly walked towards the door. "I got to go now," he said anxiously.

He left, and Mattie quickly followed behind him. He was too cute not to kiss, and Adam was the only boy she wanted to kiss, really. He was nice and sweet and had pretty lips that didn't have crust in the corners like Perry Hutton had in his, and he was always trying to kiss on somebody. And Adam didn't have big purple greasy lips like his brother Moses who'd tried kissing her once, too. She had to slap him across the face before he'd even let her go.

"Adam?" Mattie grabbed him by the elbow. Adam stopped, but refused to look at her. Mattie giggled and stepped in front of him, trying to force him to look at her. "I thought you said I was pretty?"

He nodded but still wouldn't meet her eyes. "You are."

Mattie stood close to him. She liked this game, flirting with him and making him so nervous he could hardly talk at all. Adam's crush on her was bigger than Texas, and coming from him, made it sweeter than if it had come from any other boy because he was forbidden. He was too old. Dumb. Retarded. He was putty in her hand, and the most handsome man she'd ever seen. And he had put her safely on a pedestal, out of reach even from himself.

"I thought you said you wanted to make me happy?" she whispered, staring up at him.

Adam swallowed hard. That's surely what he wanted. It was why he ate sandwiches when he wasn't hungry and gulped down glasses of milk, knowing he hated the way it tasted. His eyes darted down to hers, and Mattie smiled. Lord, why did she have to go and do that? he wondered, feeling his heart melt down into his stomach.

She reached up and put her hand behind his head, then pulled his face to hers like she'd seen women do in the movies. "It's all right, Adam," she said sweetly before closing her eyes and pressing her lips to his. The sensation sent a shiver through him he hadn't expected, but welcomed. Adam followed suit and closed his eyes too. The kiss was pillow-soft, light as air, and as sweet as cotton candy.

Mattie pulled away first. "I liked that. Did you?"

Adam looked surprised she'd asked the question. "I . . . did."

She pulled his face to hers again, only this time Mattie slowly slipped her tongue in between his lips. Adam's head began to spin, and it took all the strength he had not to let his knees buckle underneath him. Her tongue mated with his. He tasted like peanut butter, and he tasted like Adam.

Adam walked home in a daze. He was so immersed in thought he nearly passed by his own house, then turned and sat down on the steps, waiting for his mother to come home. Mattie's flavor still lingered on his lips, and he swore he'd never brush his teeth for as long as he lived. He didn't think it was possible for him to love her more than he already did, but now he knew better. His love for her was bottomless and endless, and as much as she'd ever need, he'd give it to her.

Mattie had strange ideas that didn't always make sense to him, but it didn't matter. She knew what to do better than he did, and he trusted her. Before he left she told him he was her boyfriend, and Adam trusted that he was. She told him that she would never kiss another boy, and that he could never kiss another girl, and he trusted that she knew what was best. Mattie told him that they were a secret and that nobody could know he was her boyfriend, not even his momma.

"Folks wouldn't understand, Adam," she said, smiling. Mattie smiled at him all the time and that made everything right.

He swore he'd never tell a soul that he was her boyfriend.

Then I'll Meet My Long-Lost Friend

Gwennie Gordon's chin dropped at the sight of Roberta Brooks coming into her store. Nearly twenty years had passed since she'd last seen that woman, and Roberta wore every one of those years like war wounds. She had to have put on a good seventy pounds, Gwennie surmised. Roberta's pieface had grown so full, it seemed to have melted into her shoulders, and wisps of gray distinctively outlined the edges of her hairline. Somewhere she was still there, though, the young tomboyish girl who'd been the spitting image of Bobby Lewis when she was a child, but who'd taken on her momma's appearance somewhere around the time she married that Brooks boy. The one she killed.

Roberta still hadn't become accustomed to the stares, but she refused to come out from under her shroud of indifference. Back in the home nobody stared because they were all afraid of what they'd see—reflections in a crazy mind, whether it be theirs or someone else's. Staring was rude behavior as far as she was concerned, but fools in Bueller had no idea how to act. So she ignored them and went on about her business as if they didn't matter, which they didn't.

"Pardon me," the man with the curly hair said, accidentally bumping into Roberta. Roberta looked up at him and grunted something he couldn't quite make out. It was her all right, Danny thought as he watched her shuffle up and down the aisles of the small store. She'd looked right at him, though, and didn't even recognize him. Part of him was relieved.

"Danny?" his wife whispered over his shoulder. "You know her?"

He'd known her years ago, back when secrets reigned in his life. She'd been the only person in the world he'd shared them with. The pretty girl so set on marrying Charles Brooks had disappeared into that woman with the thick ankles and angry frown on her face.

"No," he said softly. "I thought I did."

Abominations don't disappear like magic. And girl-boys didn't fade away either just because they had a woman clinging to them. Roberta caught sight of Danny out of the corner of her eye.

Still got that swish in his hips, but his woman don't seem to mind.

Roberta laughed out loud, but then her bottom lip gave way to a quiver. She'd missed him something terrible since the day he left. Still did.

She glanced smugly at Gwennie, then went about the business of her shopping. Eventually her presence spread through the store and others followed Gwennie's lead and stared, but Roberta ignored them, too.

"These fresh?" she muttered to herself, examining the tomatoes. Roberta turned up her nose and put one in her basket. "Don't look fresh to me." When was the last time she'd been shopping? She tried to remember. Many years had passed since she'd been allowed to pay good money for rotten tomatoes and hard bread.

Count yo' blessin's, Roberta.

Yes, Lawd. Count 'em all . . . one by one . . . by—

Roberta had stopped trying to shake the voices from her head years ago, stopped running from what she could never outrun, no matter how fast or how far away. It had taken her years to understand that she couldn't outrun something living inside her because wherever she'd go, it would be right there with her, out of breath and as tired as she was.

Look at that one there. she thought, glancing in the direction of a woman cowering in the corner, staring wide-eyed at Roberta. She was mad enough to shout, "Whatchu lookin' at?" but Roberta pressed her lips together instead and turned her back on the nosey heffa.

Getcho bread and go, baby.

They got candy too. Remember candy?

Roberta smiled and hurried over to the counter where rows of candy sat like prizes at a carnival, just waiting for her to pick which one she wanted.

"There's too many," she mumbled, licking her lips. "Which one to choose?"

Count yo' blessin's, Roberta.

Sara studied the woman carefully from the next aisle, trying to see the remnants of a younger one hidden behind the hard lines and dark circles around her eyes. The one who might have smiled at her from across the road the day Adam almost died, and the day Charles did die. Was that Roberta Brooks? She stared at the woman in the store hard enough to burn a hole in her, hoping she'd have her answer and dreading the truth together.

Roberta turned to where Sara stood and all of a sudden, she knew she'd come face-to-face with Charles's wife, a stranger, and a kindred spirit. They'd shared more than any two women on earth had shared, without even knowing for certain what the other looked like. Their souls were connected by the ugliest circumstances and would remain so until death. Sara understood the depth of this revelation, but from the blank stare in Roberta's eyes she obviously had no idea.

She waited until Roberta paid for her groceries and left, and then Sara crept warily past the condemning stares, paid for her own groceries, and left soon after. Without thinking her eyes searched the street for Roberta, but there was no trace of her. A strange sense of sadness filled her. All of them had been responsible—Sara, Roberta, even Charles. Especially Charles . . . but how could she blame a dead man and the man she loved? Sometimes it was hard not to envy him, because he never had to live with the results of his sins. Roberta had lived with them for twenty years in a kind of hell too terrible to imagine. And Sara had suffered too, raising a man who'd never fully be a man, a fool who'd been punished for crimes that weren't his.

Woman Dead Down Home

Why you wait till the las' minute, Ernestine?" Florence shouted to her best friend sitting next to her, twisting and screaming in labor. Ernestine had called her up frantic in the middle of the night, scared to death that she'd have to have this baby by herself at home.

"I was waitin' on EJ," she whined. "He said he was gonna be home soon and . . . awwwwww! 'Flo? Do somethin'! Pleeeease!"

Florence floored the gas pedal on Ma Meryle's '48 Plymouth, hoping it would somehow sprout wings and fly through the air like one of those fancy airplanes. But at best, she was only pushing forty miles per hour. The nearest hospital was more than an hour away, and the only midwife in town, Mrs. Carter, didn't answer the door when they knocked.

"I am doin' somethin', girl!" Florence was livid. "I'm drivin'! And you know that sonavabitch ain't no good! He ain't never where he say he gonna be and I told you not to mess with his ass! Didn't I?"

"I ain't gonna make it, 'Flo!" Ernestine warned, squirming next to her. "I swear I ain't gonna make it to no hospital!"

Florence was so scared, she wanted to cry. "Lord, don't let that baby come now!" she prayed. "Please! Don't let it come now!"

"Oh God! Oh my . . . 'Flo!"

Roberta swung open the door, ready to cuss out the mothafucka' banging on it this time of night. She clutched possessively to an old wooden cane she had hidden behind her back and swore she'd swing it if they didn't get the hell off her porch.

"Who the hell is it?" she screamed through the door.

Florence hadn't wanted to come here, but desperation had taken that old Plymouth, turned it around as if by magic, and parked itself right in front of the house. Ma Meryle had told her Roberta had been taught to be a midwife years ago.

"Awww!" Ernestine wailed again.

"We need yo' help!" Florence yelled back. "Can you help us, please?"

"Please!" Ernestine reiterated, clutching at her stomach, nearly doubled over in Florence's arms.

Roberta hesitated for a moment, then cracked open the door enough to peek through. Standing on her porch were two women, young, one of them about to shit out a child at any moment. She stepped back hesitantly to let them both in.

Florence provided support for Ernestine as they came inside.

"We ain't got nowhere else to go!" she said desperately. "Please! Help us," she begged.

Roberta's mind revved under her doubt and confusion, and

soon enough an inventory of tasks came spewing out of her mouth, from years of being under Martha's tutelage. It was automatic, instinctive, which surprised her more than anybody in the room because she thought she'd made it a point to dismiss all that mess as soon as she'd moved out and married Charles. But nobody seemed to want to let her forget. It was the second time since she'd been home that some young desperate girl would need her to deliver a child, and the second time she'd reluctantly given in and done it.

Roberta took hold of Ernestine and practically carried her to the back room of the house, where she'd thrown Martha's old mattress until she could drag it outside and get rid of it. She helped the girl onto the bed, then turned and barked orders to Florence.

"Put a pot of water on the stove to boil, and get me some towels out the closet in my room."

Florence stood stunned by the sound of efficiency coming from the woman.

"Go on, gal!" Roberta shouted over her shoulder. She pulled up a stool to the foot of the mattress, lifted up Ernestine's gown, and ripped off her panties.

"This chil' comin', all right," she muttered more to herself than to Ernestine. "And he ain't 'bout to wait on me at all." She laughed.

A wave of adrenaline rushed through her. All of a sudden Roberta felt like she was riding in a fast car or even flying, free and sure of herself for the first time in years. The whole notion dismayed her that she could possibly find joy in midwifing, but it wasn't joy. It was power, control, maybe even destiny, that she should be adept at the one thing she'd loathed her whole life. There was a twisted irony in it all, quite possibly another curse cast upon her by Miss Martha herself. Roberta laughed again. She had to give that old bitch some credit, though. Martha surely knew how to condemn a soul and condemn it good!

Roberta watched over the young woman and her child until they'd both drifted off to sleep, then came out into the parlor where Florence sat, biting her nails. *Sorry-ass girl hadn't been a bit of help,* Roberta thought bitterly. Not that it mattered. She'd gotten the task done well enough.

"They all right?" Florence said, standing quickly to her feet.

Roberta sat down in the old rocking chair and sighed. "They sleepin'," she said matter-of-factly. "They be fine in the mornin'. You can come back to get 'em then."

She picked up her purse and started to leave.

"And bring thirty dollars with you when you come." Roberta looked her in the eye. "That's how much I charge fo' my services," she explained.

Roberta stared at her hands and saw that they were dirty. She needed to bathe and wash off the filth of some other woman's pussy covering her hands. She looked around the room impatiently, hoping this girl would hurry up and leave.

"Thirty dollars," she repeated. "Bring it with you when you come get her in the mornin'."

Roberta got up and left Florence sitting there alone. A few minutes later Florence heard the water running in the bathtub. She left, quietly closing the door behind her.

The spirit of deja vu haunted her now. Roberta stood at the edge of the wooded area in back of the house and stared down at the X she'd drawn on the top of the mound of dirt covering the young woman's afterbirth, then walked around the grave three times while reciting the Lord's Prayer like Martha had taught her, like she'd done all those times when she was young. No use messing with tradition, she thought, smiling. The last thing Roberta needed were ghosts of dead babies haunting her too. The Good Lord knew she already had enough ghosts to contend with.

"Our Father, who art in heaven, hallowed be thy name—"

Pillow for His Head at Night

The door was locked when Adam came home. Moses always locked it on Saturdays when Momma was at work, and Adam knew why. He went around to the side of the house and sat in the ground underneath the window of the bedroom he shared with his brother. The bed creaked and bumped against the wall the way it always did when Moses had a girl in the room. Moses had lots of girlfriends, and he always locked them in the house with him and took them to his room on Saturdays, when Momma was at work.

Voices sifted out through the window screen and lighted on Adam's ears, moans and groans and whispers from Moses and the girl he was with. Sometimes Adam could tell by the sounds coming from the girl that she liked Moses. Other girls didn't seem to want to be with him like that, but Moses wouldn't let them leave until it was time. Some girls left the house smiling and holding on tight to Moses. Other girls ran away crying. Those were the girls

Adam felt sorry for and he wanted to tell them so, but he knew better than to say anything. Moses would get mad at him if he did. He was like that sometimes—mean and a bully. Other times Moses was good and took Adam to the soda shop for rootbeer floats. It just depended on the day and Moses's mood, Adam concluded.

His brother had told him once when they were small and out fishing, "I hate you, Adam. But I love you too. Sometime I don't know which one I feel the most."

"W-why, Moses?"

Moses shrugged, " 'Cause—I don't know. Sometimes I wanna hit you so hard—hard 'nuff to make yo' nose bleed or to black yo' eye. You jus' make me feel like that."

"I-I-I'm sorry."

"It ain't yo' fault. That's jus' how you are, is all. You can't help it. I don't think you can help it."

"I c-c-could if you t-tol' me what to do."

Moses laughed, "You too slow to know what to do. Even if I tol' you, you wouldn't know how to do it. 'Sides, I don't think I know what to tell you 'cept stay out of my way when I get mad. 'Specially when I get mad witchu. Or else I might hurt you bad."

Adam was confused. "B-b-but, how you gon' hurt m-me, if you l-love me too?"

"Me and you—we ain't nothin' alike. Sometimes it's like we ain't even brothers."

"B-b-but we is brothers, M-M-Moses. Momma s-s-said—"

"Momma say a whole lotta things, 'specially bout you. She don't say much bout me, less she fussin' bout somethin'."

"S-s-she fuss all the t-t-time bout you. B-b-but ssshe l-l-love you. I hear her say that to you."

"She say it, but I don't think she mean it like when she say it to you."

"H-h-how come?"

"Cause she never look me in the eye when she say. I think you got a bite, boy! Pull, Adam! Pull him in!" Moses grabbed the rod from Adam's hands and yanked the hook out of the water.

"Damn!" He shook his head. "He got away." Moses handed the fishing rod back to Adam. "Bait yo' hook again, Adam, and pay attention next time. You ain't never caught a fish and we ain't leavin' here today 'til you do. I promise."

It took all afternoon, but Adam did finally catch a fish. Moses jumped up and down as much as Adam did, and he hugged Adam so hard he took his breath away.

"I knew you could do it, Adam! I knew it!"

That's how Moses was, though, Adam thought, smiling. He loved Adam sometimes, and other times he didn't. Adam figured it was because Moses was so big, and people that big could act anyway they wanted and nobody would fuss at them about it because they were scared of them. That's what Adam thought.

The girl that day liked Moses. Adam heard them whispering, and the girl giggled at something Moses said. It was probably Darlene. She was older than Moses and even older than Adam, and she always did like Moses a lot. Lots of girls did, but not every girl.

Adam's thoughts drifted back to Mattie. His thoughts always went back to Mattie, and he didn't mind one bit. He and Mattie had done it too, twice, but he'd never tell and neither would Mattie. The first time it was awful.

"I tol' my momma I didn't feel good. So she let me stay home."

He fussed at her for that. "It ain't r-r-right to fib to yo' m-momma, Mattie."

Sometimes he had to remember that Mattie was so young, only fourteen. She knew more than he did about a lot of things, because she was just smart, but sometimes she did the kinds of things kids tended to do, and he'd have to let her know it wasn't right. Lying to her momma wasn't right at all.

Mattie sat on his lap and kissed him like she always did. "I like kissing, don't you? I especially like kissing you."

Whenever she said things like that, his face would get hot and all he could do was grin.

He'd hurt Mattie without meaning or trying to, and that hurt him. But he hadn't been able to help himself. He couldn't stop, even though he knew he should've, and even though he'd wanted to.

"It hurts, Adam," she whispered into his ear. "It hurts bad."

But something wouldn't let him stop pushing himself in and out of her. He wanted to, but he couldn't . . . he just didn't know how.

Adam loved her too much to hurt her and he wished he'd never done it after that first time. He wished he'd never been born so that he couldn't do it, but Mattie had kissed him until he was so hard in his pants, he feared he might bust out of them and he wanted to go home. Adam had stood up and told her, "Mattie! I need to go."

He was embarrassed and didn't want her to see him like that, but she'd told him, "If you leave, Adam Tate, I ain't never talkin' to you again."

He believed her, so he stayed.

"I never done this before. Have you?" she asked, staring into his eyes.

Adam shook his head and watched Mattie lie down in bed, untie her robe, and then she was naked to him. His eyes grew wide.

"Adam," she whispered, "take your clothes off and lay on top of me."

She was warm and softer than anything he'd ever felt before in his life. All he wanted to do was to lie there, and grow old there, and maybe even die there with her. That would've been enough, but he knew her momma would be home soon, and she probably wouldn't like seeing the two of them naked together in one of her beds.

Mattie started to move underneath him, kiss his neck and shoulders, and eventually his mouth. He liked the way she moved, pushing her hips up and down against him and slowly spreading her legs so that he wouldn't have to put all of his weight down on her because he was bigger than she was. Adam knew he'd smash her if he put all his weight down on her. He felt his body begin to mold to hers, like they had melted and become the same person. She moved, and he moved too. And without even thinking about it, he slipped down to the moist, soft spot between her legs and felt her move again, this time against the part of him that was hard, and it sent chills through him like it was wintertime, only he wasn't cold.

"Go slow, Adam, 'kay?" Mattie whispered in his ear. "Go slow so it don't hurt so bad."

He nodded and tried his best to go slow, so he wouldn't hurt her so bad. He tried his best.

When it was over, Adam held her tight and told her how sorry he was for not being able to go slow, and for hurting her, and he hoped she wasn't so mad that she'd never talk to him again. He'd probably jump off a bridge if she stopped speaking to him. Mattie dried his tears and kissed his lips, and then smiled.

"You did fine, Adam," she said, trying to reassure him. "That's jus' how it is for girls. At least, that's what I hear. It always hurts girls, but not boys."

"B-B-But I didn't . . . mean to, M-Mattie," he cried.

"I know. The next time it won't hurt as much, and then the time after that and the time after that we jus' have to keep doing it. Okay?"

He nodded. "Okay."

And that's why he loved her so much, because Mattie was nice to him, because she loved him back.

Mattie told him that it hadn't hurt so bad. Adam believed her. He believed everything she told him

"How you feelin', baby?" Agnes asked, pressing her hand against Mattie's forehead.

Mattie smiled. "I'm feeling better, Momma. I just think my monthly's coming, that's all."

Agnes headed into the kitchen and Mattie followed. "Did you soak in a hot bath like I tol' you?"

"Yes, ma'am," Mattie said, leaning against the door frame. "And it made me feel much better."

"Good 'nuff fo' you to go to school in the mornin'?" Agnes asked teasing her.

Mattie nodded. "Yes, ma'am. I think so."

Doggone His Soul

Roberta Brooks was midwifing again, and even though women were hesitant, they trickled in. Poor ones mostly, and desperate, young ones, but it didn't matter to Roberta as long as they paid. Not all of them came to give birth to children. Some came to get rid of them, and Roberta skillfully mixed the abortive medicine Martha had made for Nadine all those years ago, this time to perfection.

Most of her time was spent in her garden. She tended to it carefully, weeding and watering it, taking better care of her garden than she'd taken care of her own children. Roberta had never had patience for children, though, not the way she had for her garden. It was pretty and didn't cry or need titty milk to live. Taking care of her garden eased her mind and calmed her nerves. Sometimes for no reason her hands shook, her palms sweated, her heart beat too fast and hard in her chest, and Roberta wanted to scream at the top of her longs for no other reason than to scream.

But tending her garden calmed her nerves and made her feel better.

The bottoms of her feet itched so bad she'd scratch them raw. At first she tried soaking them in an oatmeal bath, and then Epsom salts, hoping it would ease the discomfort, but none of those things worked. They itched so bad one night Roberta couldn't sleep, so she left the house barefoot and went outside for bit. Without thinking, she walked a short ways down the road in front of the house. The air was cool and the sky glistened with stars hanging brightly over her head. Crickets called her name from a distance and sang a song she recognized but couldn't recall its name. All of a sudden she realized that the soles of her feet had stopped itching. Roberta looked down at them and laughed. From that night on, she let them carry her to wherever it was they'd been itching to go.

Her feet carried her to places in Bueller she'd never go to on her own, both familiar and unfamiliar. Once, on her way home from the market, they turned left instead of right and Roberta ended up at the old abandoned barn where she and Charles had first made love. She slowly opened the door and saw that the blanket they'd lain on was still there, crumpled and faded in the corner, tattered and worn at the edges over the years. It reminded Roberta of herself. She sank down to her knees and stared at the place they'd been, then saw their ghosts writhing around on the ground, twisted together in knots, whispering something inaudible.

"Charles was such a fine man," she uttered lovingly.

Time crept by and she sat staring into space, seeing images that took her back to a time where anything was possible.

Another time her feet carried her to the old tree where she and Danny used to talk for hours about nothing at all except their feelings, maybe their dreams. She thought about him from time to time. Roberta didn't miss him, in the beginning, but she missed him now, and she'd loved to sit with him again under that tree to tell him about the things she'd seen, heard, and done. Danny thought being raped by his stepfather was such a horrible thing. Roberta knew things more horrible than that, but she brushed those thoughts aside most of the time.

Adam didn't push her as high as she'd liked, because he was afraid she would fall. "I wanna go higher, Adam!" Mattie begged, kicking her legs. "C'mon now!"

Adam shook his head stubbornly. "Nope. I-I ain't l-l-lettin' you fall!"

Mattie dragged her feet until the swing finally stopped. "Well, then let's go inside."

Adam dug his hands into his pockets. "Ain't y-yo' momma gon' b-b-be home soon?"

She climbed off the swing and stood close to him. "We could do it fast."

"Naw, l-l-las' time we did it f-f-fas' you said it hurt."

"It hurt a little bit, but not as much as the first time. Besides, I told you we need to practice so it'll stop hurting altogether." She stood up on her tiptoes, kissed his lips, then grabbed him by the hand and led him inside. They had an hour before her mother would be home, which was more than enough time.

This time, Roberta's feet had turned down West Garrett instead of Willow Road. Roberta stood stunned in the distance, watching the young couple giggling and kissing in back of a house she didn't recognize. "Why y'all bringin' me this way?" she'd asked her feet, obediently following them, and finally stopping where they'd planted her. The couple hadn't seen her, and hurried inside the house. Roberta had never seen the girl before, but she knew for certain who the boy was, and that revelation stopped her heart and brought tears to eyes that had been bone-dry for years.

"Charles," she mouthed, staring blankly at the place he'd been standing.

Even from where she stood, she'd known it was him—Charles Brooks—alive and visiting young women, kissing them, holding them . . . loving them, the way she'd always wanted him to love her. Roberta had wanted to call out to him, *"Charles? Whatchu doin' here, Charles?"* but words refused to come out of her mouth, and soon enough he'd disappeared inside that house with the dark-skinned girl holding his hand. Maybe it wasn't him, she thought, trying to reconcile her thoughts. Maybe he'd been just a boy who looked like Charles.

No, too many things were similar—his build, the broad shoulders, and the way he didn't quite stand up as straight as he should've, the way he walked and how he flowed like water with each step he took. Charles had always walked like he was dancing, ready to spin a girl around on the floor and dip her low and deep. But even from as far away as she was, she recognized his face, singed with dark spheres burned into it for eyes.

Roberta pinched herself viciously on the arm to make sure she was awake because sometimes she had dreams about him, looking the way he used to look the way that boy had looked. Pain radiated through her arm and she knew that this was no dream. Charles was here, in Bueller, or maybe he'd never really left. There was something wrong. Charles shouldn't have been back in Bueller. She'd angrily watched him melt away years ago one night when he'd called out another woman's name instead of hers. Or maybe that had been a dream too—a terrible dream she'd mistaken for real. Roberta shook her head and turned to go home. No, something was terribly wrong. Her hands shook uncontrollably, and Roberta clamped them together around her purse the whole way home, to hold them still.

Ha! Ha! And you thought you cut that devil?
You didn't cut him, gal!
Or, maybe you did . . .
And maybe he been born again!

In the weeks that followed Roberta finally learned the boy's name. Fool, they called him.

"Fool! Come get this watermelon and carry it home to yo' momma."
"Fool! You see Moses? I been waitin' fo' him fo' mo' than an hour?"
"Fool! (laughing) What's one plus one?"

Fool smiled at her once. Roberta bit her lip and turned the other way. He looked too much like her husband for it to be right.

He bumped into her another time. "'S-s-scuse me, m-ma'am." The touch from him charred her skin. She hurried home and doused it with water, hoping to put out the smolder before it set her ablaze.

Before long she realized who this boy really was. He was Charles's spirit, come back to life. He'd been sent back to haunt her from his grave. The boy's eyes were blacker than black, blacker than Charles's had been, and they were void of any semblance of soul whatsoever.

He got dead man eyes, Roberta. He got monster black eyes.
You bes' look out, gal! He gon' sneak up on you.
Kill you . . . he will. Make you pay.

"Pay fo' what?" she asked out loud, sitting up late one night in her room. "Pay fo' what?"

Fo' killin' the soul that's in him.

"I'm scared, Moses," Wilma whispered, staring at Roberta measuring and mixing ingredients in the kitchen.

Moses sat slumped on the sofa next to Wilma and shrugged indifferently.

Dumb-ass girl, he wanted to say. But he figured it was best to keep his mouth shut. Otherwise, she'd start up again with all that crying and carrying on.

"If my momma and daddy find out, they'll kill me," she kept saying over and over again.

She'd come crying to his house before he left to pick up his momma from work. "I missed my cycle, Moses! I'm pregnant! What are we gonna do?"

We? He wondered why he needed to do anything. Hell, he wasn't the one pregnant. And what made her so sure it was his?

"I can't have no baby now. I can't finish school if I have to take care of a baby," she cried.

Moses ended up using fifty dollars of his hard-earned money that he'd been saving for a new clutch to finally shut the girl up. Now here he was, watching all his money being mixed and poured into a jar by some old crazy woman who Wilma said could take care of it. For fifty dollars, she'd damn well better take care of it, he thought.

Roberta had seen this boy before. The big one that had trouble crawling all over him walking around with a chip on his shoulder as big as a tree stump. She'd seen him with Charles's ghost—his old self reborn into his new self. The one they called Fool. They were kin—brothers, she'd heard. They didn't resemble each other much at all.

Do he know that Charles come back from the dead, Roberta?

"I don't think he do," she answered out loud.

Roberta tightened the lid on the mason jar before handing it to the idiot girl sitting in her house, relishing the thought of how much money she'd made off of other fools just like her.

That boy looked like he was in a hurry to leave. He looked like he thought he was too good to be sitting up in Roberta's house, sprawled out on the sofa like an ugly stain.

"I reckon I'll be seein' that other boy in here soon, too."

Moses looked perturbed that she seemed to be speaking to him. "Beg yo' pardon?"

"Fool. That what they call him? Y'all kin. Ain't you?"

Don't be messin' with that boy, Roberta. He a mean one.

"Oh, I ain't 'fraid of him." She stared hard at him.

Moses glared at the crazy woman but didn't bother to respond.

Roberta laughed. "Well, fuck you, too, boy! Lookin' at me like you done lost yo' damn mind."

"We need to go, Moses," Wilma whispered, and grabbed hold of his arm. The two stood and started to leave.

"He makin' plenty babies like you, I s'pect. Him and that li'l girl, the dark one, her momma dress up like a doll. You know the one I mean?"

Moses stopped and turned to Roberta. "Whatchu sayin'?"

Roberta could see that he was annoyed, but she could also see that she'd peaked his interest by the mention of his brother and that little girl.

"You already know, boy. That Fool and the girl you was slidin' up on not too long ago. Pretty bows in her hair—but she wouldn't even talk to you from what I could see. She talk to him, though, when nobody's lookin'. She talk to him all the time. I reckon she doin' other things with him, too," Roberta had a wicked twinkle in her eyes, watching that boy pretend he wasn't squirming like a snake on the inside. "She a chil', you know—playin' grown folks' games." Roberta's gaze shifted to Wilma, standing timidly in the doorway, "But then, I s'pose that's why so many of 'em end up here."

"Thank you for the—the—" Wilma faltered.

"My money is all the thanks I need, girl."

"We really need to go, Moses." Moses followed her out the door.

"Fool or no fool, he gon' beat you to that one, son! Ain't he?" She laughed as they left.

Roberta sure enough had pissed that boy off. It hadn't taken much, though. She'd known from the moment she'd laid eyes on him that he was the kind who let his bad temper get the best of him. His kind was a fighter—and a lover, too, drinking up all them girls with his eyes every time one happened to pass by him. He was a good-looking boy, so she knew he had no problem getting girls, and she suspected she might as well get used to seeing him and his money from now on. That little girl running around with Fool didn't want him, though. Roberta had seen the way the girl turned up her nose at him and rolled her eyes every time he said her name. But she wasn't rolling her eyes at that other boy. Just like Roberta had never rolled her eyes at Charles.

Or Nothing I Can Say

Agnes tried to blink away the truth of what she saw trembling in her doorway. Mattie's blouse was ripped at the sleeve, and she held the front of it closed together in her fist. Tracks of tears streaked her face and blood trickled from the corner of her mouth.

"Mattie?" Agnes asked, baffled. She'd been home for hours, looking frantically for this girl who should've been home long before. Agnes had seen signs that Mattie had come in from school. Her books were on the kitchen table where she always put them, and Agnes had called out absently.

"Mattie King! If you don't come get these books off my kitchen table and put 'em in yo' room—"

But Mattie wasn't in the house. Agnes waited impatiently, knowing she was going to lay into that girl as soon as she set foot in the house. Hours passed and eventually anger turned into worry, and worry into panic as she searched through the neighborhood knocking on doors and asking, "You seen Mattie?"

No one had, until now. Agnes saw her, and she knew that the worst had happened.

She closed the door behind her and turned to Mattie. Night had already fallen. Agnes stared at the girl and then swallowed hard. "Where you been, and what happened?"

Mattie's blank stare fixed on the mantle across the room. Framed pictures lined the shelf above the fireplace, pictures of her father before he died and of Mattie growing up over the years from a snaggletooth six-year-old to the young woman she'd become. Everything had changed so much after he'd passed away. All of a sudden their rock was gone, and Mattie and her mother were left behind riding the wave of life, clinging desperately together, hoping the other was half as strong as he'd been. *If he'd been here,* Mattie thought, *maybe none of this wouldn't have happened.*

"Mattie?" Agnes's voice trembled and tears filled her eyes. "Tell momma what happen, baby?"

Blurred images of him flashed through her mind, tearing into her, making her pay for the way she'd been carrying on. The side of her face throbbed from where he'd hit her. Mattie tasted blood. He'd crushed her, pushing himself heavily on top of her so she couldn't breathe. And finally he'd spliced into her, knowing she hadn't wanted him to, knowing she hadn't been ready for him. She wanted to vomit at the memory of his hands, and his mouth gaping open and swallowing her, almost completely. Mattie opened her mouth, but words wouldn't come because they were buried under the heavy bed of lies and deceit she'd built over them these past few months. She'd snuck that boy into the house and done things with him she had no business doing, lying to her mother and even to him, telling him that everything they were doing was all right, when she knew in the back of her mind that it wasn't. *Good girls don't do those things.*

Her thoughts drifted back to earlier in the day. She'd rushed in from school, dropped her books on the table, and began making sandwiches and putting them in a paper sack, getting ready for their date. Adam had said he'd bring the blanket, and she trusted he wouldn't forget it. Mattie filled her father's old thermos with cold milk and hurried out the back door to meet with Adam. She'd been looking forward to this all week. It had been his idea, which she found sweet. Usually she had to be the one to think of special things for them to do, but this time, he'd told her, he wanted to take her someplace nice, on a real date, to show her how much he loved her. But she already knew that he did.

Mattie and Adam spread their blanket near the river, but not too close. "I-I-I seen a w-water . . . water mocas-sin in there the other day," he'd told her. As usual Adam ate heartily, but Mattie had hardly touched her food. She hadn't been feeling well at all lately. "I might be getting the flu or something," she explained to him, rubbing her stomach and frowning. "My stomach been real upset and stuff."

Adam looked concerned and pressed his hand gently against her stomach too. "You m-make sho' you tell yo' m-m-momma so she can g-get you s-some medicine."

After they'd finished eating Adam and Mattie lay back on the blanket, gazed up into the sky, and laughed at the shapes the clouds had made.

"Look!" she said, pointing. "There's a pirate ship."

Adam strained to see what she saw, but he never could. He pretended he did, though, and Mattie couldn't help but be touched by his efforts.

"I-I see a dog!" he laughed, pointing. And he really did too.

Adam put his hand on her stomach again, then rolled over, lifted himself up on his elbow, and kissed the front of her blouse. He looked up at her and smiled.

Mattie rubbed her hand over his head and giggled. "That make it feel a whole lot better," she teased.

Adam's kisses traveled up to her chest, then he carefully unbuttoned her blouse and kissed the mounds of her breasts. Mattie cringed slightly at how tender they were. Her period must've been coming, she concluded. Maybe that's why she felt sick all the time. Finally, Adam's kisses met her lips. He crawled on top of her, careful not to press all of his weight against her, and kissed her passionately until he felt himself rise and harden in his jeans.

Adam looked into her eyes. "Y-you ain't feelin' good?"

Mattie and shook her head. "Naw, I ain't."

With that he rolled off her and lay next to her, holding her hand in his.

The time soon came for them to leave. Adam kissed her one last time, gathering up the blanket and what was left of the sandwiches.

"C'mon, I . . . I'm gon' . . . walk you home."

Mattie shook her head. "That's all right, Adam." He was such a gentlemen. If other boys were like him, she thought, girls would be a whole lot better off.

"N-naw, I got to walk . . . you home," he insisted.

"I got here by myself, and I can get home by myself. Besides, it's late and my momma's gonna be home soon. If she sees you walkin' me home, she ain't never gonna let me out of the house again." Her mother was adamant that Mattie wasn't allowed to date boys until she turned sixteen, and if she ever found out her daughter had been with Fool, she'd punish her for the rest of her life. Mattie hadn't even told Doris, her best friend, because no one else would've understood what they meant to each other. When it was just the two of them it was a precious thing that she could savor any way she wanted. Other people would've insisted on turning it into something to laugh at and make ugly, and they might've even gone as far as to call her names, too. She definitely didn't want that.

She watched him turn and wave before he walked away and hurried to button her shirt, knowing she had to make it home before her mother did.

She hadn't heard him creep up behind her, and before she had a chance to scream, Moses covered her mouth with his hand and forced her down to the ground.

"Awww, you gon' give it up to his crazy ass but you won't even give me the time of day, huh?" he growled, ripping away her panties and wrestling to free himself from his pants.

Mattie kicked and tried to scream. She begged him to stop but Moses wouldn't listen. He smelled like whiskey, and fire blazed in his eyes.

"I'm gon' sho' you how it's done, girl!" he laughed wickedly. "I'm gon' show you how a real man fuck!"

Mattie's hand flew up and hit him on the side of the face.

"Bitch!" he grunted, hitting her back.

Moses ripped into her.

How come you don't talk to me, girl? You think you too good? He'd asked her that everytime he saw her and Mattie turned up her nose at him, rolled her eyes, giggled, and whispered something to her friend she was always with. But she hadn't turned up her nose at Adam—Fool—had she? She raised her skirt for his dumb ass like he was better than Moses. Everybody always thought that Fool was better than Moses.

Fool is such a nice boy, Moses. How come you can't be mo' like him?

"He the sweet one. That big one, there, he foul. Plum foul."

"Don't be silly, boy. I love you as much as I love yo' brother. He jus'—special, Moses. Adam is special."

Agnes bathed her daughter, pulled her nightgown over her head, and then put her to bed. Mattie lay awake and stared out the window, trying not to hear the muffled sounds of her mother's crying coming from the other room.

She'd asked her again and again, "Mattie . . . who did this?"

Mattie held the truth inside her. Moses would tell about her and Adam if he were ever confronted. He might even go so far as to accuse Adam of being the one who'd done this to her. He'd been trying to get her to talk to him for a long time, but she'd always ignored him because he was uglier on the inside then he could ever be on the outside. She'd seen glimpses of it in the way he spoke to folks and treated other girls. Mattie never wanted a boyfriend like that. Adam was as different from his brother as fire was from water. She dried her face with the back of her hand, knowing she'd never be able to look at him again. Not after this. Not after what Moses had done.

"No one would understand," she whispered sadly, staring at the stars. "They jus' wouldn't."

Davis Phillips and his wife Charlene weren't rich people. It was cheaper to have that crazy midwife deliver their eighth child then come up with enough money to have it at the hospital. Roberta had delivered a number of babies and all of them had turned out fine, so surely she could manage another one, crazy or not.

Roberta was in the bedroom with Charlene, cleaning up after delivering a healthy son to the couple.

If po' folks was smart, they'd stop havin' all these damn kids.

If po' folks was smart maybe they wouldn't be po'.

"Thank you, Roberta," Charlene said, apprehensive. Roberta had hardly said much to her at all during the procedure, but she'd done a wonderful job. "I ain't never had such a easy delivery."

Roberta cut her eyes at the woman and grunted. "Hmph. You done had enough of 'em that they slide out like worms. It's no wonder it was easy."

Charlene was offended but kept quiet, fearing that Roberta might snap if she said the wrong thing.

Roberta was too busy eavesdropping on the conversation in the outer room to pay much attention to the woman lying in bed, cradling the newborn.

"Abe King was a damn good man," she heard one of the male voices mutter. "It's a shame fo' somebody to get away with some shit like this. A damn shame it is."

"Agnes say Mattie ain't said a word since it happen. The girl won't talk . . . so . . . she don't know who might've done it."

"How ol' is she now, 'bout thirteen?"

"Fourteen I think. Never been with a man 'cordin' to Agnes."

"Man! If that was my baby girl, I'd kill the mothafucka' fo' some shit like that. Kill him with my bare hands."

"I'd kill him fo' Abe, man. I sho' as hell would. Beat the shit out of his ass with that ol' bat I got out there in the shed. Wouldn't want to get my hands dirty on his raggedy ass."

Rumors had been quietly circulating for days about the young girl who'd been raped by someone, but no one knew who. Roberta had been privy to conversations not necessarily meant for ears of folks passing by because they all thought she was crazy. None of them gave much thought to a woman wandering around in circles muttering to herself, arguing with voices inside her own head. Roberta might as well have been invisible.

She was smarter than they gave her credit for, though, but didn't see a reason to let people know that. Nothing she did was any of their business anyway. After all, they'd gossiped at her expense for more years than she cared to remember, so in her mind they owed her anonymity. She'd managed to piece together what they'd been talking about. That girl Mattie, the pretty one, dressed up every day with her hair tied up in pretty ribbons, had been raped by someone in town, only no one knew who. They'd been speculating since it happened, blaming everyone from faceless strangers passing through town in brown sedans to schoolboys caught with their pants down with some fast girl laying spreadeagle in her momma's bed, fucking dicks no longer than her little finger. Mattie was no different, although she'd been smarter than the rest of them, Roberta concluded. She'd been slick as ice, sneaking that boy, Fool— *damn if he don't look like Charles*—into her house whenever her momma was gone.

Poor Mattie King. They'd all said it so much it got on Roberta's nerves. Maybe that girl had been raped, but then maybe she hadn't. She certainly didn't deserve all the concern she'd been getting from folks. Roberta would've told them all that but she knew they wouldn't listen because she was crazy, and not good for much except delivering babies.

That boy had haunted her dreams ever since she laid eyes on him, though. He'd come into her room at night, stood over her, and stared down at her while she lay terrified in bed with the covers pulled up to her chin, casting his coal-black eyes on hers. They set her on fire, but she didn't dare move. She just lay there, helpless, trying to squeeze her eyes shut, praying he'd go back to hell, only to wake up and find the sun streaking across her bed. But it was him, though. She knew it, and she'd swear it on the Bible, too, if anyone asked her to. Maybe that girl was raped, and maybe she wasn't. Maybe that boy had done it too, but probably not. He needed to disappear, though. She knew that for certain. He needed to be done with once and for all, so that she could finally get a good night's rest.

"I'd kill him fo' Abe, man. I sho' as hell would."

She carefully emptied the basin of afterbirth into a large plastic bag and packed up her things. The men she heard talking nodded to her, and Davis placed fifty dollars in the palm of her hand. Roberta went to the door and pulled it open, but before leaving she turned around and told them what she'd seen. It wasn't a lie, either. It was just what she'd seen.

"I saw that boy, Fool? I saw him flittin' 'round with that girl a time or two. I ain't sayin' he did it. But I saw him flittin' 'round that King girl . . . a time or two."

Roberta let the door close quietly behind her, knowing full well she'd set a match to a fire just begging to start. She hurried home to bury that woman's afterbirth before it got too late. Most folks would never put too much stock into anything she said. Roberta wasn't right in the head. Everybody knew that, including her—especially her. But it would all come together nice and neat once people started to put it all together. She hadn't been the only one who'd seen that boy pining over that girl. Other folks had seen it too, when Mattie King would turn around and angrily yell at that boy to *"quit followin' behind me and leave me alone, boy!"* Roberta knew she never meant it, but nobody else did. They'd sew together the quilt of condemnation because they needed an answer to a terrible question that needed answering, and needed justice for a girl unjustly violated. She'd planted the seed, but they'd water it and stand back to watch it grow. Fool had been the one. Or at least, he'd do.

Fell Down on My Knees

He'd hidden behind the house in his usual place, waiting to see if Mattie would come outside, but she never did. Adam hadn't seen her in two days. The last time he had, she'd told him that she hadn't been feeling well. He hoped she was all right, but it was hard not to worry about her. He walked along the narrow path behind the bushes, heading around the tree at the end of her yard and out onto the road, when he was startled to see Mrs. King, Mattie's mother, staring at him from the porch. He stopped abruptly, and then waved.

"H-how you this evenin', M-M-Miss King?" he asked, grinning, hoping she wouldn't ask him why he was coming from behind her house. Mattie had told him that it was best to keep their love a secret, especially from her momma.

"She wouldn't ever let me see you again, Adam. Momma might keep me locked up inside the house from now 'til I'm an old woman if she find out."

A lump formed in his throat. Agnes didn't wave back or say a word. She just stared at him with her mouth hanging open, like she knew. Adam hoped she didn't know. And he hoped she wouldn't keep Mattie locked away from him because it would break his heart. He turned and walked away, then looked tentatively over his shoulder and waved again.

She hadn't wanted to believe it. Davis Jones had come to her earlier that day, repeating the story he'd heard from Roberta Brooks to Agnes about Fool followin' after Mattie. Fool had never been a troublemaker. He'd never been anything but polite and considerate and eager to help. Folks had mentioned to her that they thought he might have a crush on Mattie, but Agnes had dismissed it, thinking that he was too harmless for it to matter. But what had he been doing, coming from behind the house? she wondered. Agnes went inside to Mattie's room where Mattie was asleep and gently touched her shoulder.

"Mattie?" she asked softly.

Mattie's eyes fluttered open.

Agnes sat down on the side of the bed and smiled. She rubbed her warm hand across her daughter's forehead and down her cheek. "How you feelin', baby?"

Mattie shrugged.

Agnes cleared her throat and considered her words carefully before she said them. Mattie hadn't told her anything about what had happened, and Agnes needed to know who'd done this to her baby. She needed to know how to help her.

"I jus' saw Fool comin' from 'round back of the house." She explained carefully, examining Mattie's expression for any indication that the mention of his name would would confirm or deny her suspicions. Mattie stared blankly at her mother.

"He been botherin' you, honey?" she asked, trying to hide the quiver in her voice. "They say he been followin' 'round behind you . . . botherin' you sometimes." Agnes smiled, weakly. "That true?"

It was true. Adam could be dumb at times. So dumb he'd nearly given away their secret, and then she would have had to scold him in front of everybody. She wished she'd never met him. She wished she could turn back the clock to that day in her backyard. If she could do it all over again, she'd curse him and tell him to keep the hell away from her. That's all she'd ever had to do, even if it meant hurting his feelings. Then her life would be the way it was before, and Moses wouldn't have put his filthy hands on her, and Agnes wouldn't be sitting on the edge of her bed trying not to cry.

"Please, baby," Agnes pleaded. "Tell me somethin'."

Mattie bit down on her bottom lip. Maybe it was time to tell her something, anything, and everything. Tears filled her eyes because she loved Adam. Keeping him a secret might not have been the right thing to do, but it hadn't have been wrong either. If she told about Adam, then she could tell about Moses, and it would all make sense and cleanse the palate of her conscience and maybe things could go back to normal. Maybe they could be the way the were before she'd ever met Adam, and—

"He . . . he—" Tears burned in her eyes and escaped down her cheeks. *He's been so sweet to me, momma.* She wanted to say. *His name is Adam, not Fool, and he's a good boy.* The words lingered on the tip of her tongue. *Adam wanted to walk me home, but I wouldn't let him. If I'd let him, maybe—*

Mattie turned over on her side and cried. None of those things mattered anymore. None of them were as precious to her as they'd once been, and Adam could just as well have fallen off the side of the world.

*   *   *

Agnes quietly closed the door behind her as she left Mattie's room and went into the parlor to gather her thoughts. A few minutes later she picked up the phone and dialed Davis and Charlene's number.

"Hello, Charlene," Agnes said, biting back tears. "How you and that baby doin'?" The sound of Charlene's voice sounded like a bird chirping in her ear. Agnes heard her, and yet she didn't, but she responded in customary fashion. "That's good. I'll be by there when I can." She dabbed at her nose with a handkerchief. "Well . . . I don't know. I ain't sho' how she doin' at this point, but I'm prayin'. Yes. Yes, I 'preciate yo' prayers too. Thank you so much. Is Davis home? May I please speak to him fo' a moment? Yes, dear. I'll see you soon." The sound of Davis's voice bought clarity back to her thinking. He'd been one of her husband's best friends, and he and his wife had been there for her and Mattie, long after Abe had died.

"Davis?" Agnes tried to be cheerful. "I'm . . . we fine. Yes." She cleared her throat. "I been talkin' to her. I saw the boy comin' out from behind my house this afternoon. Naw . . . he looked like he was surprised to see me. I didn't say nothin' to him. I jus'—well, I asked her if it was true . . . if he had been botherin' her the way everybody says. She jus' . . . cried, Davis. That's all she could do."

Agnes hung up the phone. The last words he said to her were, "Don't worry, Agnes. We gon' handle it."

It was late, and Adam should've been in bed, but he'd been so worried about Mattie lately, he couldn't even close his eyes to sleep. His mother had been asleep for hours when he decided to sneak out of the house and go for a walk, to clear his head. As usual, Moses hadn't come home from work. Mrs. King had seen Adam, but all he'd done was say hello to her. She couldn't get mad at him about that, and neither could Mattie. It wasn't like he'd told her about the two of them or about the things they'd done, or that they loved each other. So she couldn't be mad at him. Adam walked down the center of Wabash Road with so much on his mind, one thought quickly flashing to another, coming so fast, that in his confusion he had to stop and scratch his head for a moment. That happened sometimes. He'd think about too many things at once and would end up getting them mixed up together until none of it made sense. Then he'd have to take a deep breath, close his eyes, scratch his head, and start all over again. He was so busy trying to clear his mind, he almost didn't hear the car coming up behind him. The headlights got his attention, and Adam moved over to the side of the road to get out of the way. The car surprised him, then slowed down next to him until it finally stopped.

"Get in the car, boy." Adam leaned down and looked into the car, recognizing Clyde Jones behind the wheel and Walter Haskins sitting next to him.

Adam waved and smiled, then climbed into the backseat like he was told, thinking how nice it was of them to stop and offer him a ride. He'd walked farther than he'd intended, and a ride home this time of night sure was appreciated.

"H-h-how y'all doin' this evenin'?" he asked, politely. "Y-y'all doin' alright?"

Neither man answered and Adam leaned forward thinking that maybe they hadn't heard him. "I-I say . . . y'all doin' alright?"

The two men looked at each other, fixed their eyes back on the road, but never answered Adam.

He sat back and decided he should just keep quiet the rest of the way home.

Clyde drove in the direction of Adam's house, but then suddenly turned down old Parker Road. Why'd they turn here? he wondered. That old Parker house was empty and nobody was home. Adam remembered they'd moved back when he was a little boy, and he knew nobody would be home. Maybe Clyde didn't know that.

"Clyde?" Adam asked, concerned. "Ain't nobody home no mo', Clyde." Again Clyde didn't respond. Adam leaned forward and tapped him lightly on the shoulder. "Them Parker's . . . left a while b-b-back. I 'member . . . when they left. I-I think I was . . . s-six."

Suddenly Walter reached into the back of the car and hit Adam hard in the face with his fist. "Shut the fuck up, Fool!"

Adam grunted, then fell back in the seat, cupping his hands around his nose. Pain shot through his head, and he looked down into his hands and saw that they were filled with blood. He stared stunned at Walter. Why had he hit him like that? Why'd he hit him for no reason at all? Adam wanted to ask but Walter glared at him, pressing his lips together with his fist balled up, like he was about to hit him again. Adam crouched back in the corner of the backseat. Minutes later Clyde slowed down and parked the car in front of the barn behind the house, got out, opened up the back door, and grabbed Adam by the collar.

"W-what's wrong, Clyde?" Adam asked, finally giving in to the fear setting in. Clyde ignored him and dragged him into the barn.

It was dark inside, except for an old kerosene lantern sitting on a rainbarrel in the corner. Adam's face was throbbing, and his eyes watered from the blow. Clyde's brother Davis stood rigid, slapping the fat end of the wooden bat against his palm. Adam wiped the blood from his hands onto his coveralls. The look on Davis's face was enough to scare him even more than he already was. He'd seen Davis Phillips mad before, and he could tell by looking at him he was mad now. And mad at him.

"Evenin' D-Davis," Adam said, nervously, wiping a trickle of blood from his nose. Walter had broken it, he could tell. Adam tried to breath through it but couldn't. Moses had broken his nose once, but he'd done it accidently. Walter hadn't done it accidently.

Davis walked slowly over to him with a crooked smile twisted across his lips. He stood in front of Adam for a moment, then suddenly swung the bat into the air and brought it down hard against the side of Adam's knee.

"Aaaagh!" Adam screamed, clutching his leg, crumbling down to the ground.

Davis leaned down and growled in Adam's ear. "That girl's daddy was like a brother to me, boy! You mess with one of his, you mess with one of mine!"

Adam looked up into Davis's angry face. Confusion spread over him like a fever and he had no idea why this was happening. "W-w-what's the m-matter, D-Davis?" Adam asked, desperately. "What's w-wrong?"

"Did you put yo' hands on that girl?" Davis asked through clenched teeth. He pointed the small end of the bat in Adam's face. "And don't you lie to me, Fool! I'll know if you lyin'."

Adam didn't understand what he was talking about. Davis had hit him, and Walter had hit him, which made no sense at all. He didn't need to be out here this time of night. Adam needed to be home. He should've stayed home.

He gritted his teeth and struggled through excruciating pain to try and get to his feet.

"Answer him!" He heard Clyde yell before kicking him in his ribs with the toe of his boot.

"Umph!" Adam grunted.

"Did you mess with that gal?"

Adam protectively covered his ribs with his arm. He wanted to run. He'd always been so fast when he ran, but the pain was too much for him to even stand up, let alone run. What . . . gal? What gal were they all accusing him of touching? Mattie? They must've been talking about Mattie because that's the only girl he'd ever touched.

"Som'bitch!" Walter screamed, kicking Adam over and over again, stomping him down to the ground. "How you gon' do that to that gal? How you gon'—"

"That's a'nuff, Walter!" Davis shouted. "We got to hear him say he did it!"

Waves of pain washed over Adam's entire body and the taste of blood pooled in his mouth. He needed to spit but couldn't. Adam's coughs sprayed blood into the air as he slowly rolled over, face down on the ground, feeling it pour from his mouth.

Davis knelt down over him. "Did you touch that gal, Fool?" He said in a low growl. "Tell the truth, boy. Ain't no sense in lyin'."

Adam felt his eyes begin to roll up in his head. Had he touched that gal? He'd touched Mattie, and that was the truth.

Don't ever tell nobody, Adam. They wouldn't understand the way we do.

He'd touched her in the most delicious ways. He'd touched like he'd always dreamed he could touch a woman, and his appetite for her had been insatiable and endless and he knew he'd die if he was never able to touch her again.

Don't tell nobody . . .

"No . . . suh, Davis," Adam whispered.

Clyde roughly pulled him up by his collar. Adam grimaced in agony. "You sayin' you didn't rape that gal, Fool? 'Cause her momma saw you creepin' round the house, and the midwife say she saw you too." His nostrils flared like an angry bull's.

Rape? Adam had never heard that word before—rape. Was that what he'd done with her? Had it been rape that had felt so good to him? Had it been rape he'd poured into her from him that left him trembling and crying into her shoulder? Had he raped Mattie, putting his tongue into her mouth, and suckling on her small, erect nipples like he'd seen babies do? Was that what it was called? He'd heard Moses call it something else—fuckin'—gettin' some—pussy. But he'd never heard rape. It rhymed with grapes, and Mattie had been sweet and juicy like purple grapes. Juice running down his chin—sweet girl—pretty and purple dark like grapes. Rape.

"Yes, I did," he whispered, loud enough for them all to hear. Clyde dropped him to the ground and all three men began beating him viciously until the world turned dark.

Moses had been out drinking with his friends when he'd heard what Davis and Clyde were going to do.

"The midwife say he been messin' with that girl," one of them had said. "She said she'd seen him foolin' with her all the time, and Davis said they gon' get him, man. That's all we heard. Said somethin' 'bout the Parker place, but that's all we know."

Guilt ate away at him and threatened to run him off the road, but Moses wouldn't let it.

"Slow down Moses, man!" his friend Sid said. "You gon' kill us fo' we get there!" Moses had been drunk, pissed off, and mean as hell. He'd always been as mean as hell, for no other reason than it was what he'd chosen to be from birth. His ass was big enough to get away with it, and it never mattered who got in the way. Mattie had gotten in the way of him and Adam. Her black ass had just gotten in the way, and now, Davis, Clyde, and Walter's chicken ass were about to get in the way too. Nobody messed with his brother and got away with it. Moses pounded on Adam if he chose to, but he'd kill any other motha' fucka' who tried. God help them if they hurt his brother. Or God damn them. He didn't care which. That was up to God.

Moses sometimes wondered if he could kill a man with his hands. Until that night, he'd never known for certain. Three dead men lay crumpled in that old barn tonight, but there was no remorse in Moses Tate. Remorse had visited him so infrequently, he wondered if he'd even recognize it if it did. Heads had been crushed as easily as walnuts, and Adam lay up against him, barely breathing and bleeding from everywhere.

"We need to get the fuck outta here, man!" One of his friends said, anxiously. "Moses! Let's get him and go, man!"

"Hold on, Adam," Moses said in a raspy voice. "I'm gon' get you home to Momma. I'm gon' get you—" Moses felt himself crying.

Adam's eyes fluttered open for a moment, and he stared out at the road, wondering if it led to heaven—or hell, before finally closing his eyes to sleep.

I Mean, the Devil's Gonna Git You

The grey sky weighed down heavy, threatening a storm, while the wind blew against her back, pushing her closer and closer to her destination looming in the distance.

Sara was beyond tired. The last few days had take a heavy toll on her, leaving dark circles under her eyes. The years had sapped their share of her strength, too. Being a woman alone, raising two boys on her own, had been harder than she'd made it look. Living under a microscope and pretending not to notice had been hard, too. People never openly spoke about her and Charles to her face, only in hushed voices behind her back, as if they were sparing her the humiliation of it all, somehow. She'd been covered in a bed of gossip, true and untrue, for longer than she cared to remember, feigning indifference to side glances of folks who'd heard that "she was the woman who he'd been cheatin' with Roberta's man" and that "she'd even had the nerve to have a baby by him."

Her feet scuffled under her, barely able to hold her up on legs that should've sat down and rested a long time ago, but now was not the time. Moses had offered to drive her there, but she'd told him to stay behind. Moses needed to be home, and Sara was the one who'd had to fight this battle. The good Lord knew, Moses had fought his own. He'd never told her what happened, but then, he didn't have to. Three men were found dead, bludgeoned to death on the old Parker property, men she'd known, maybe even liked and respected, men who'd helped her from time to time with repairs needed around the house. One of the men had even sold Moses his truck. He'd taught the boy to drive and showed him how to change tires and oil and rebuild carburetors. If she remembered right—Clyde, that was his name— he'd even take the boys fishing from time to time. All dead. The papers said their skulls had been crushed. Moses never said a word when he came home that night. She was glad he hadn't. A mother's instincts told her it was best for him not to say anything at all. And they also told her that Adam hadn't been the type of boy to rape a girl. Doubts crept in and out about both her sons, though. Doubts she knew she'd wrestle with until the day she died.

Sara stared up at the door at the top of the steps, then took a deep breath. Slowly she walked up the creaking stairs, praying her strength would hold out long enough for her to say what she had to say, whatever that was. She hadn't really known what that would be. Sara had walked all that way without giving much thought to what she'd say to the woman. Perhaps it would be enough to just look her in the eyes. Maybe all she needed was the recognition and to admit that she knew what this woman had done, intentionally or not. Exhaustion caused her to pause at the top before taking another step towards the door and knocking to seeing what was hidden in this woman's face. She'd waited long enough. Maybe she'd waited too long. But she was finally there, and a sense of relief slowly began to build inside her. This would be over soon, and that was all she'd ever wanted.

"They say the midwife, the crazy one? They say she tol' 'em he did it." Moses had told her that.

Roberta stood at the door, staring insolently at the woman who looked like a limp cat-o'-nine-tails. The woman's dress hung on her and looked like it belonged to someone else. Her hair was wild on her head, blown into chaos by the wind that had worked up over the course of the afternoon and brought the storm clouds with it. She stared back at Roberta with lazy eyes, sunk deep into her head and as red as the roses growing in Roberta's front yard.

"What is it?" Roberta asked impatiently, clutching her shawl closer to her. This fool had better hurry up and say something or get the hell off her porch, she thought angrily.

Sara stared at the woman for a moment and saw, clearly as if the day had passed twenty minutes ago instead of twenty years ago, the face of the woman standing across the road on the day Adam nearly died and Charles was killed. It had been her. Of course it was, Sara concluded, and it was clear that Sara had done the right thing by coming—for retribution of her own.

Roberta smacked her lips and rolled her eyes. "I said, whatchu want?"

Roberta's indignant tone fueled the small flame burning somewhere in Sara's soul and made her angry. It took all the strength she had left to draw back her shoulders and lift her eyes to stare squarely into Roberta's. There was nothing menacing about this woman anymore. For years Sara had lived in fear of her—fear and guilt. She'd betrayed Roberta by having an affair with Charles. He'd betrayed her too. And for that, they'd both suffered— Charles in death and Sara in life. But Roberta hadn't been so innocent either. She'd been a betrayer in her own right and as guilty as either of them, daring to take the power of life into her own hands and declare herself to be God. She'd killed Charles and had gotten away with it, too, walking around a free woman, back to the life she'd left before she'd been sent away. For the second time she'd tried to kill Adam, and for the second time Sara had resurrected her son.

"Roberta," her name had never crossed Sara's lips before now. "My name is Sara—Sara Tate."

Sara waited for a response, an expression, some sign from Roberta that she'd known who she was, but none ever came. Roberta just stared blankly at her, tapping her foot impatiently.

"My price has gone up to fifty dollars if you want me to deliver a baby, and fifty-five if you want me to get rid of one," she said indifferently.

"Adam is my son," Sara said proudly. From the look on her face, Roberta had no idea what Sara was talking about, or maybe she hadn't heard her. Sara cleared her throat and said it louder, "Adam is my son."

Roberta shrugged her shoulders.

No. She had no idea, Sara concluded. Roberta didn't even know his name, but she'd wanted him dead because . . . why? It took a second for the answer to come to her—because he was the spitting image of his father. Charles and Adam could've been twins, they looked so much alike. That's what Roberta had seen in him, and that's why she'd wanted him dead. Then . . . and now.

"Charles Brooks was his daddy," Sara said carefully, making sure Roberta could hear every word. Making sure she understood.

Suddenly Roberta stopped tapping her foot. All the color washed out of her round face, and Sara knew she finally understood.

"They call him Fool 'round here—but his name is Adam. Charles gave him that name."

Roberta's heart beat fiercely in her chest.

She the one! 'Member? Look close, gal! She the one—in the garden—she had yo' husband.

"I want you to know," Sara explained triumphantly, "he ain't dead, Roberta. My boy ain't dead."

Roberta stepped back and shook her head. She'd heard them say they'd kill him. She knew she'd heard it, and she knew that if they did, everything would be as it should've been. But somebody had been killed. Who? Folks all over town were talking about it, and she thought they were talking about—

"You lyin'!" she hissed at Sara. It didn't matter who she was, or what that bastard's name had been. Roberta knew who he really was. He was Charles! He was Charles come back—

Got black eyes like him. Like Charles. Like—Mr. Bobby.

They'd killed that boy because Roberta had slept like a baby the night before, and the night before that, too. She'd slept good and hard, knowing full well he would never be again. She knew it! And this bitch was standing here on her porch lying through her teeth. Roberta grabbed the door and slammed it full force in Sara's face.

Sara started to laugh, and then the tears came. "He ain't dead, Roberta!" she yelled through the door. "You couldn't kill him when he was a baby, and you can't kill him now!" Tears flowed in rivers down her cheeks and her laughter turned to hysteria. "So you see . . . long as he alive . . . long as me and Charles's son is alive . . . Charles gon' be alive too! And ain't nothin' you can do 'bout it! Ain't nothin' you can do!"

* * *

Roberta slid down the door to the floor and clutched her shawl tight around her. That foolish woman outside her door was just trying to scare her, that was all. She was talking nonsense and Roberta would have no part of it.

I don't think he dead, Roberta. I don't think he is. Do you?

It Was Only a Dream

2002

John King had come full circle, around the world and a thousand different lifetimes, it seemed. All for the sake of ending up back in Bueller, sitting in a small room with an old, disfigured man, slow in thinking and even slower in moving, listening to old Sam Cooke songs he'd copied and recorded on a CD and brought down to Adam for his birthday, along with a new CD player.

Adam sat in his chair staring out the window, looking into the past, while John lay sprawled out on the bed smoking a cigarette, watching the smoke ascend and finally disappear into thin air.

He'd been coming down regularly for nearly a year, ever since he'd learned the truth about the man he'd grown up known as Fool, and as his father. Resentment of where he'd come from and how he'd gotten there had driven him miles away from his hometown, only to bring him back when he was finally ready to listen to a new version of the truth, one that was much more digestable and easy on the ears.

Fool had been Adam and Adam had been his father. Years ago, John had suspected that Adam had been like most young men. He'd met a girl, fallen in love, and looked forward to having a few kids with her and to growing old with her. Only circumstances hadn't been kind to Adam, or Mattie, the girl he loved—or John . . . the kid.

Mattie was young, too young, and probably all broken up over the bullshit she'd had to put up with. John suspected that some-one had raped that girl but he knew, like Moses somehow knew, that it hadn't been Adam. So she cut out early, before it got deep enough to drown her. He guessed, out of all of them, she'd been the brains of the family.

Adam had been broken up and pieced back together again, at least on the outside. But John figured he'd never be cool on the inside, no matter how hard you tried to sew him together. Hell, he couldn't blame him. Men can't handle broken hearts as well as women. It's just not in them. So Adam decided to die slowly, in the small room of his brother's house, growing old to Sam Cooke and holding on for dear life to the memories he still held of that girl in the place where his heart should've been.

The world had passed him by, but Adam didn't seem to mind or notice. Sara Tate had succumbed to cancer years ago. She died with her sons by her side and not so unhappy that she couldn't still smile and light up a room or a man's heart. Roberta's chil-dren, John's half-brother and sister, had done well for themselves. The boy, Charles Jr., played pro football, had long since retired, and was living with his family in California. Elizabeth had gotten married, moved to Dallas, and even had children and grandchil-dren of her own. And Roberta—Roberta was resting, or so one hoped.

*   *   *

Adam glanced over at John. Sometimes, he had to pinch himself to make sure he wasn't dreaming and that he really did have a boy—a son who belonged to him. John was strong, handsome. "M-my momma . . . use to t-t-tell me . . . I was . . . handsome too," he said out loud, not necessarily to John.

John nodded. "Yeah, I remember you telling me that."

Adam leaned forward and pressed the repeat button on his new CD player John had bought for him and taught him how to work.

"I . . . ever show you a p-picture of my momma?"

John smiled. Adam had showed him the same picture a hundred times, but it was all good. "You always show me a picture of her," he teased.

Adam missed the humor as usual, or decided to ignore it. John could never really be sure which.

"She . . . was a p-pretty woman." Adam sat back, smiling. "R-real pretty. L-l-like yo' momma was. M-Mattie was pretty too. She was."

John remembered. He'd grown up seeing pictures of Mattie all over his Momma Agnes's house, and she had been a very pretty girl.

"I . . . I . . . look like . . . my daddy, though. M-my momma say I l-look jus' like him."

"Yeah. You told me that too. He was a good looking dude?" John asked lightheartedly.

"That's w-w-what she say. S-say he was . . . the f-finest man she ever did see and that I-I look jus' like him." Adam turned to John and stared at him with the eye that hadn't been permanently closed shut by Davis, Clyde, and Walter, that night in the barn. "B-back 'fo' I got beat up." he said sadly. "Back then I . . . I look like you. A whole l-lot like you. M-me and you c-c-could be twins if you w-wasn't my boy," Adam boasted.

"So, that must mean I look like your daddy too." John said thoughtfully, knowing how much the connection meant to Adam. "If you look like him, and I look like you, then I must look like him too."

Adam smiled, then he laughed and scratched his head. "I . . . I reckon . . . that's how it go, son." He sat back in his chair and stared out the window again. "I . . . reckon it is."

John smiled, inhaled on his cigarette, and blew a puff of smoke over his head. "I reckon it is."